the Zabîme Sisters

the Zabîme Sisters

by ARISTOPHANE
translation & afterword by
MATT MADDEN
lettering by
NICHOLAS BREUTZMAN

First Second
NEW YORK & LONDON

THIS MODEST WORK IS DEDICATED TO THE DIVINE,
TO THE ONENESS WHOSE DOMAIN IS EVERYTHING
AND WHICH CAN BE FOUND IN EACH OF US.
A TOKEN OF MY DEVOTION.

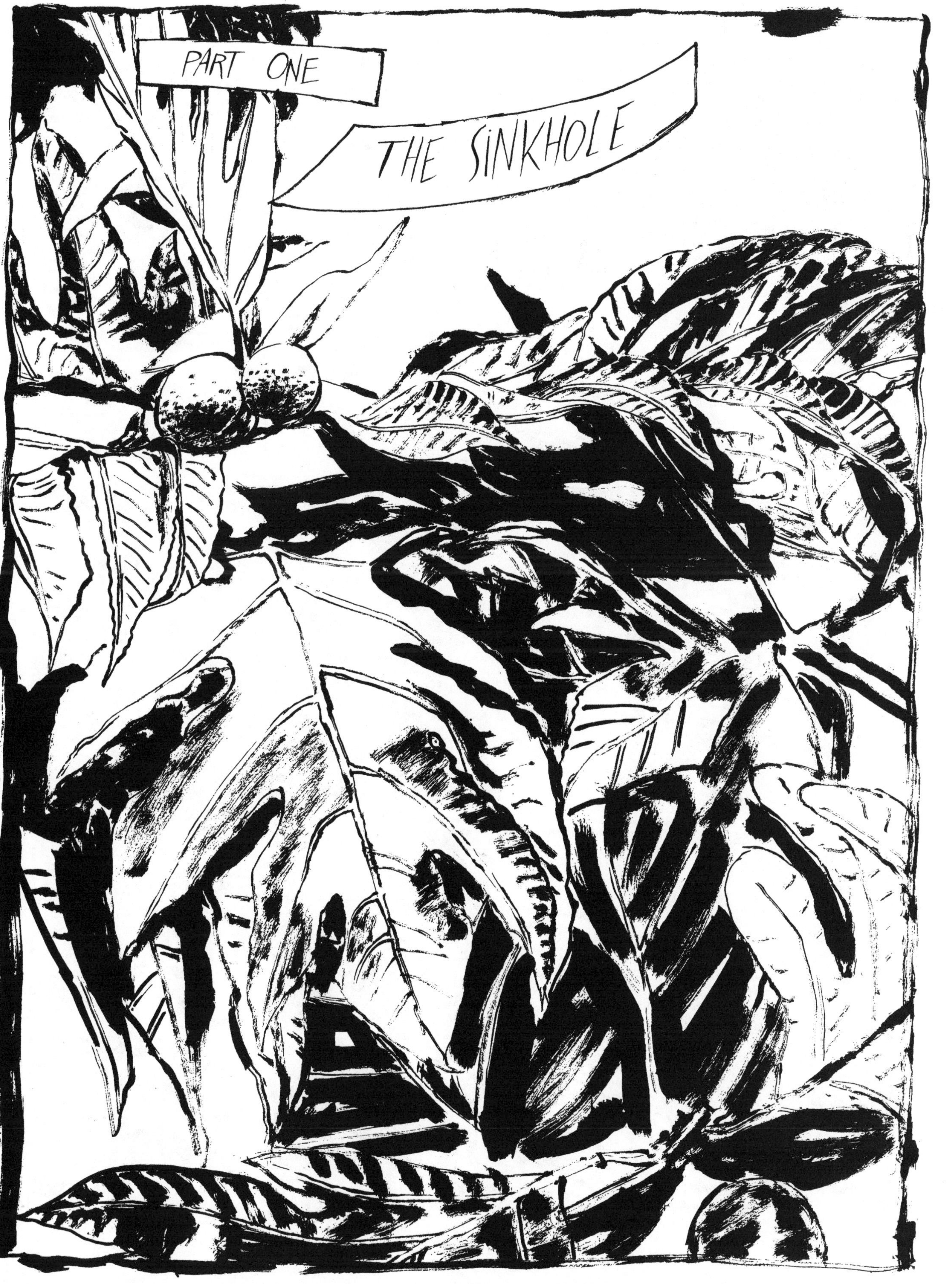
PART ONE
THE SINKHOLE

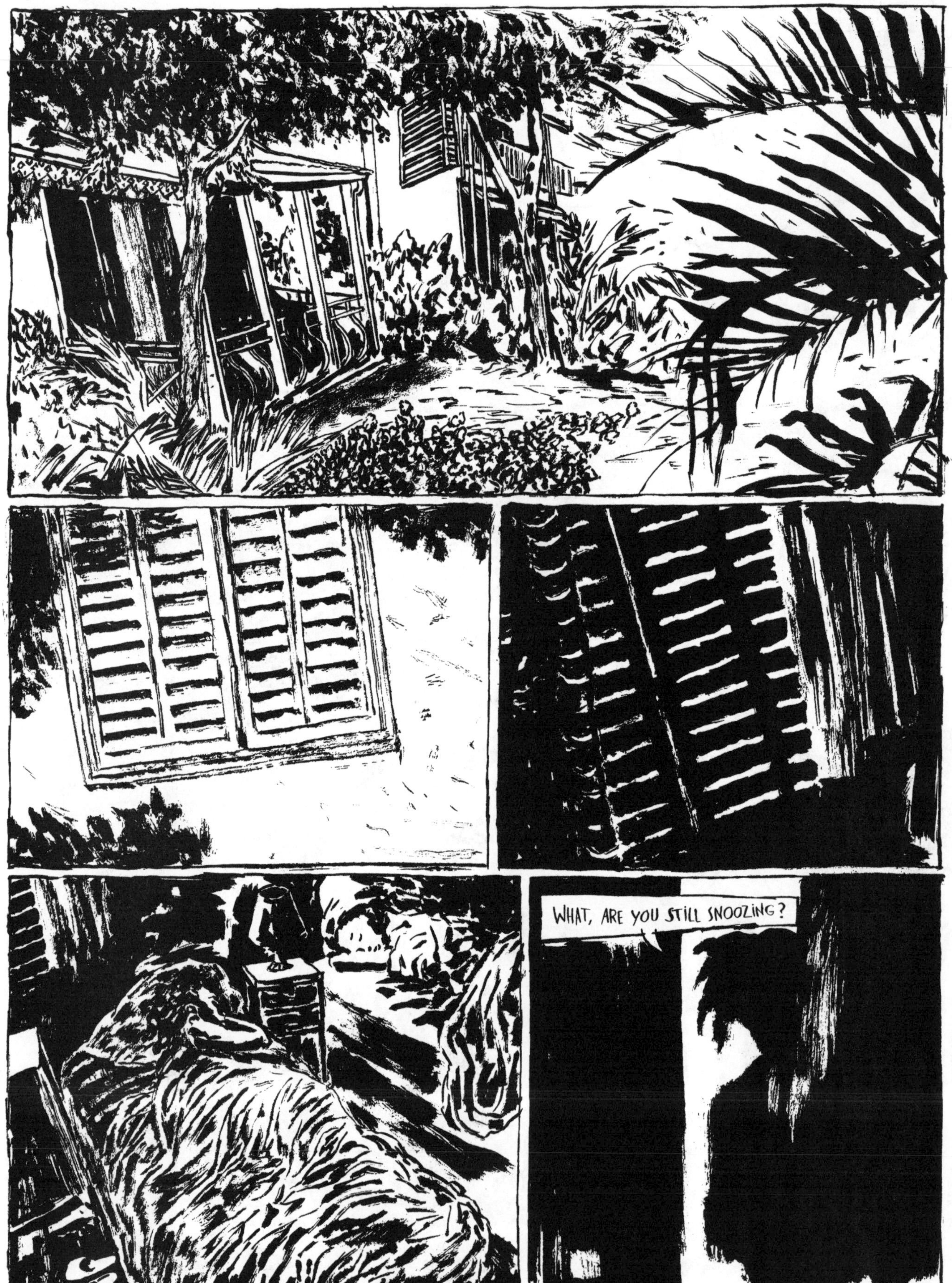
WHAT, ARE YOU STILL SNOOZING?

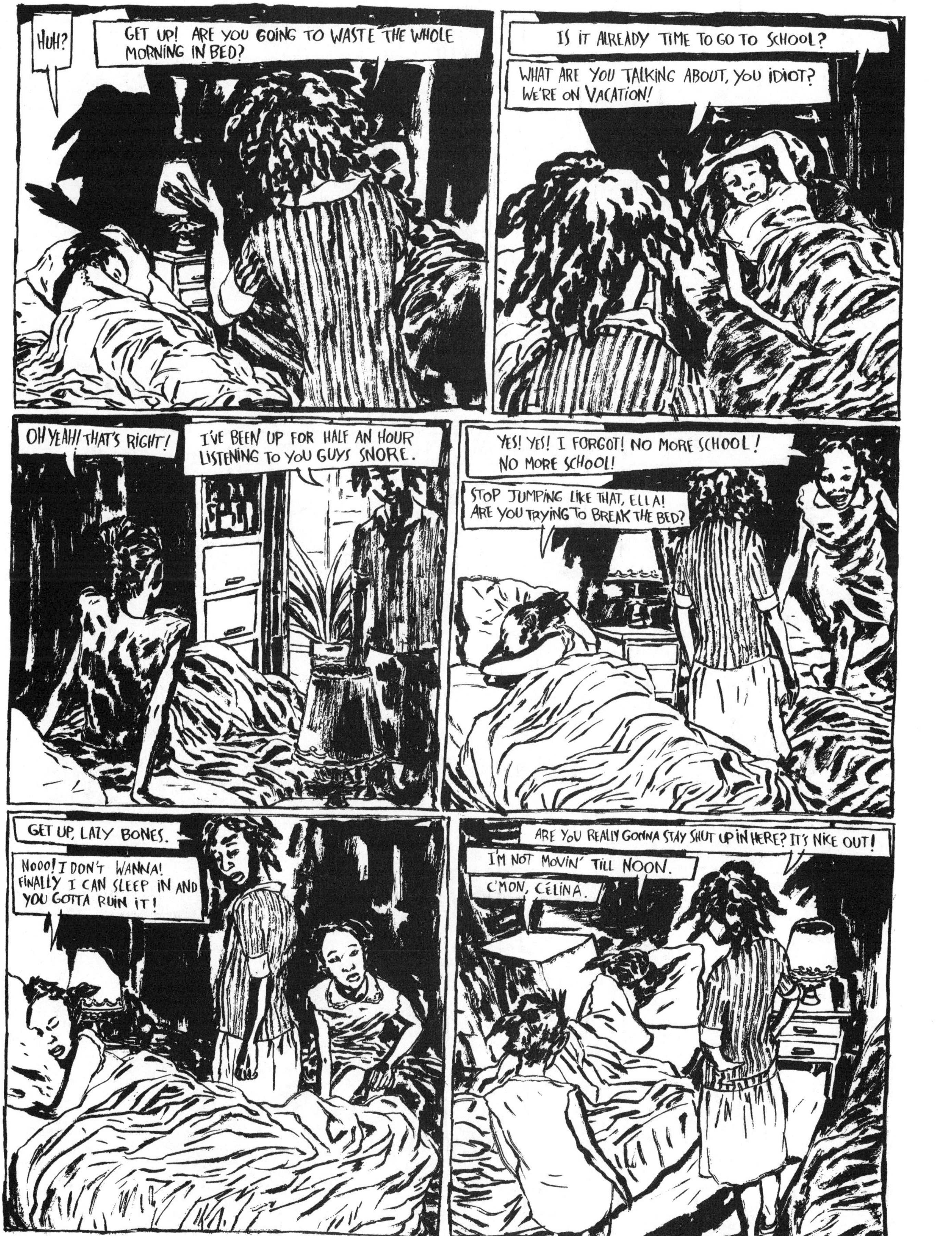
HUH?
GET UP! ARE YOU GOING TO WASTE THE WHOLE MORNING IN BED?
IS IT ALREADY TIME TO GO TO SCHOOL?
WHAT ARE YOU TALKING ABOUT, YOU IDIOT? WE'RE ON VACATION!
OH YEAH! THAT'S RIGHT!
I'VE BEEN UP FOR HALF AN HOUR LISTENING TO YOU GUYS SNORE.
YES! YES! I FORGOT! NO MORE SCHOOL! NO MORE SCHOOL!
STOP JUMPING LIKE THAT, ELLA! ARE YOU TRYING TO BREAK THE BED?
GET UP, LAZY BONES.
NOOO! I DON'T WANNA! FINALLY I CAN SLEEP IN AND YOU GOTTA RUIN IT!
ARE YOU REALLY GONNA STAY SHUT UP IN HERE? IT'S NICE OUT!
I'M NOT MOVIN' TILL NOON.
C'MON, CÉLINA.

CÉLINA GOT UP AFTER MAKING THEM BEG HER. SHE TOOK PARTICULAR PLEASURE IN BEING PLEADED WITH AND IN FEELING INDISPENSABLE.

WHEN SHE GOT THIS ATTENTION FIRST THING IN THE MORNING, SHE FELT ESPECIALLY CONTENT.

YOU'RE NOT EATING ANYTHING?

DID YOU THINK I WAS WAITING FOR YOU? I WAS JUST ABOUT TO LEAVE WITHOUT YOU!

YOU WOULDN'T!

I WOULD SO.

WELL HOW ABOUT THAT? AND WHERE ARE THE THREE OF YOU PLANNING ON GOING WITHOUT EVEN ASKING FOR MY PERMISSION?

WE'RE GOING TO THE RIVERBANK, MAMA.

AND WHEN WERE YOU GOING TO TELL ME?

BUT WE JUST DID.

YOU AREN'T GOING ANYWHERE. THERE'S WORK TO DO AND I NEED YOUR HELP.

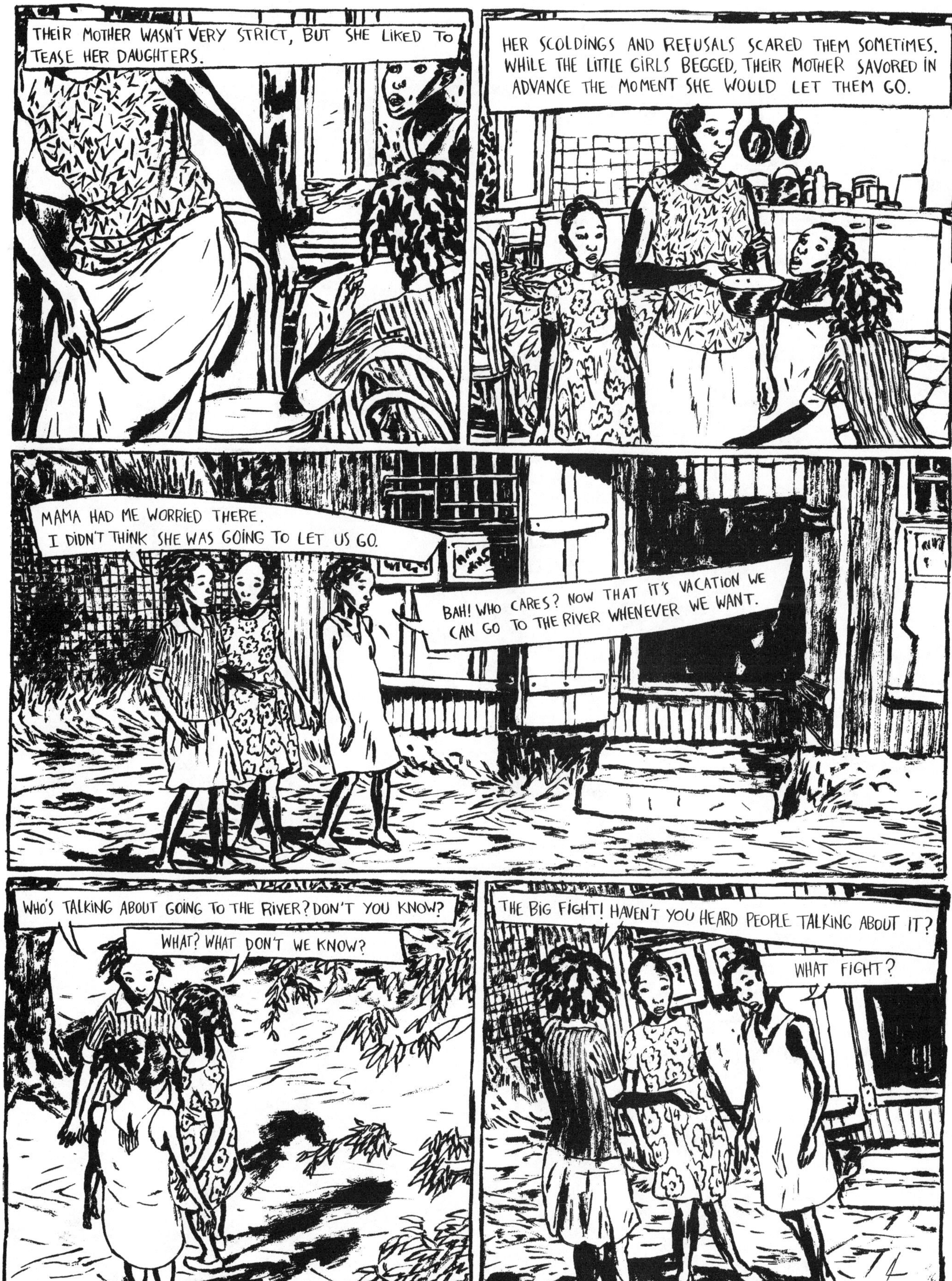
THEIR MOTHER WASN'T VERY STRICT, BUT SHE LIKED TO TEASE HER DAUGHTERS.
HER SCOLDINGS AND REFUSALS SCARED THEM SOMETIMES. WHILE THE LITTLE GIRLS BEGGED, THEIR MOTHER SAVORED IN ADVANCE THE MOMENT SHE WOULD LET THEM GO.
MAMA HAD ME WORRIED THERE. I DIDN'T THINK SHE WAS GOING TO LET US GO.
BAH! WHO CARES? NOW THAT IT'S VACATION WE CAN GO TO THE RIVER WHENEVER WE WANT.
WHO'S TALKING ABOUT GOING TO THE RIVER? DON'T YOU KNOW?
WHAT? WHAT DON'T WE KNOW?
THE BIG FIGHT! HAVEN'T YOU HEARD PEOPLE TALKING ABOUT IT?
WHAT FIGHT?

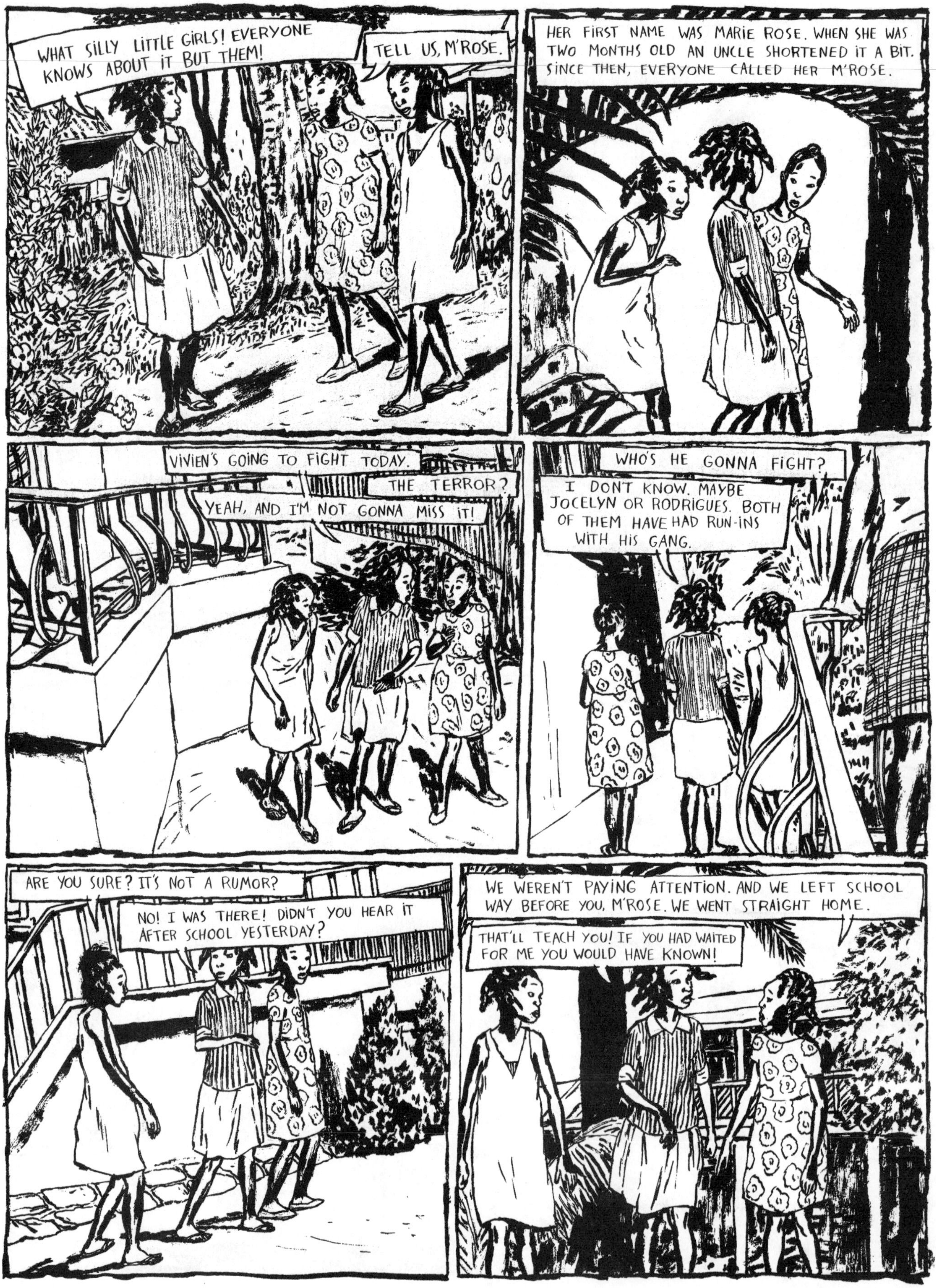
WHAT SILLY LITTLE GIRLS! EVERYONE KNOWS ABOUT IT BUT THEM!
TELL US, M'ROSE.
HER FIRST NAME WAS MARIE ROSE. WHEN SHE WAS TWO MONTHS OLD AN UNCLE SHORTENED IT A BIT. SINCE THEN, EVERYONE CALLED HER M'ROSE.
VIVIEN'S GOING TO FIGHT TODAY.
THE TERROR?
YEAH, AND I'M NOT GONNA MISS IT!
WHO'S HE GONNA FIGHT?
I DON'T KNOW. MAYBE JOCELYN OR RODRIGUES. BOTH OF THEM HAVE HAD RUN-INS WITH HIS GANG.
ARE YOU SURE? IT'S NOT A RUMOR?
NO! I WAS THERE! DIDN'T YOU HEAR IT AFTER SCHOOL YESTERDAY?
WE WEREN'T PAYING ATTENTION. AND WE LEFT SCHOOL WAY BEFORE YOU, M'ROSE. WE WENT STRAIGHT HOME.
THAT'LL TEACH YOU! IF YOU HAD WAITED FOR ME YOU WOULD HAVE KNOWN!

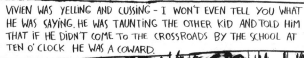

TELL US, M'ROSE, WHAT HAPPENED?

WELL, THE TRUTH IS, THERE WERE SO MANY PEOPLE I COULDN'T SEE MUCH, BUT I HEARD IT.

VIVIEN WAS YELLING AND CUSSING - I WON'T EVEN TELL YOU WHAT HE WAS SAYING. HE WAS TAUNTING THE OTHER KID AND TOLD HIM THAT IF HE DIDN'T COME TO THE CROSSROADS BY THE SCHOOL AT TEN O'CLOCK HE WAS A COWARD.

AND WHAT DID THE OTHER KID SAY?

HE DIDN'T SAY ANYTHING. OR MAYBE HE DID, BUT I COULDN'T HEAR IT BECAUSE EVERYONE WAS YELLING.

I BET VIVIEN WAS SHOUTING LOUDER THAN EVERYONE, AS USUAL.

NOT JUST THAT: HE WAS WAVING HIS ARMS IN THE AIR LIKE A MADMAN!

I COULDN'T SEE HIM, BUT I SAW HIS FISTS FLYING AROUND IN THE AIR. HE EVEN HIT SOMEONE IN THE EAR BY ACCIDENT.

HE'S ALWAYS STARTING SOMETHING.

THAT OTHER KID'S GONNA GET CLOBBERED. NO WAY AM I GONNA GO SEE THAT.

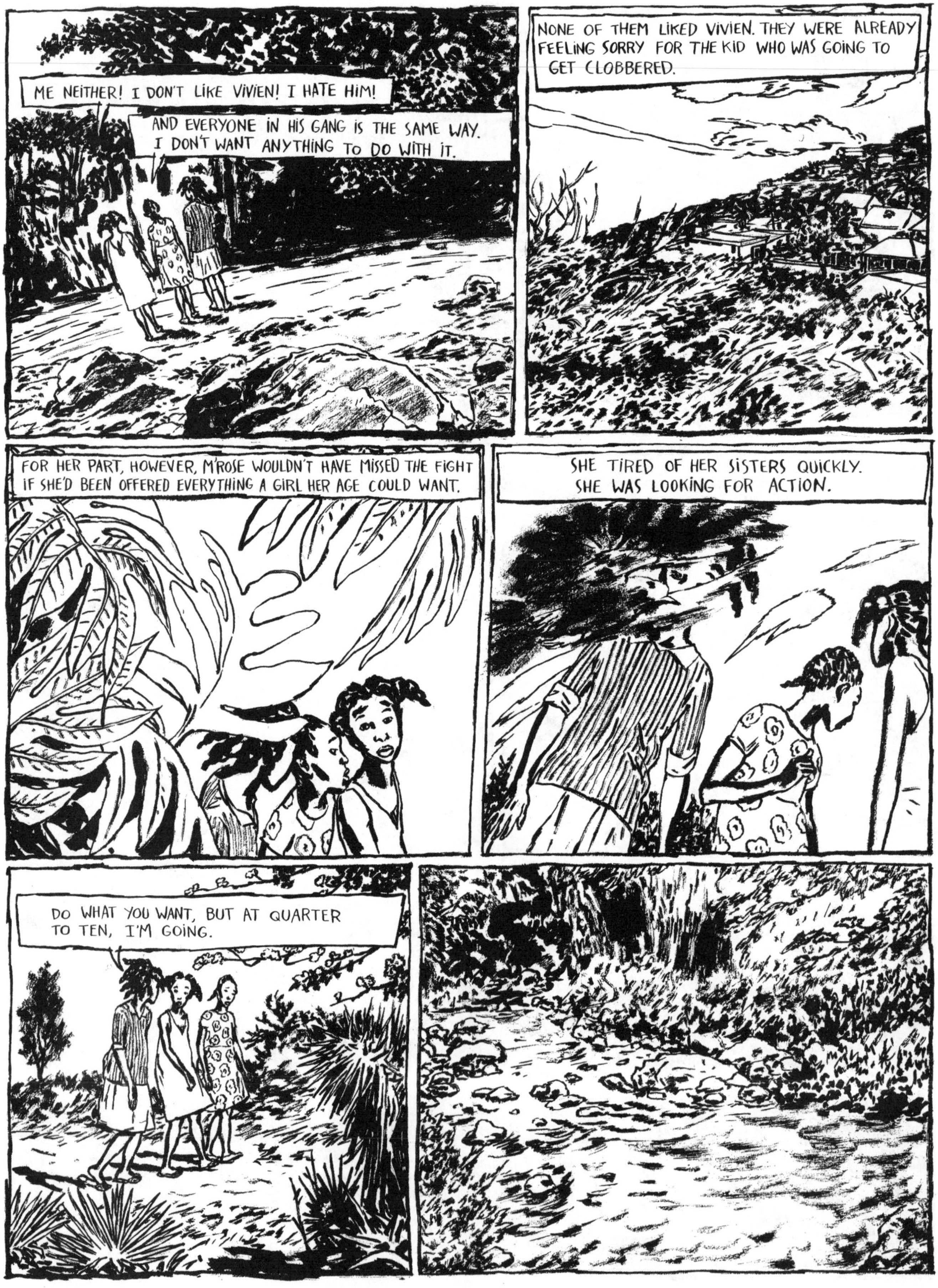
ME NEITHER! I DON'T LIKE VIVIEN! I HATE HIM!
AND EVERYONE IN HIS GANG IS THE SAME WAY. I DON'T WANT ANYTHING TO DO WITH IT.
NONE OF THEM LIKED VIVIEN. THEY WERE ALREADY FEELING SORRY FOR THE KID WHO WAS GOING TO GET CLOBBERED.
FOR HER PART, HOWEVER, M'ROSE WOULDN'T HAVE MISSED THE FIGHT IF SHE'D BEEN OFFERED EVERYTHING A GIRL HER AGE COULD WANT.
SHE TIRED OF HER SISTERS QUICKLY. SHE WAS LOOKING FOR ACTION.
DO WHAT YOU WANT, BUT AT QUARTER TO TEN, I'M GOING.

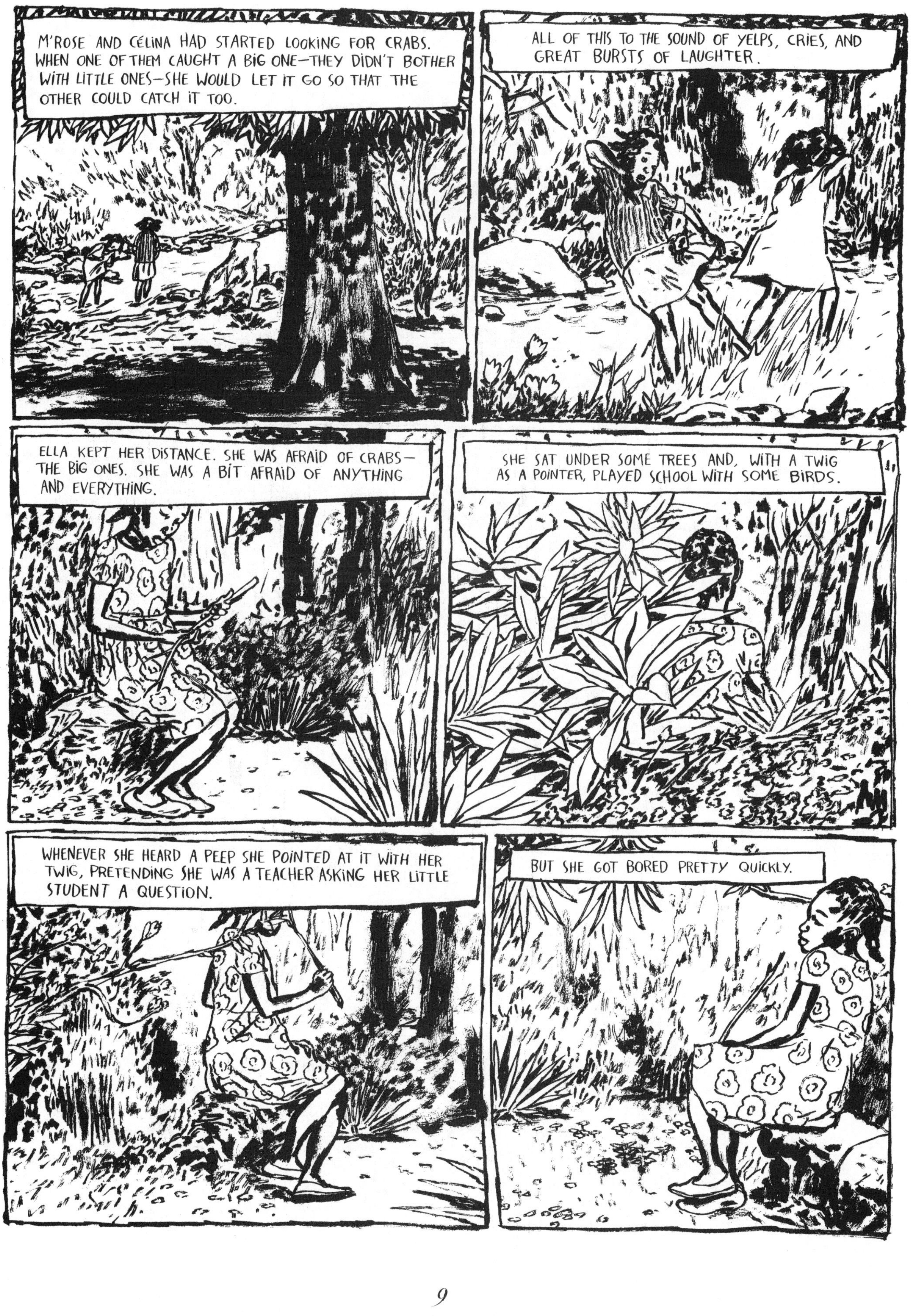
M'ROSE AND CÉLINA HAD STARTED LOOKING FOR CRABS. WHEN ONE OF THEM CAUGHT A BIG ONE—THEY DIDN'T BOTHER WITH LITTLE ONES—SHE WOULD LET IT GO SO THAT THE OTHER COULD CATCH IT TOO.
ALL OF THIS TO THE SOUND OF YELPS, CRIES, AND GREAT BURSTS OF LAUGHTER.
ELLA KEPT HER DISTANCE. SHE WAS AFRAID OF CRABS—THE BIG ONES. SHE WAS A BIT AFRAID OF ANYTHING AND EVERYTHING.
SHE SAT UNDER SOME TREES AND, WITH A TWIG AS A POINTER, PLAYED SCHOOL WITH SOME BIRDS.
WHENEVER SHE HEARD A PEEP SHE POINTED AT IT WITH HER TWIG, PRETENDING SHE WAS A TEACHER ASKING HER LITTLE STUDENT A QUESTION.
BUT SHE GOT BORED PRETTY QUICKLY.

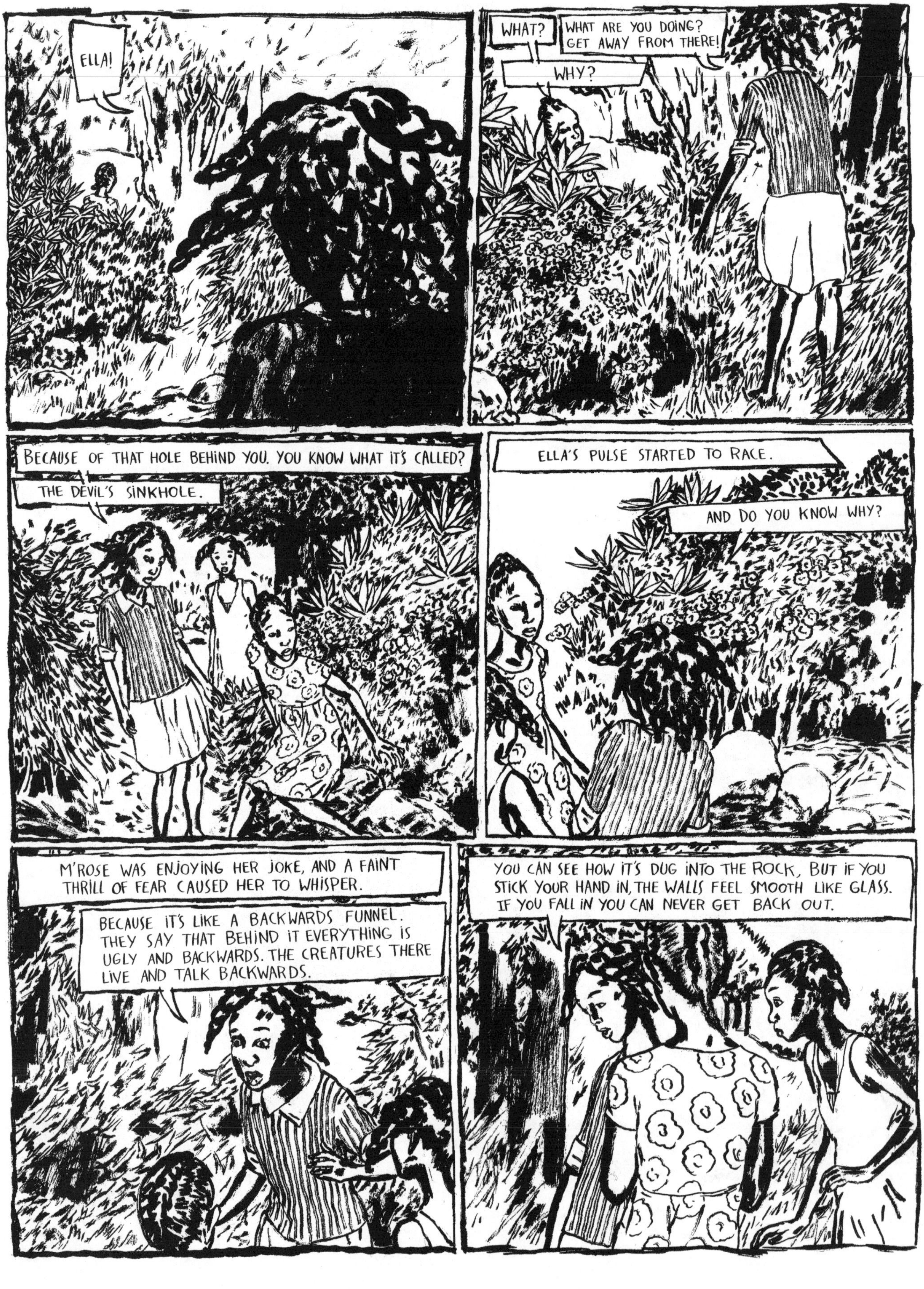
ELLA!
WHAT?
WHAT ARE YOU DOING? GET AWAY FROM THERE!
WHY?
BECAUSE OF THAT HOLE BEHIND YOU. YOU KNOW WHAT IT'S CALLED?
THE DEVIL'S SINKHOLE.
ELLA'S PULSE STARTED TO RACE.
AND DO YOU KNOW WHY?
M'ROSE WAS ENJOYING HER JOKE, AND A FAINT THRILL OF FEAR CAUSED HER TO WHISPER.
BECAUSE IT'S LIKE A BACKWARDS FUNNEL. THEY SAY THAT BEHIND IT EVERYTHING IS UGLY AND BACKWARDS. THE CREATURES THERE LIVE AND TALK BACKWARDS.
YOU CAN SEE HOW IT'S DUG INTO THE ROCK, BUT IF YOU STICK YOUR HAND IN, THE WALLS FEEL SMOOTH LIKE GLASS. IF YOU FALL IN YOU CAN NEVER GET BACK OUT.

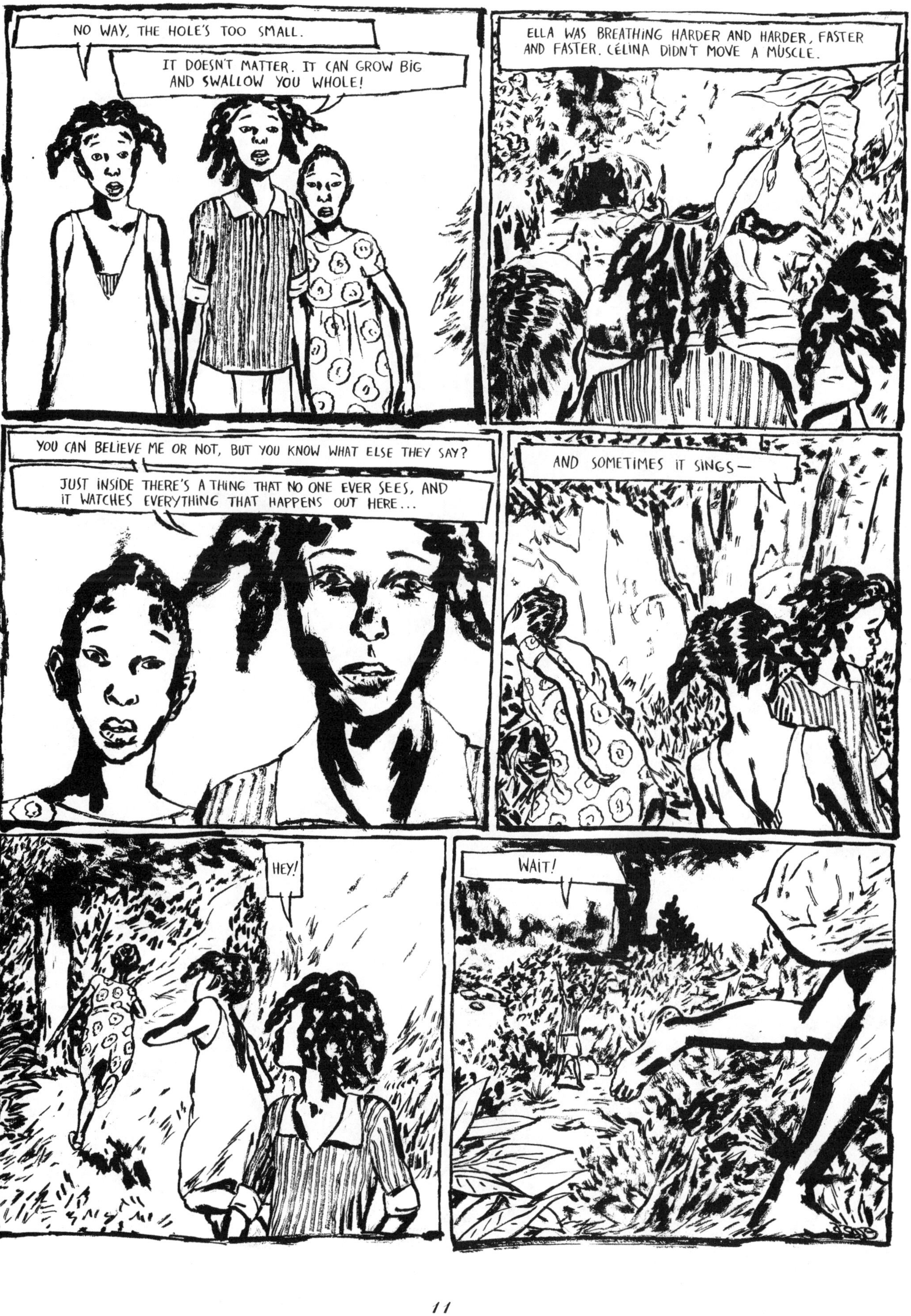
NO WAY, THE HOLE'S TOO SMALL.
IT DOESN'T MATTER. IT CAN GROW BIG AND SWALLOW YOU WHOLE!
ELLA WAS BREATHING HARDER AND HARDER, FASTER AND FASTER. CÉLINA DIDN'T MOVE A MUSCLE.
YOU CAN BELIEVE ME OR NOT, BUT YOU KNOW WHAT ELSE THEY SAY?
JUST INSIDE THERE'S A THING THAT NO ONE EVER SEES, AND IT WATCHES EVERYTHING THAT HAPPENS OUT HERE...
AND SOMETIMES IT SINGS—
HEY!
WAIT!

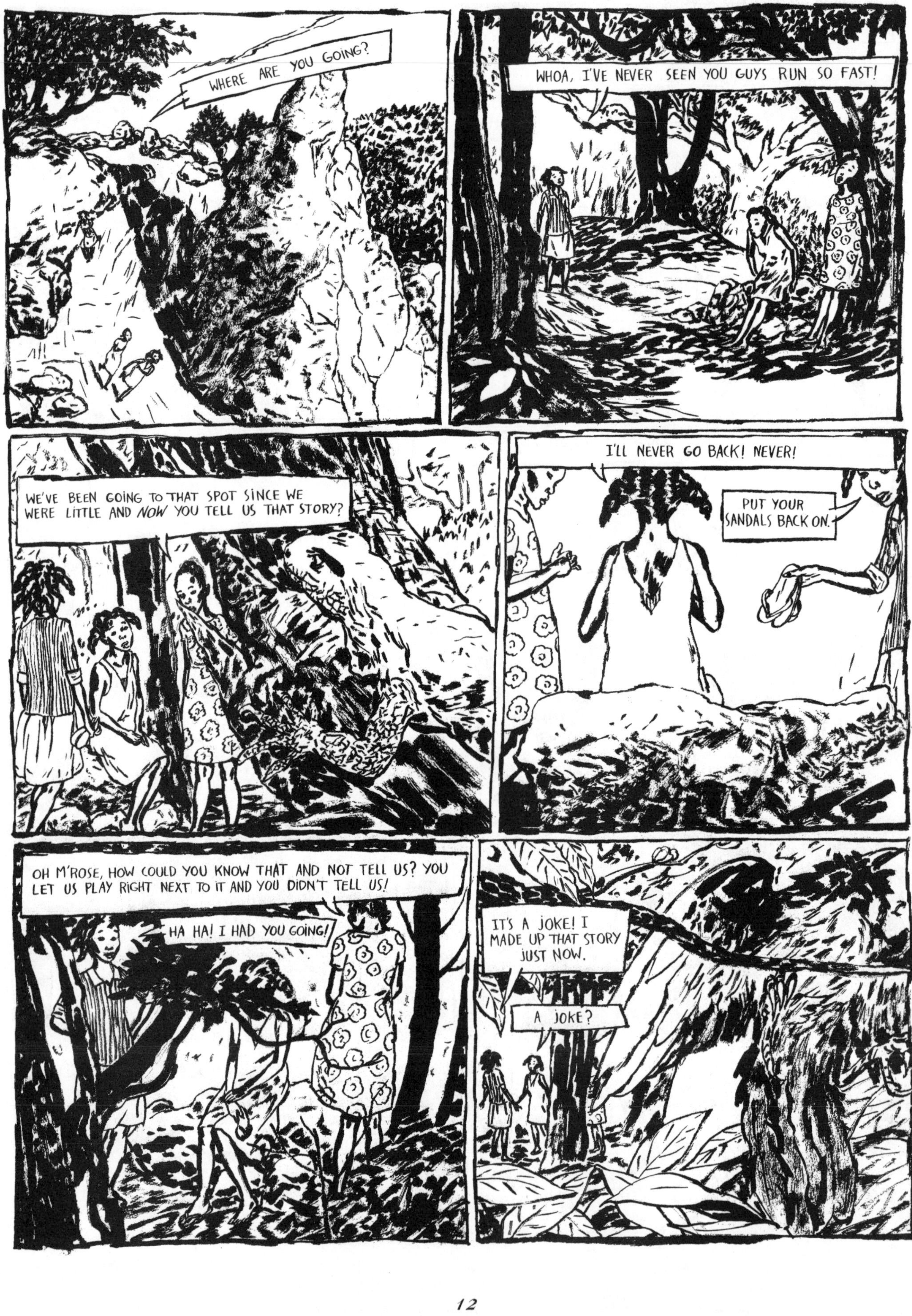
WHERE ARE YOU GOING?
WHOA, I'VE NEVER SEEN YOU GUYS RUN SO FAST!
WE'VE BEEN GOING TO THAT SPOT SINCE WE WERE LITTLE AND *NOW* YOU TELL US THAT STORY?
I'LL NEVER GO BACK! NEVER!
PUT YOUR SANDALS BACK ON.
OH M'ROSE, HOW COULD YOU KNOW THAT AND NOT TELL US? YOU LET US PLAY RIGHT NEXT TO IT AND YOU DIDN'T TELL US!
HA HA! I HAD YOU GOING!
IT'S A JOKE! I MADE UP THAT STORY JUST NOW.
A JOKE?

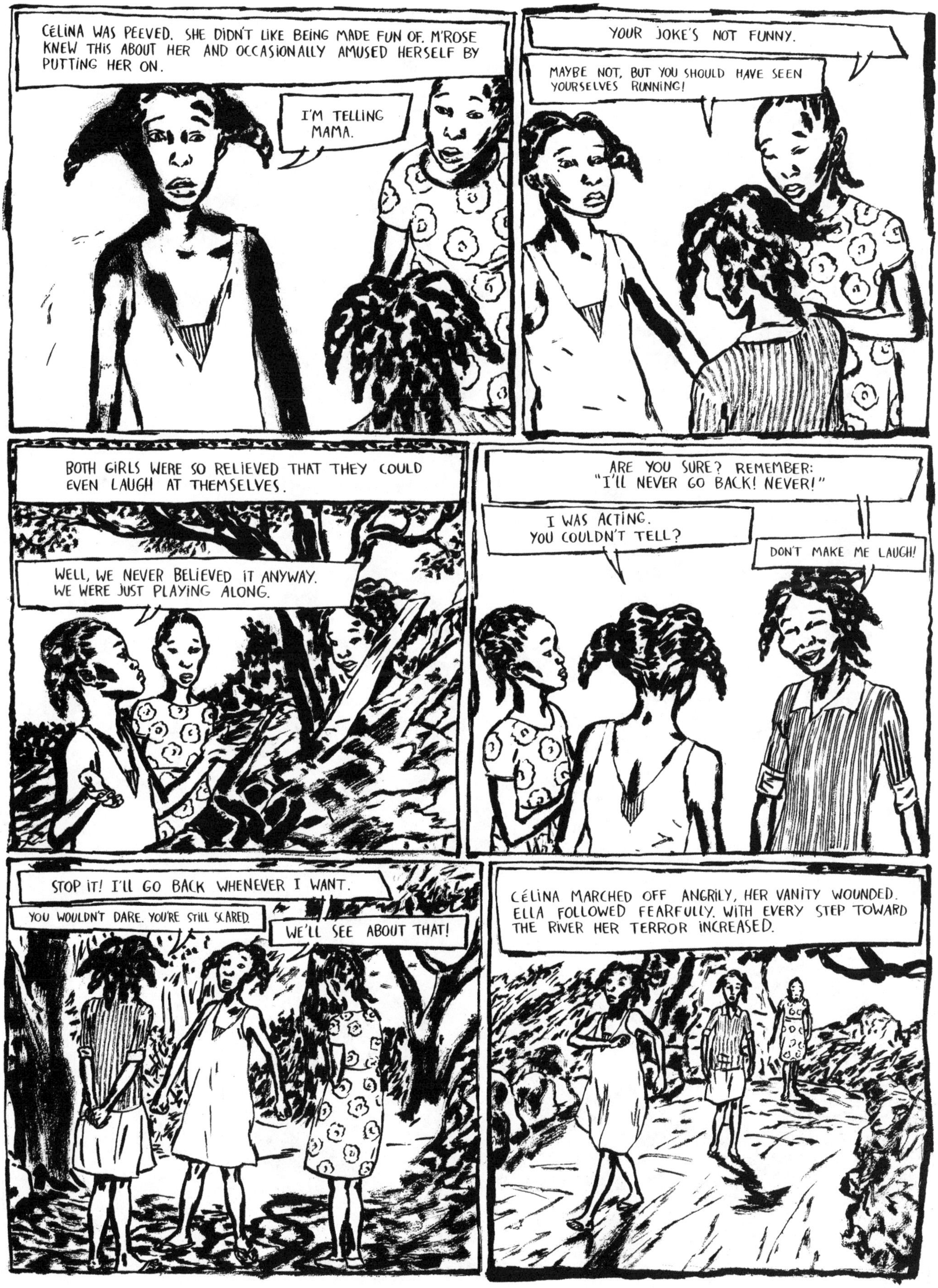
CÉLINA WAS PEEVED. SHE DIDN'T LIKE BEING MADE FUN OF. M'ROSE KNEW THIS ABOUT HER AND OCCASIONALLY AMUSED HERSELF BY PUTTING HER ON.
I'M TELLING MAMA.
YOUR JOKE'S NOT FUNNY.
MAYBE NOT, BUT YOU SHOULD HAVE SEEN YOURSELVES RUNNING!
BOTH GIRLS WERE SO RELIEVED THAT THEY COULD EVEN LAUGH AT THEMSELVES.
WELL, WE NEVER BELIEVED IT ANYWAY. WE WERE JUST PLAYING ALONG.
ARE YOU SURE? REMEMBER: "I'LL NEVER GO BACK! NEVER!"
I WAS ACTING. YOU COULDN'T TELL?
DON'T MAKE ME LAUGH!
STOP IT! I'LL GO BACK WHENEVER I WANT.
YOU WOULDN'T DARE. YOU'RE STILL SCARED.
WE'LL SEE ABOUT THAT!
CÉLINA MARCHED OFF ANGRILY, HER VANITY WOUNDED. ELLA FOLLOWED FEARFULLY. WITH EVERY STEP TOWARD THE RIVER HER TERROR INCREASED.

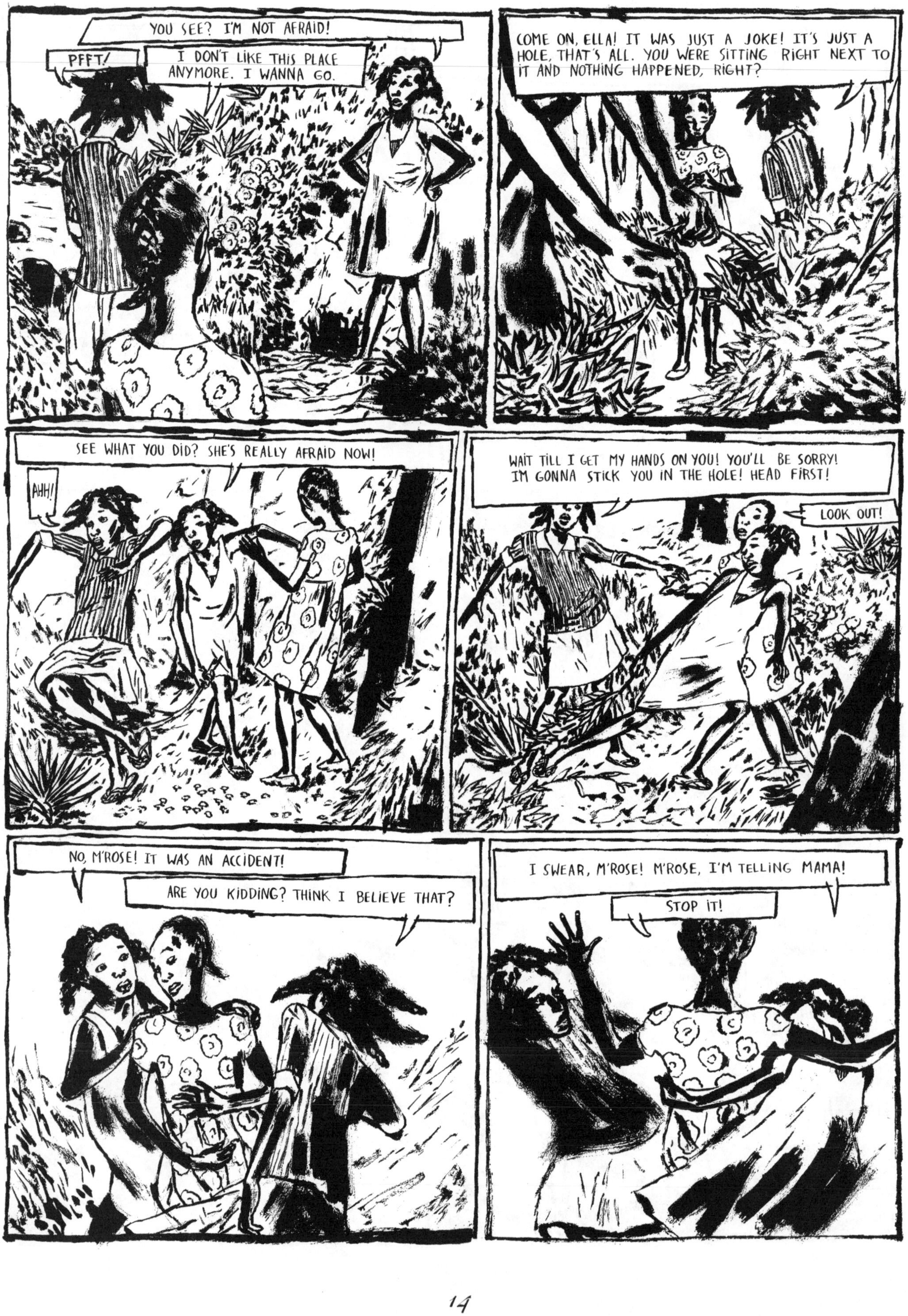

YOU SEE? I'M NOT AFRAID!
PFFT!
I DON'T LIKE THIS PLACE ANYMORE. I WANNA GO.
COME ON, ELLA! IT WAS JUST A JOKE! IT'S JUST A HOLE, THAT'S ALL. YOU WERE SITTING RIGHT NEXT TO IT AND NOTHING HAPPENED, RIGHT?
SEE WHAT YOU DID? SHE'S REALLY AFRAID NOW!
AHH!
WAIT TILL I GET MY HANDS ON YOU! YOU'LL BE SORRY! I'M GONNA STICK YOU IN THE HOLE! HEAD FIRST!
LOOK OUT!
NO, M'ROSE! IT WAS AN ACCIDENT!
ARE YOU KIDDING? THINK I BELIEVE THAT?
I SWEAR, M'ROSE! M'ROSE, I'M TELLING MAMA!
STOP IT!

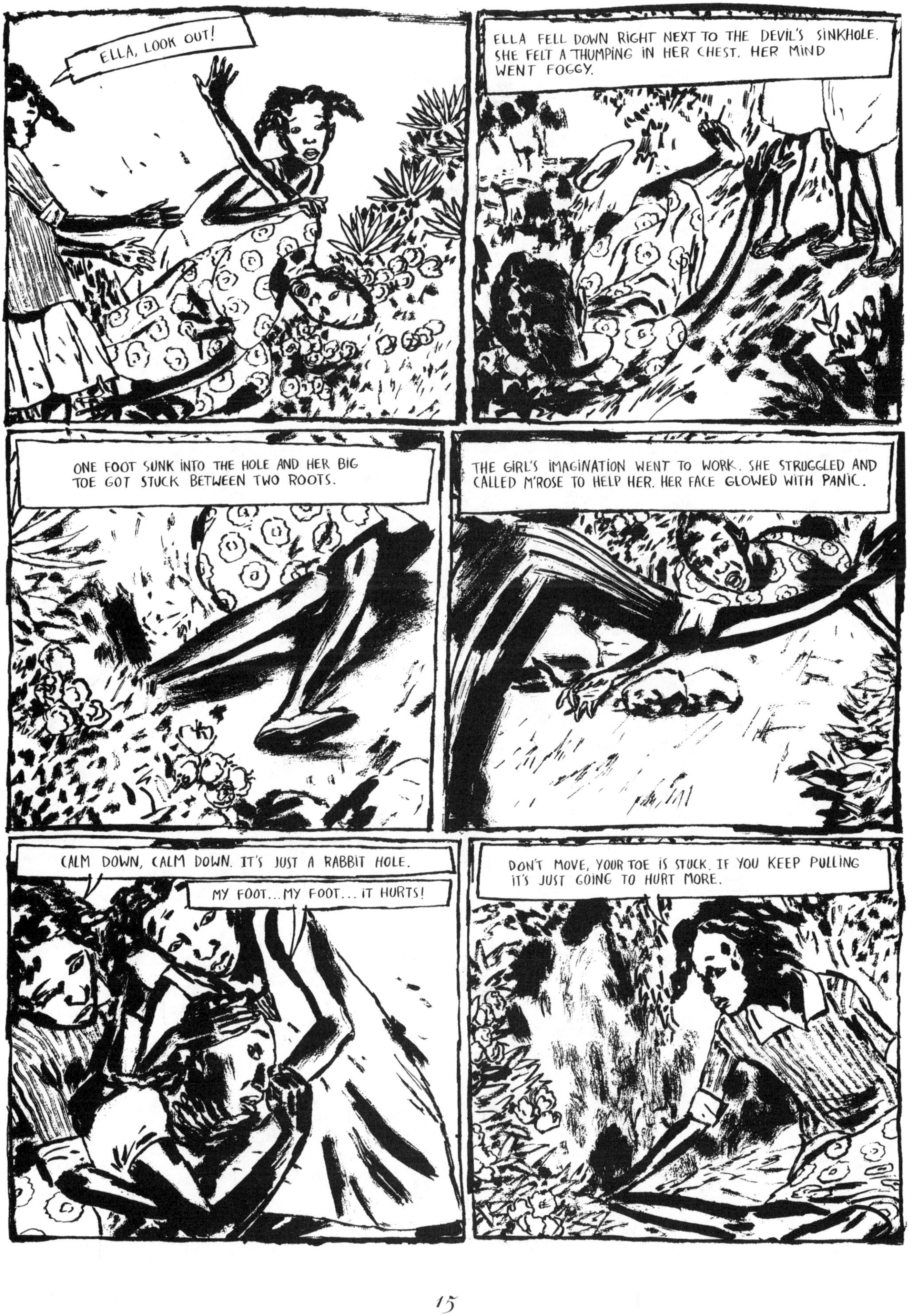
ELLA, LOOK OUT!
ELLA FELL DOWN RIGHT NEXT TO THE DEVIL'S SINKHOLE. SHE FELT A THUMPING IN HER CHEST. HER MIND WENT FOGGY.
ONE FOOT SUNK INTO THE HOLE AND HER BIG TOE GOT STUCK BETWEEN TWO ROOTS.
THE GIRL'S IMAGINATION WENT TO WORK. SHE STRUGGLED AND CALLED M'ROSE TO HELP HER. HER FACE GLOWED WITH PANIC.
CALM DOWN, CALM DOWN. IT'S JUST A RABBIT HOLE.
MY FOOT... MY FOOT... IT HURTS!
DON'T MOVE, YOUR TOE IS STUCK. IF YOU KEEP PULLING IT'S JUST GOING TO HURT MORE.

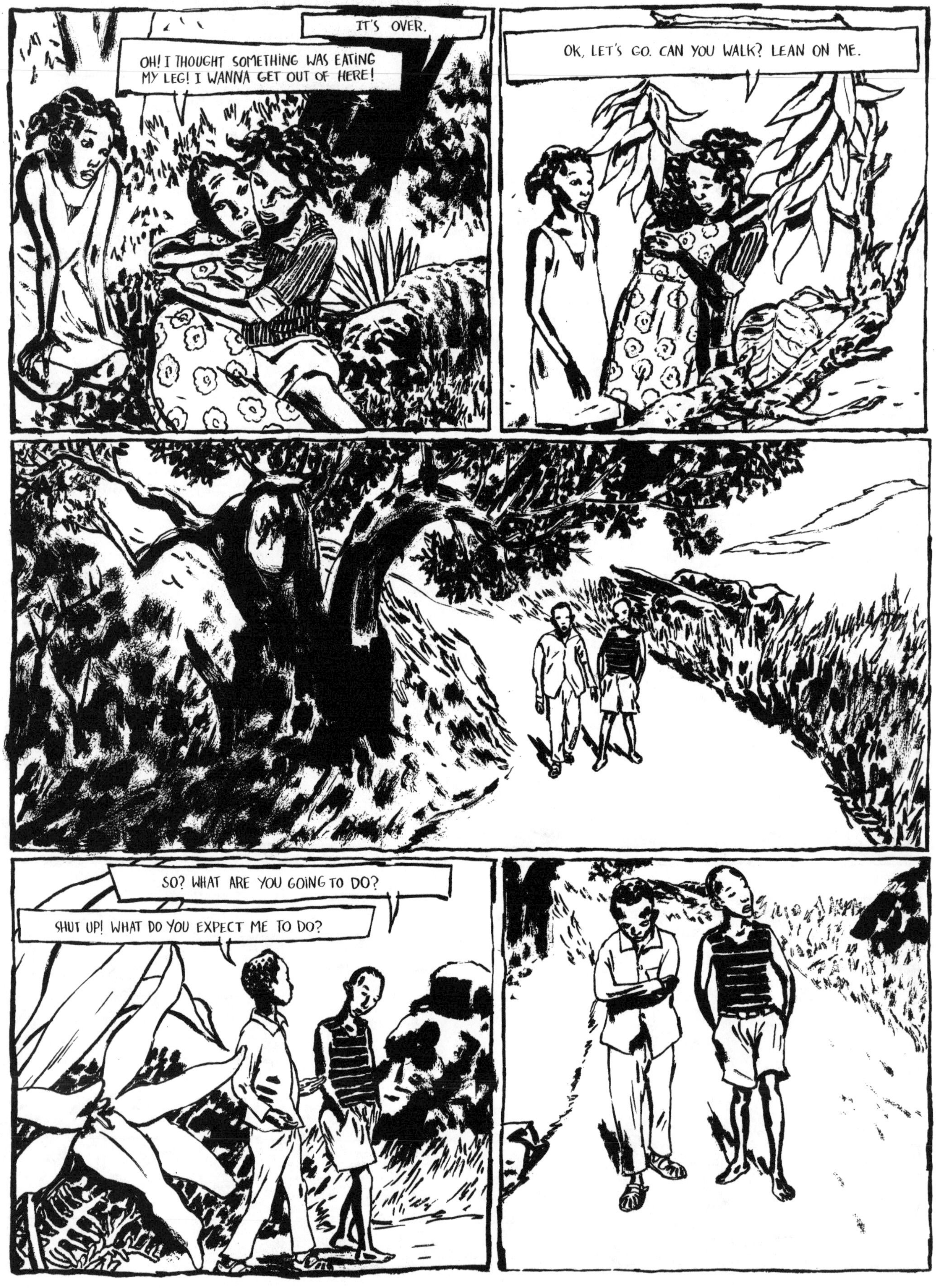
IT'S OVER.
OH! I THOUGHT SOMETHING WAS EATING MY LEG! I WANNA GET OUT OF HERE!
OK, LET'S GO. CAN YOU WALK? LEAN ON ME.
SO? WHAT ARE YOU GOING TO DO?
SHUT UP! WHAT DO YOU EXPECT ME TO DO?

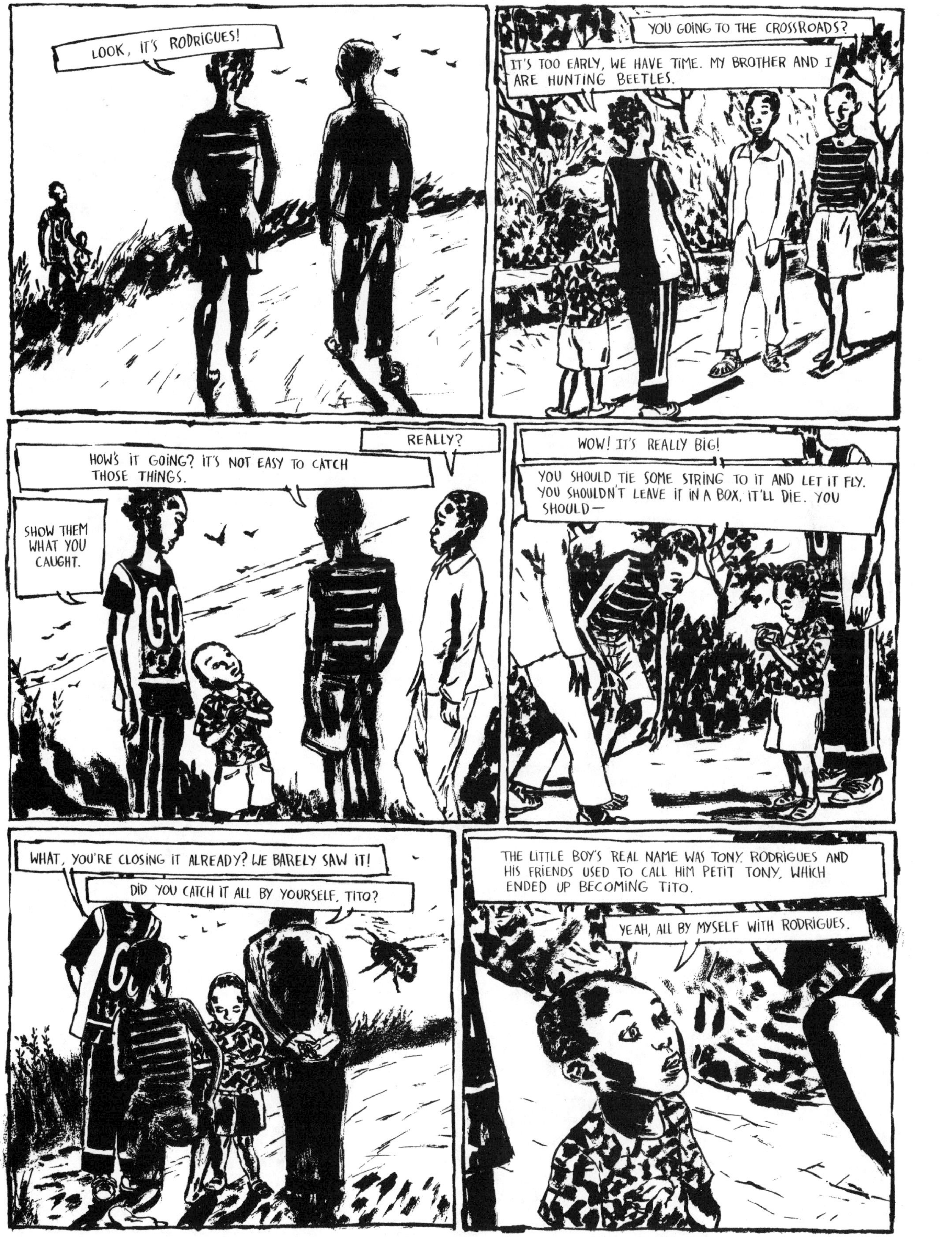
LOOK, IT'S RODRIGUES!
YOU GOING TO THE CROSSROADS?
IT'S TOO EARLY, WE HAVE TIME. MY BROTHER AND I ARE HUNTING BEETLES.
HOW'S IT GOING? IT'S NOT EASY TO CATCH THOSE THINGS.
REALLY?
SHOW THEM WHAT YOU CAUGHT.
WOW! IT'S REALLY BIG!
YOU SHOULD TIE SOME STRING TO IT AND LET IT FLY. YOU SHOULDN'T LEAVE IT IN A BOX, IT'LL DIE. YOU SHOULD—
WHAT, YOU'RE CLOSING IT ALREADY? WE BARELY SAW IT!
DID YOU CATCH IT ALL BY YOURSELF, TITO?
THE LITTLE BOY'S REAL NAME WAS TONY. RODRIGUES AND HIS FRIENDS USED TO CALL HIM PETIT TONY, WHICH ENDED UP BECOMING TITO.
YEAH, ALL BY MYSELF WITH RODRIGUES.

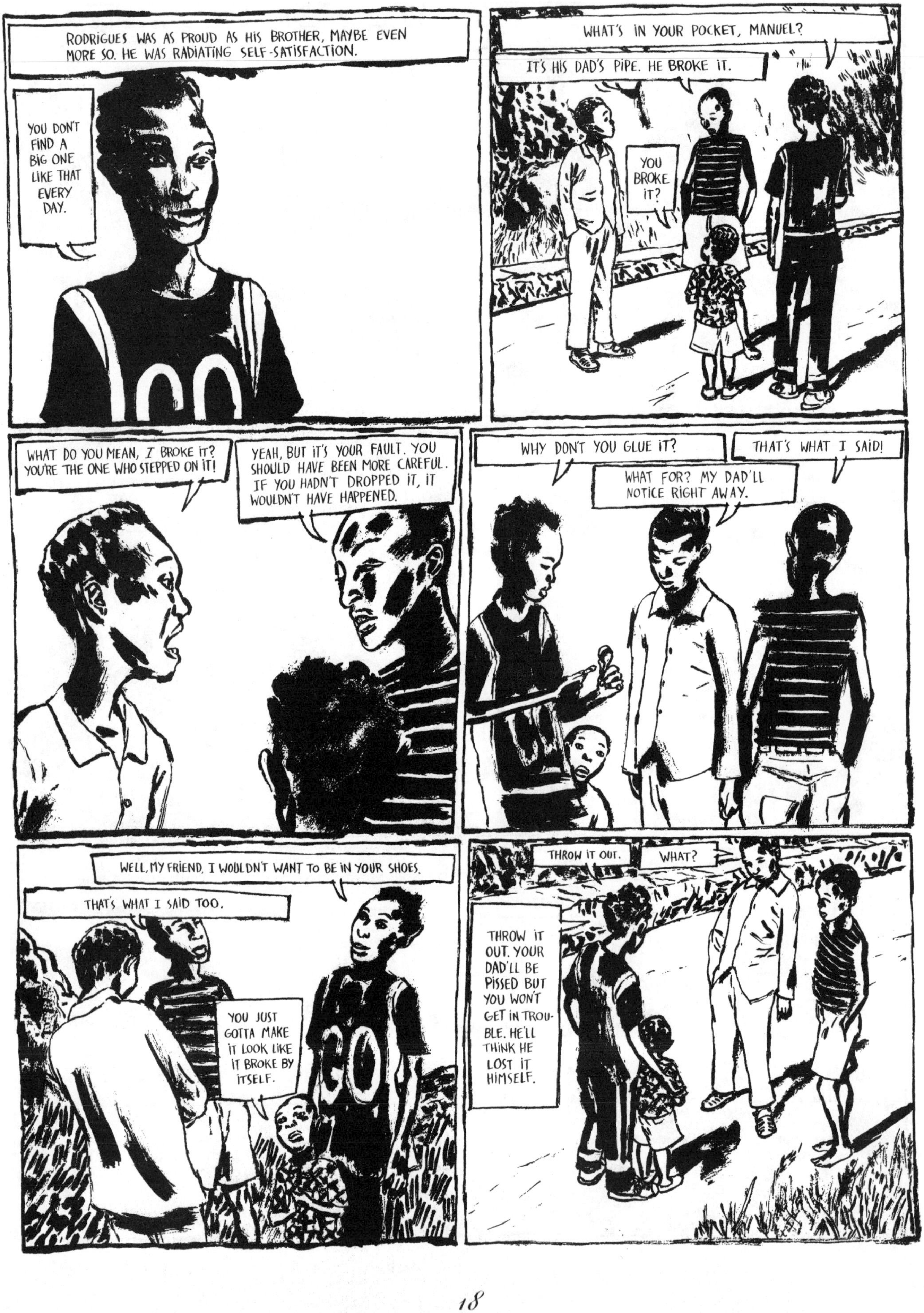
RODRIGUES WAS AS PROUD AS HIS BROTHER, MAYBE EVEN MORE SO. HE WAS RADIATING SELF-SATISFACTION.
YOU DON'T FIND A BIG ONE LIKE THAT EVERY DAY.
WHAT'S IN YOUR POCKET, MANUEL?
IT'S HIS DAD'S PIPE. HE BROKE IT.
YOU BROKE IT?
WHAT DO YOU MEAN, I BROKE IT? YOU'RE THE ONE WHO STEPPED ON IT!
YEAH, BUT IT'S YOUR FAULT. YOU SHOULD HAVE BEEN MORE CAREFUL. IF YOU HADN'T DROPPED IT, IT WOULDN'T HAVE HAPPENED.
WHY DON'T YOU GLUE IT?
THAT'S WHAT I SAID!
WHAT FOR? MY DAD'LL NOTICE RIGHT AWAY.
WELL, MY FRIEND, I WOULDN'T WANT TO BE IN YOUR SHOES.
THAT'S WHAT I SAID TOO.
YOU JUST GOTTA MAKE IT LOOK LIKE IT BROKE BY ITSELF.
THROW IT OUT.
WHAT?
THROW IT OUT. YOUR DAD'LL BE PISSED BUT YOU WON'T GET IN TROUBLE. HE'LL THINK HE LOST IT HIMSELF.

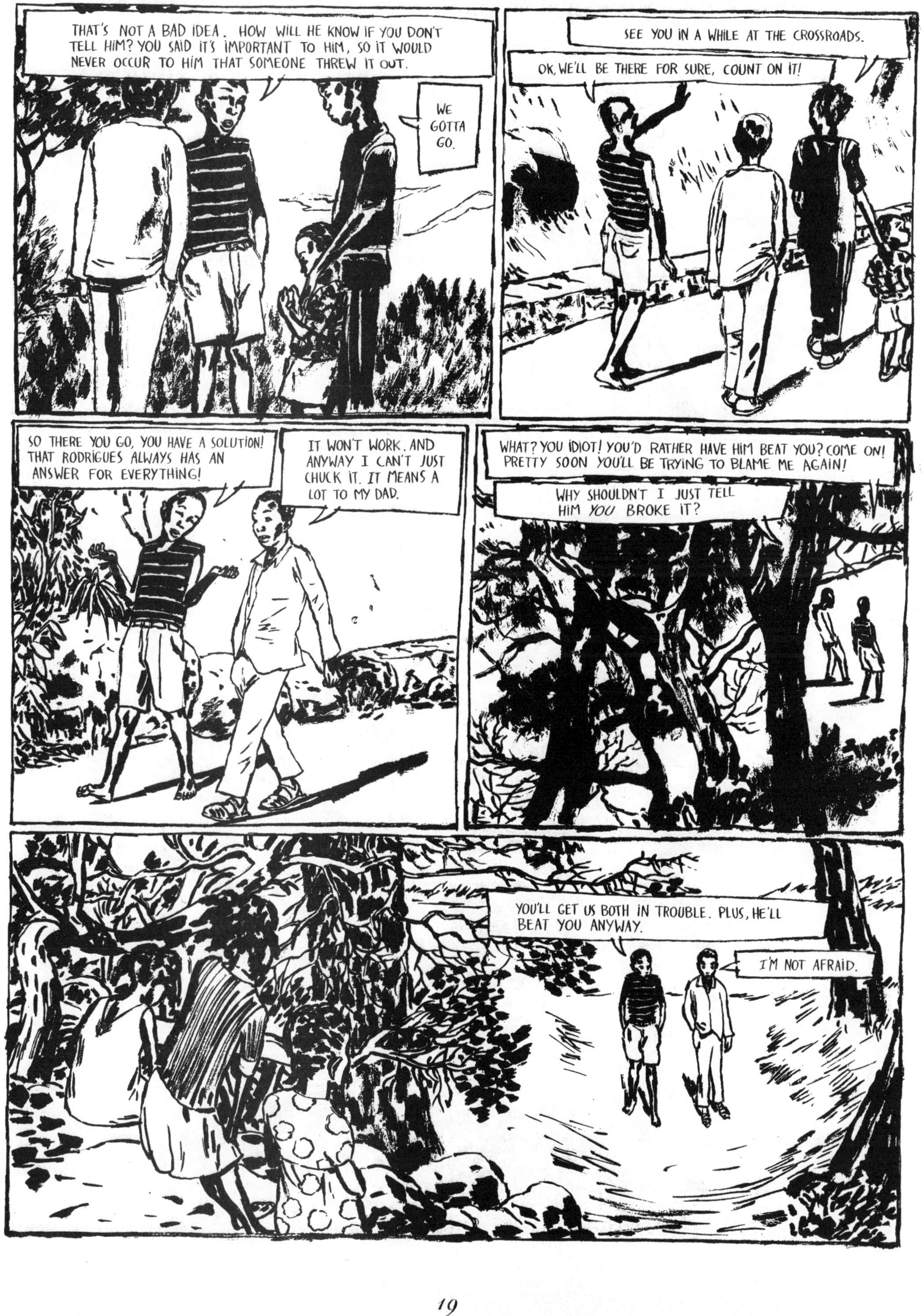
THAT'S NOT A BAD IDEA. HOW WILL HE KNOW IF YOU DON'T TELL HIM? YOU SAID IT'S IMPORTANT TO HIM, SO IT WOULD NEVER OCCUR TO HIM THAT SOMEONE THREW IT OUT.
WE GOTTA GO.
SEE YOU IN A WHILE AT THE CROSSROADS.
OK, WE'LL BE THERE FOR SURE, COUNT ON IT!
SO THERE YOU GO, YOU HAVE A SOLUTION! THAT RODRIGUES ALWAYS HAS AN ANSWER FOR EVERYTHING!
IT WON'T WORK. AND ANYWAY I CAN'T JUST CHUCK IT. IT MEANS A LOT TO MY DAD.
WHAT? YOU IDIOT! YOU'D RATHER HAVE HIM BEAT YOU? COME ON! PRETTY SOON YOU'LL BE TRYING TO BLAME ME AGAIN!
WHY SHOULDN'T I JUST TELL HIM YOU BROKE IT?
YOU'LL GET US BOTH IN TROUBLE. PLUS, HE'LL BEAT YOU ANYWAY.
I'M NOT AFRAID.

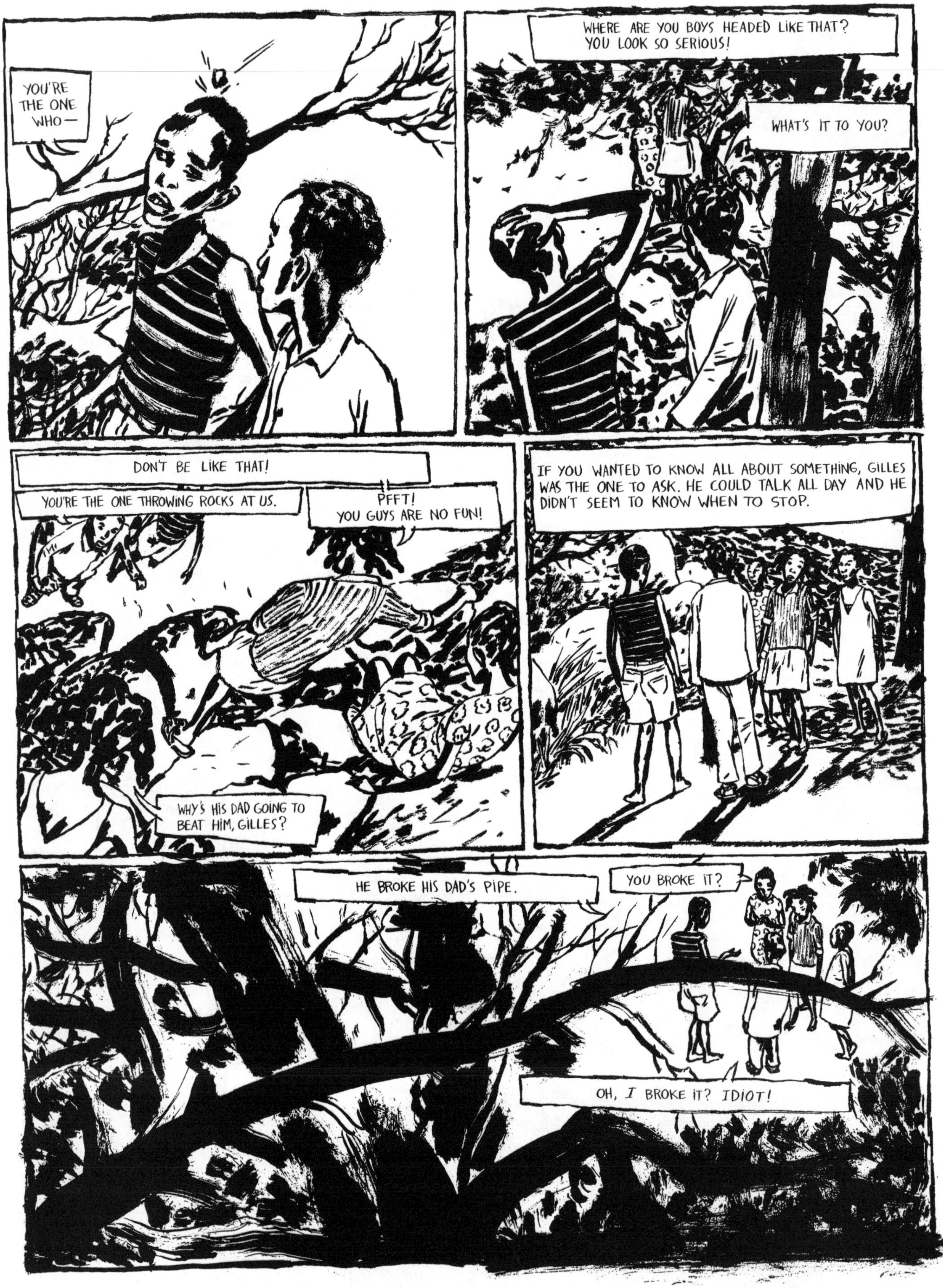
YOU'RE THE ONE WHO—
WHERE ARE YOU BOYS HEADED LIKE THAT? YOU LOOK SO SERIOUS!
WHAT'S IT TO YOU?
DON'T BE LIKE THAT!
YOU'RE THE ONE THROWING ROCKS AT US.
PFFT! YOU GUYS ARE NO FUN!
WHY'S HIS DAD GOING TO BEAT HIM, GILLES?
IF YOU WANTED TO KNOW ALL ABOUT SOMETHING, GILLES WAS THE ONE TO ASK. HE COULD TALK ALL DAY AND HE DIDN'T SEEM TO KNOW WHEN TO STOP.
HE BROKE HIS DAD'S PIPE.
YOU BROKE IT?
OH, *I* BROKE IT? IDIOT!

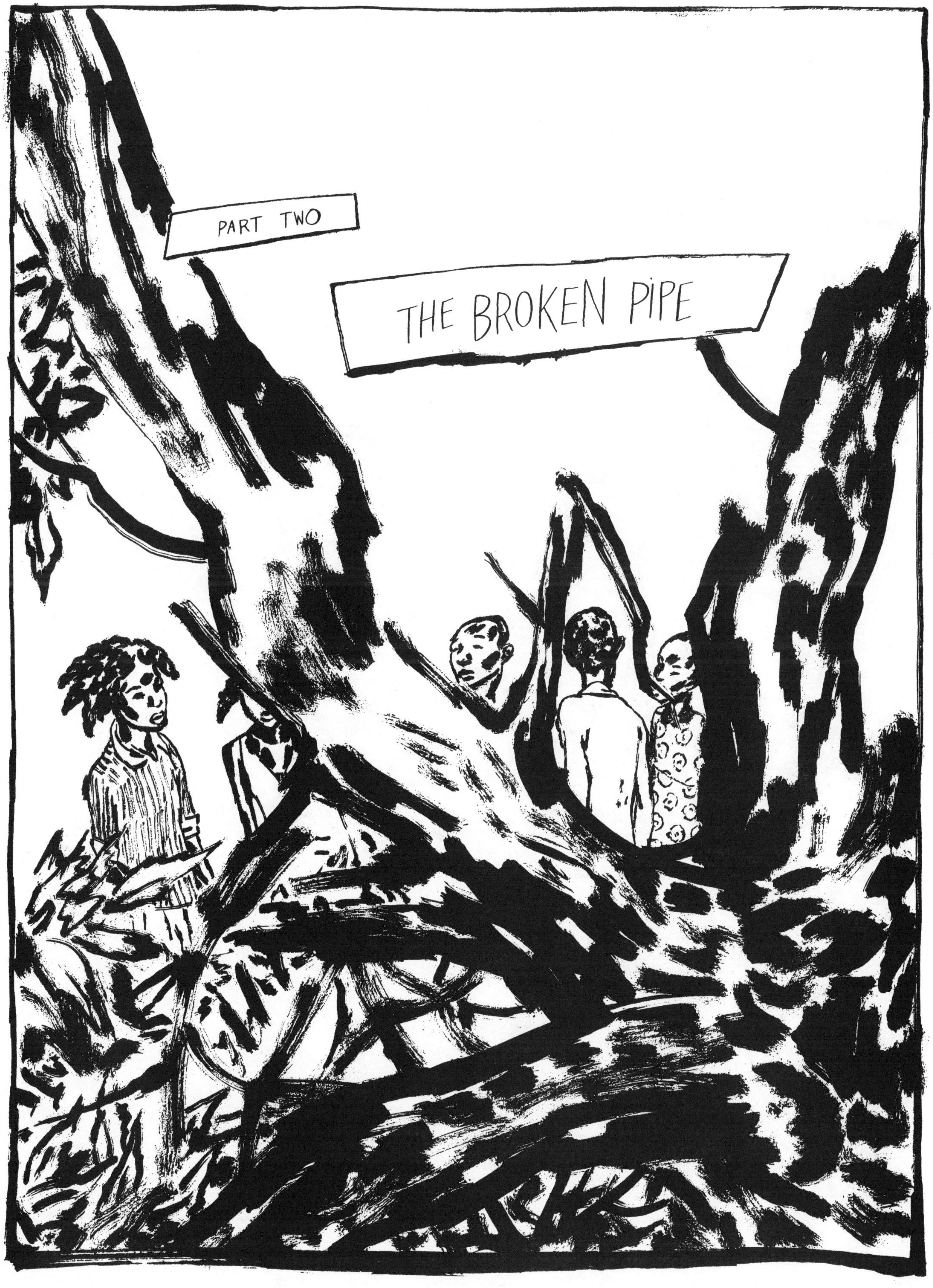
PART TWO
THE BROKEN PIPE

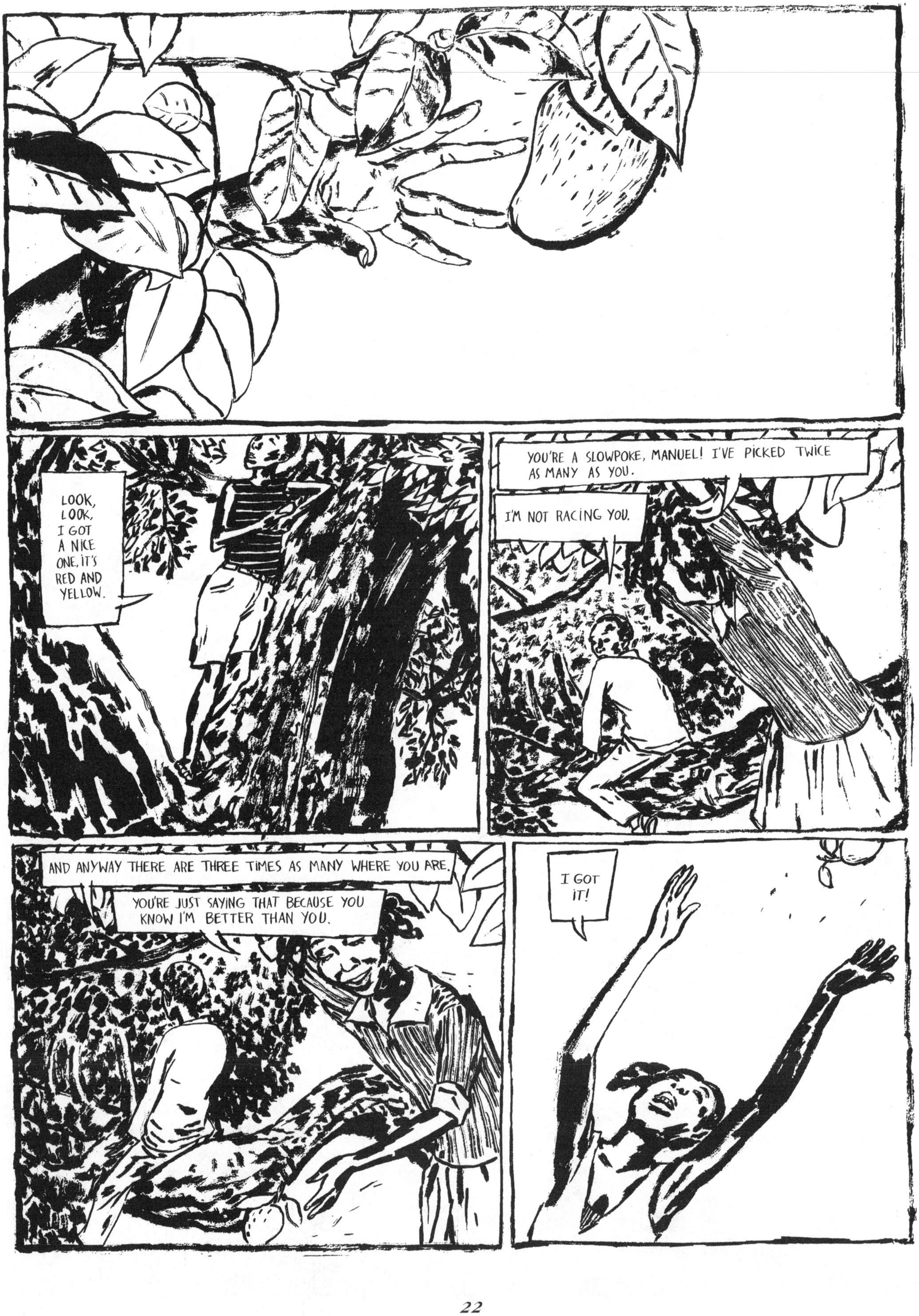
LOOK, LOOK, I GOT A NICE ONE, IT'S RED AND YELLOW.
YOU'RE A SLOWPOKE, MANUEL! I'VE PICKED TWICE AS MANY AS YOU.
I'M NOT RACING YOU.
AND ANYWAY THERE ARE THREE TIMES AS MANY WHERE YOU ARE.
YOU'RE JUST SAYING THAT BECAUSE YOU KNOW I'M BETTER THAN YOU.
I GOT IT!

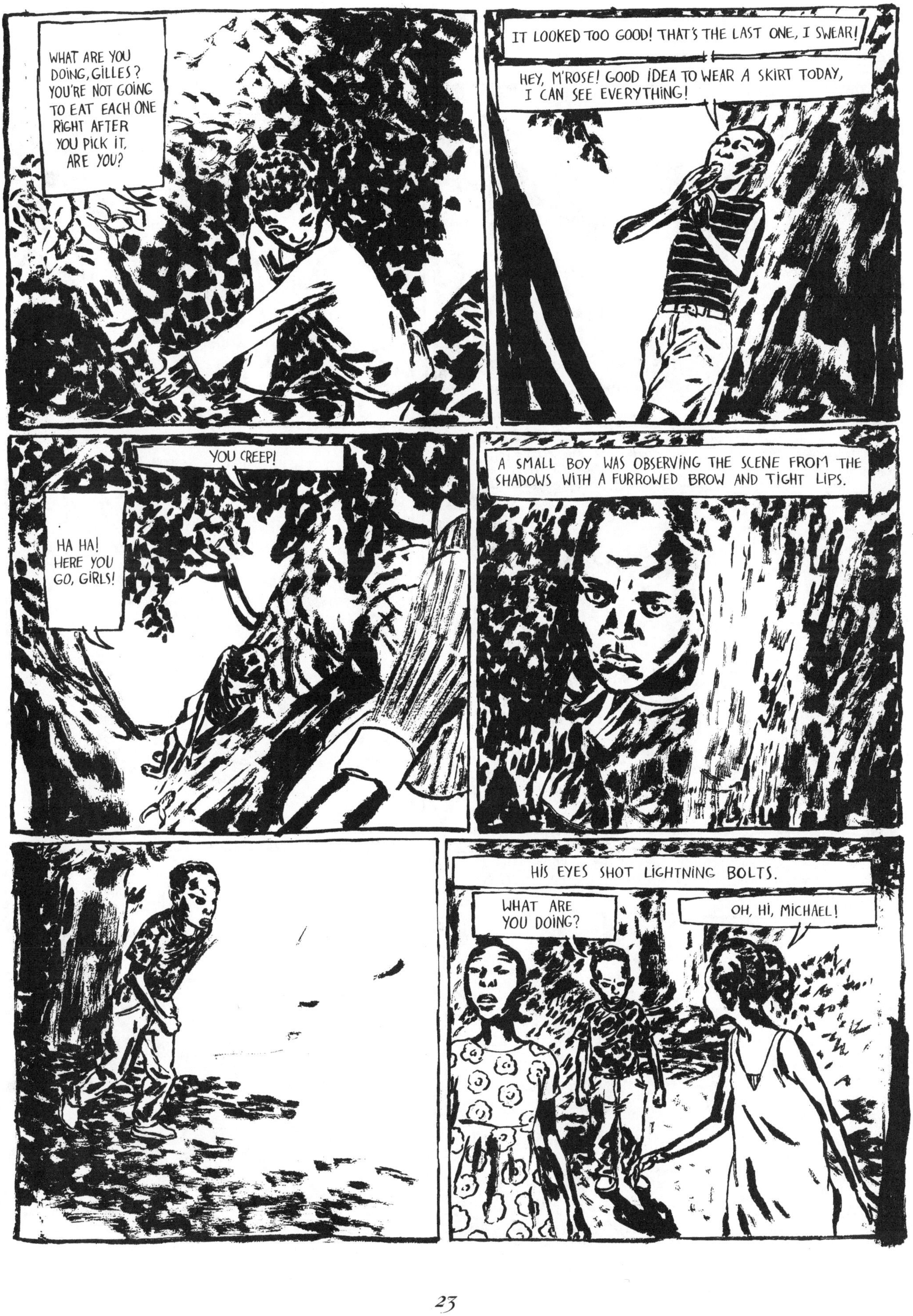

WHAT ARE YOU DOING, GILLES? YOU'RE NOT GOING TO EAT EACH ONE RIGHT AFTER YOU PICK IT, ARE YOU?
IT LOOKED TOO GOOD! THAT'S THE LAST ONE, I SWEAR!
HEY, M'ROSE! GOOD IDEA TO WEAR A SKIRT TODAY, I CAN SEE EVERYTHING!
YOU CREEP!
HA HA! HERE YOU GO, GIRLS!
A SMALL BOY WAS OBSERVING THE SCENE FROM THE SHADOWS WITH A FURROWED BROW AND TIGHT LIPS.
HIS EYES SHOT LIGHTNING BOLTS.
WHAT ARE YOU DOING?
OH, HI, MICHAEL!

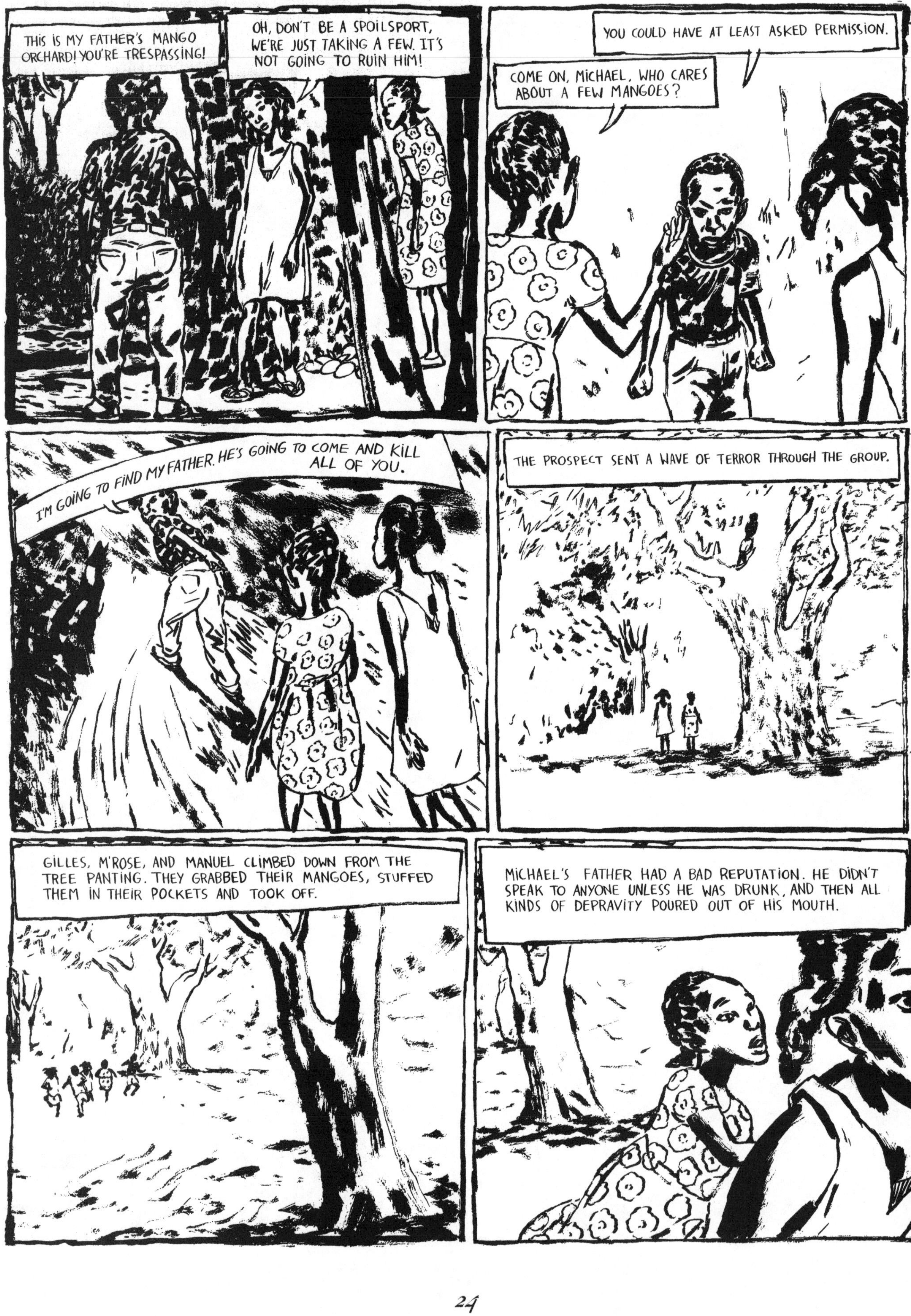
THIS IS MY FATHER'S MANGO ORCHARD! YOU'RE TRESPASSING!
OH, DON'T BE A SPOILSPORT, WE'RE JUST TAKING A FEW. IT'S NOT GOING TO RUIN HIM!
YOU COULD HAVE AT LEAST ASKED PERMISSION.
COME ON, MICHAEL, WHO CARES ABOUT A FEW MANGOES?
I'M GOING TO FIND MY FATHER. HE'S GOING TO COME AND KILL ALL OF YOU.
THE PROSPECT SENT A WAVE OF TERROR THROUGH THE GROUP.
GILLES, M'ROSE, AND MANUEL CLIMBED DOWN FROM THE TREE PANTING. THEY GRABBED THEIR MANGOES, STUFFED THEM IN THEIR POCKETS AND TOOK OFF.
MICHAEL'S FATHER HAD A BAD REPUTATION. HE DIDN'T SPEAK TO ANYONE UNLESS HE WAS DRUNK, AND THEN ALL KINDS OF DEPRAVITY POURED OUT OF HIS MOUTH.

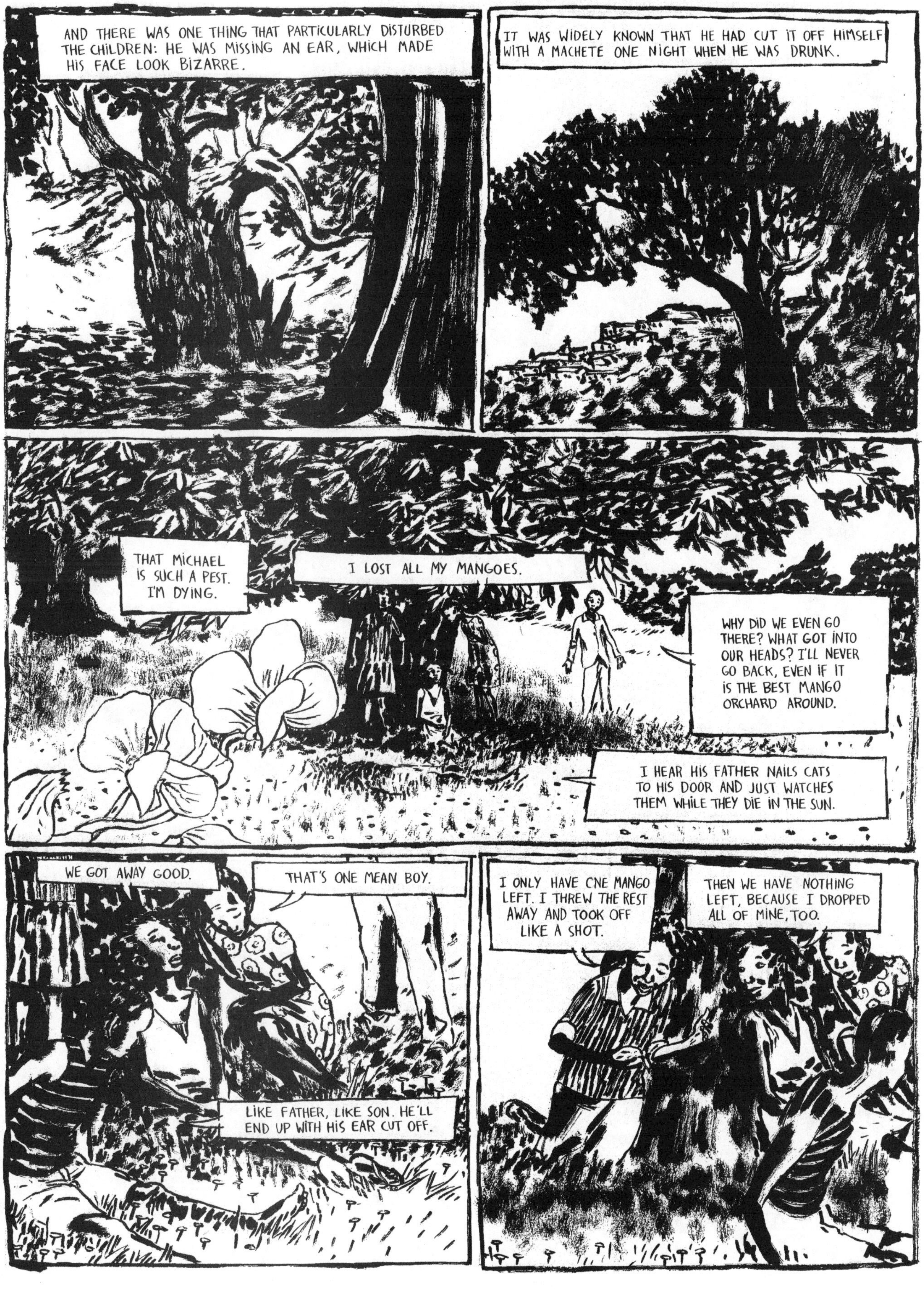
AND THERE WAS ONE THING THAT PARTICULARLY DISTURBED THE CHILDREN: HE WAS MISSING AN EAR, WHICH MADE HIS FACE LOOK BIZARRE.
IT WAS WIDELY KNOWN THAT HE HAD CUT IT OFF HIMSELF WITH A MACHETE ONE NIGHT WHEN HE WAS DRUNK.
THAT MICHAEL IS SUCH A PEST. I'M DYING.
I LOST ALL MY MANGOES.
WHY DID WE EVEN GO THERE? WHAT GOT INTO OUR HEADS? I'LL NEVER GO BACK, EVEN IF IT IS THE BEST MANGO ORCHARD AROUND.
I HEAR HIS FATHER NAILS CATS TO HIS DOOR AND JUST WATCHES THEM WHILE THEY DIE IN THE SUN.
WE GOT AWAY GOOD.
THAT'S ONE MEAN BOY.
LIKE FATHER, LIKE SON. HE'LL END UP WITH HIS EAR CUT OFF.
I ONLY HAVE ONE MANGO LEFT. I THREW THE REST AWAY AND TOOK OFF LIKE A SHOT.
THEN WE HAVE NOTHING LEFT, BECAUSE I DROPPED ALL OF MINE, TOO.

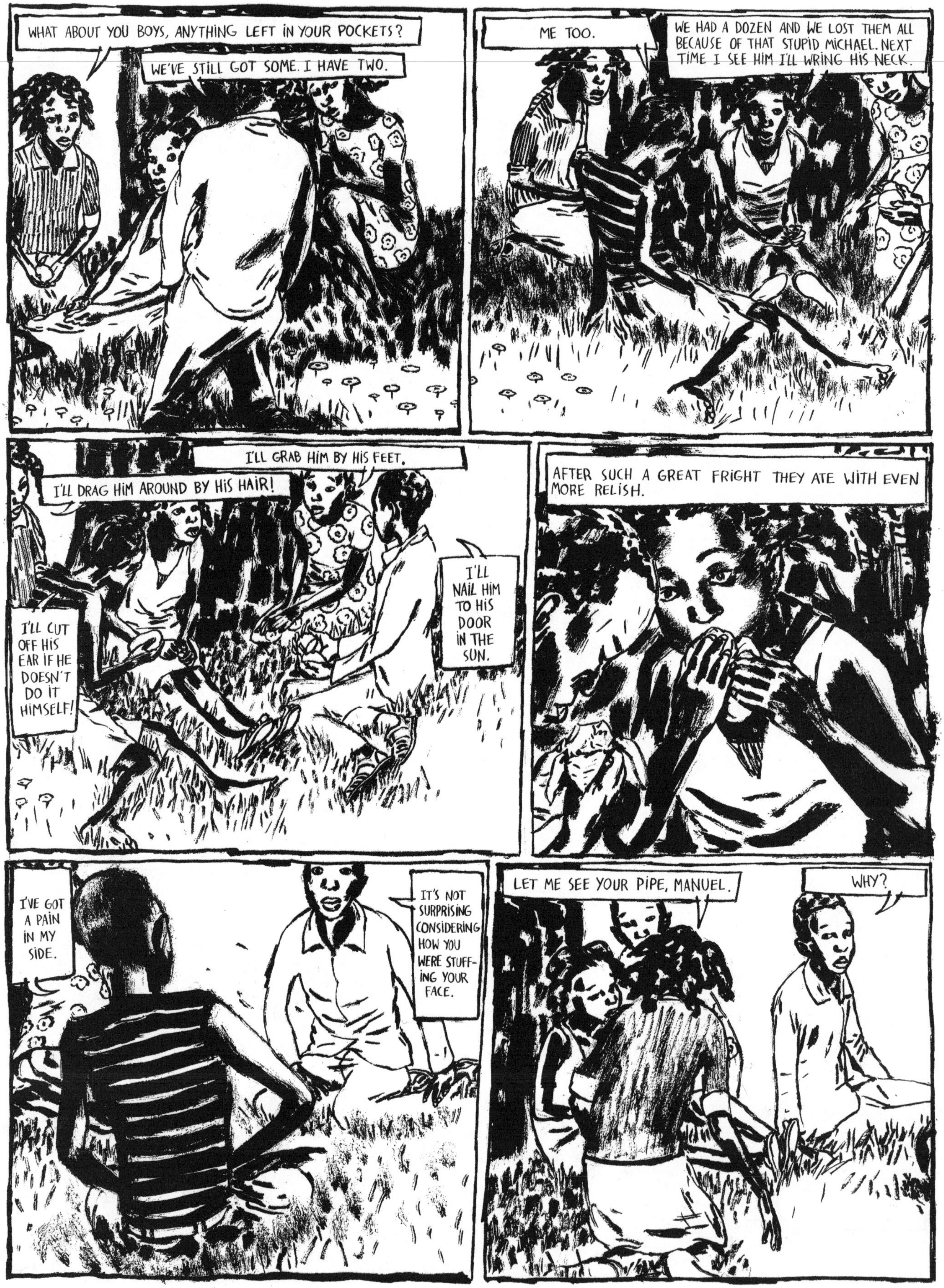
WHAT ABOUT YOU BOYS, ANYTHING LEFT IN YOUR POCKETS?
WE'VE STILL GOT SOME. I HAVE TWO.
ME TOO.
WE HAD A DOZEN AND WE LOST THEM ALL BECAUSE OF THAT STUPID MICHAEL. NEXT TIME I SEE HIM I'LL WRING HIS NECK.
I'LL GRAB HIM BY HIS FEET.
I'LL DRAG HIM AROUND BY HIS HAIR!
I'LL CUT OFF HIS EAR IF HE DOESN'T DO IT HIMSELF!
I'LL NAIL HIM TO HIS DOOR IN THE SUN.
AFTER SUCH A GREAT FRIGHT THEY ATE WITH EVEN MORE RELISH.
I'VE GOT A PAIN IN MY SIDE.
IT'S NOT SURPRISING CONSIDERING HOW YOU WERE STUFF-ING YOUR FACE.
LET ME SEE YOUR PIPE, MANUEL.
WHY?

DO YOU HAVE TOBACCO AND MATCHES?
YOU WANT TO SMOKE? I TOLD YOU, IT'S BROKEN.
LET'S SEE. MAYBE WE CAN FIGURE SOMETHING OUT.
LET HER TRY, MANUEL. IT WOULD BE DUMB TO STEAL IT AND NOT TRY IT OUT.
YOU SEE, HOLDING IT LIKE THIS. DO YOU KNOW HOW TO LIGHT IT?
SURE I KNOW!
NOT BAD. IT'S SO SIMPLE, WHY DIDN'T WE THINK OF IT?
YOU HAVE TO SUCK IN AT THE SAME TIME. OTHERWISE IT WON'T WORK.
THAT'S WHAT I'M DOING.
YOU ARE NOT! YOU WOULDN'T BE ABLE TO TALK IF YOU WERE.
THERE.
NOTHING'S COMING OUT.
YOU'RE NOT SUPPOSED TO INHALE THE SMOKE; BLOW IT OUT AS SOON AS IT'S IN YOUR MOUTH!

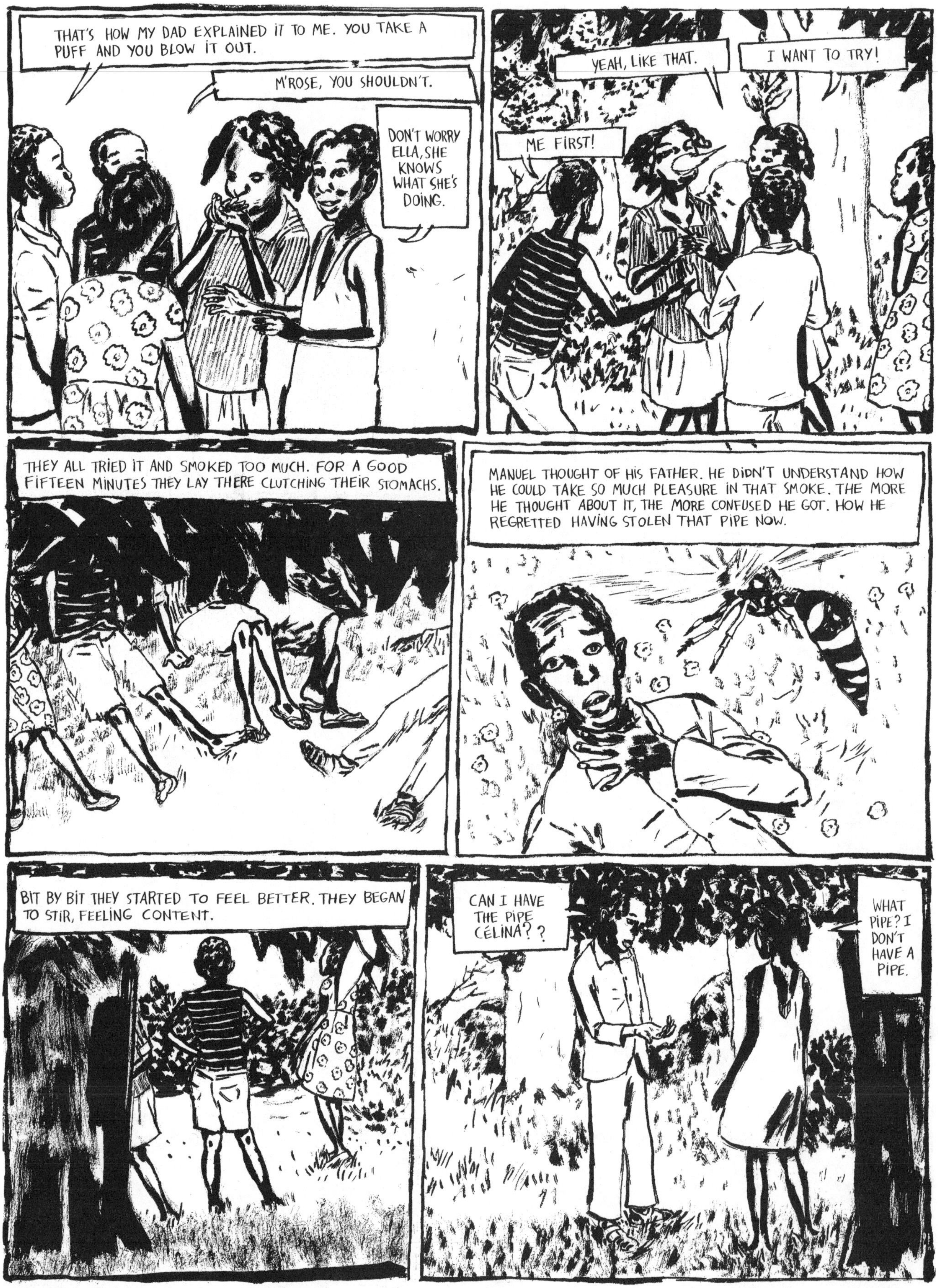
THAT'S HOW MY DAD EXPLAINED IT TO ME. YOU TAKE A PUFF AND YOU BLOW IT OUT.
M'ROSE, YOU SHOULDN'T.
DON'T WORRY ELLA, SHE KNOWS WHAT SHE'S DOING.
YEAH, LIKE THAT.
I WANT TO TRY!
ME FIRST!
THEY ALL TRIED IT AND SMOKED TOO MUCH. FOR A GOOD FIFTEEN MINUTES THEY LAY THERE CLUTCHING THEIR STOMACHS.
MANUEL THOUGHT OF HIS FATHER. HE DIDN'T UNDERSTAND HOW HE COULD TAKE SO MUCH PLEASURE IN THAT SMOKE. THE MORE HE THOUGHT ABOUT IT, THE MORE CONFUSED HE GOT. HOW HE REGRETTED HAVING STOLEN THAT PIPE NOW.
BIT BY BIT THEY STARTED TO FEEL BETTER. THEY BEGAN TO STIR, FEELING CONTENT.
CAN I HAVE THE PIPE CÉLINA? ?
WHAT PIPE? I DON'T HAVE A PIPE.

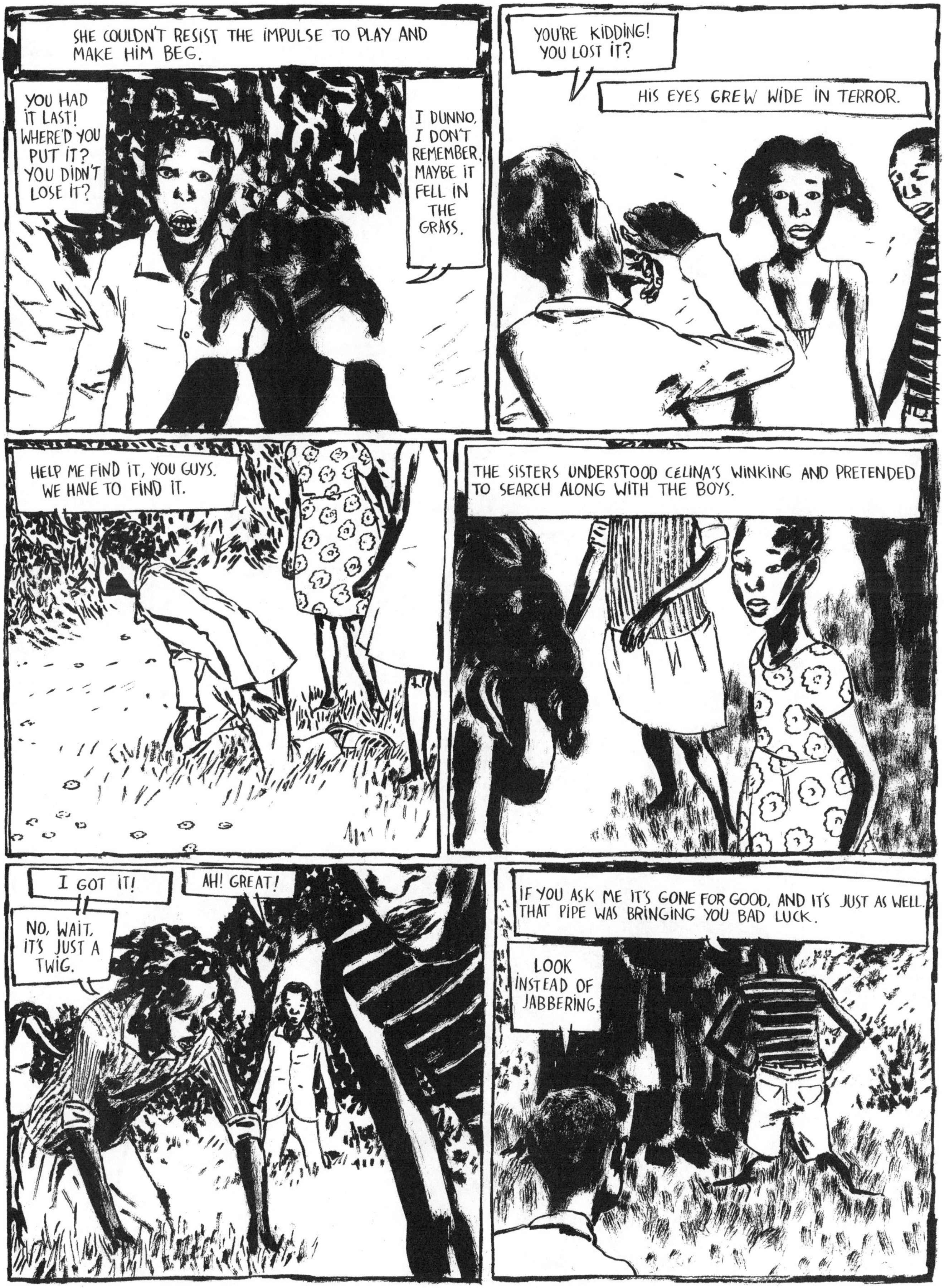
SHE COULDN'T RESIST THE IMPULSE TO PLAY AND MAKE HIM BEG.
YOU HAD IT LAST! WHERE'D YOU PUT IT? YOU DIDN'T LOSE IT?
I DUNNO, I DON'T REMEMBER. MAYBE IT FELL IN THE GRASS.
YOU'RE KIDDING! YOU LOST IT?
HIS EYES GREW WIDE IN TERROR.
HELP ME FIND IT, YOU GUYS. WE HAVE TO FIND IT.
THE SISTERS UNDERSTOOD CÉLINA'S WINKING AND PRETENDED TO SEARCH ALONG WITH THE BOYS.
I GOT IT!
AH! GREAT!
NO, WAIT, IT'S JUST A TWIG.
IF YOU ASK ME IT'S GONE FOR GOOD, AND IT'S JUST AS WELL. THAT PIPE WAS BRINGING YOU BAD LUCK.
LOOK INSTEAD OF JABBERING.

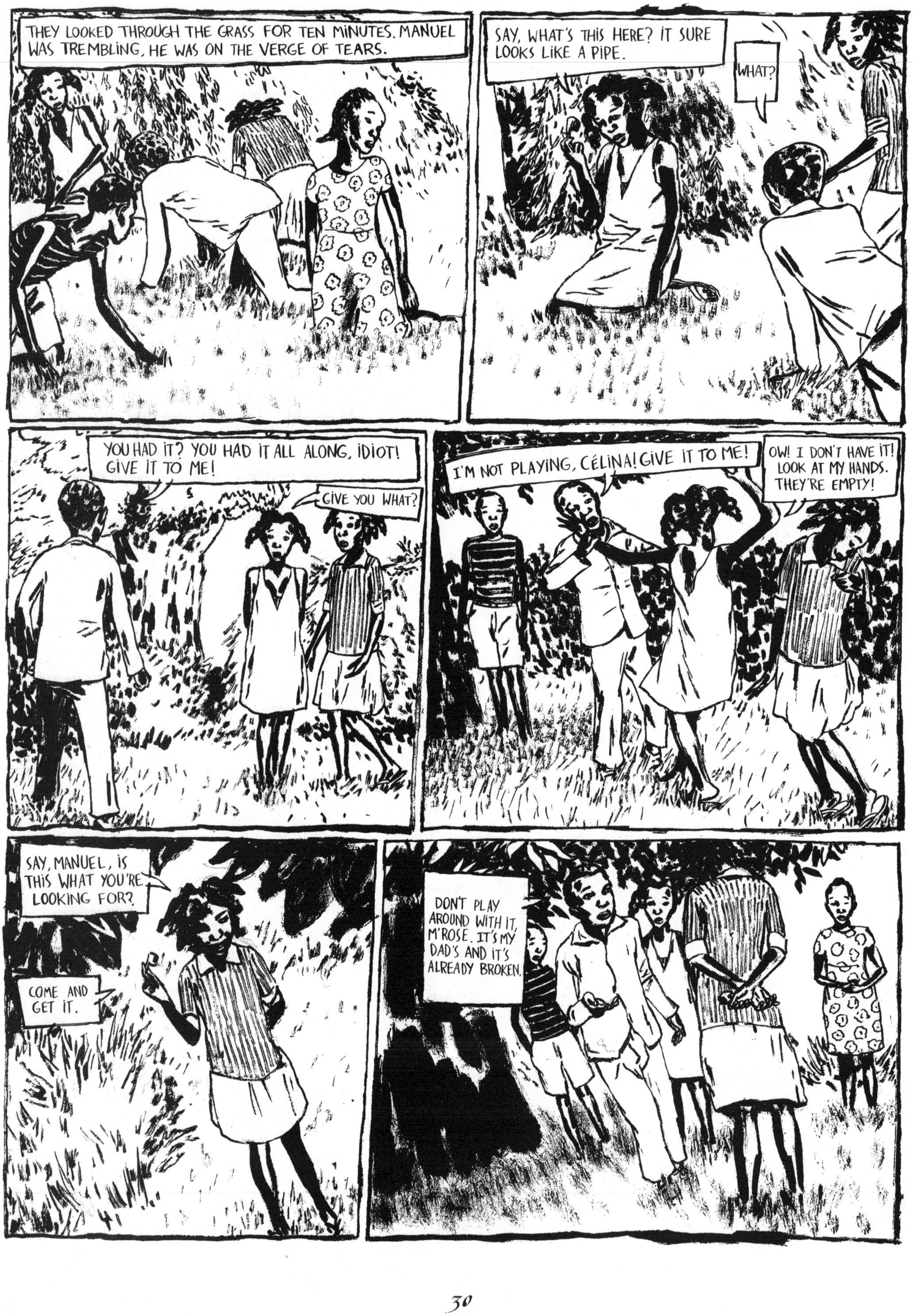
THEY LOOKED THROUGH THE GRASS FOR TEN MINUTES. MANUEL WAS TREMBLING, HE WAS ON THE VERGE OF TEARS.
SAY, WHAT'S THIS HERE? IT SURE LOOKS LIKE A PIPE.
WHAT?
YOU HAD IT? YOU HAD IT ALL ALONG, IDIOT! GIVE IT TO ME!
GIVE YOU WHAT?
I'M NOT PLAYING, CÉLINA! GIVE IT TO ME!
OW! I DON'T HAVE IT! LOOK AT MY HANDS. THEY'RE EMPTY!
SAY, MANUEL, IS THIS WHAT YOU'RE LOOKING FOR?
COME AND GET IT.
DON'T PLAY AROUND WITH IT, M'ROSE. IT'S MY DAD'S AND IT'S ALREADY BROKEN.

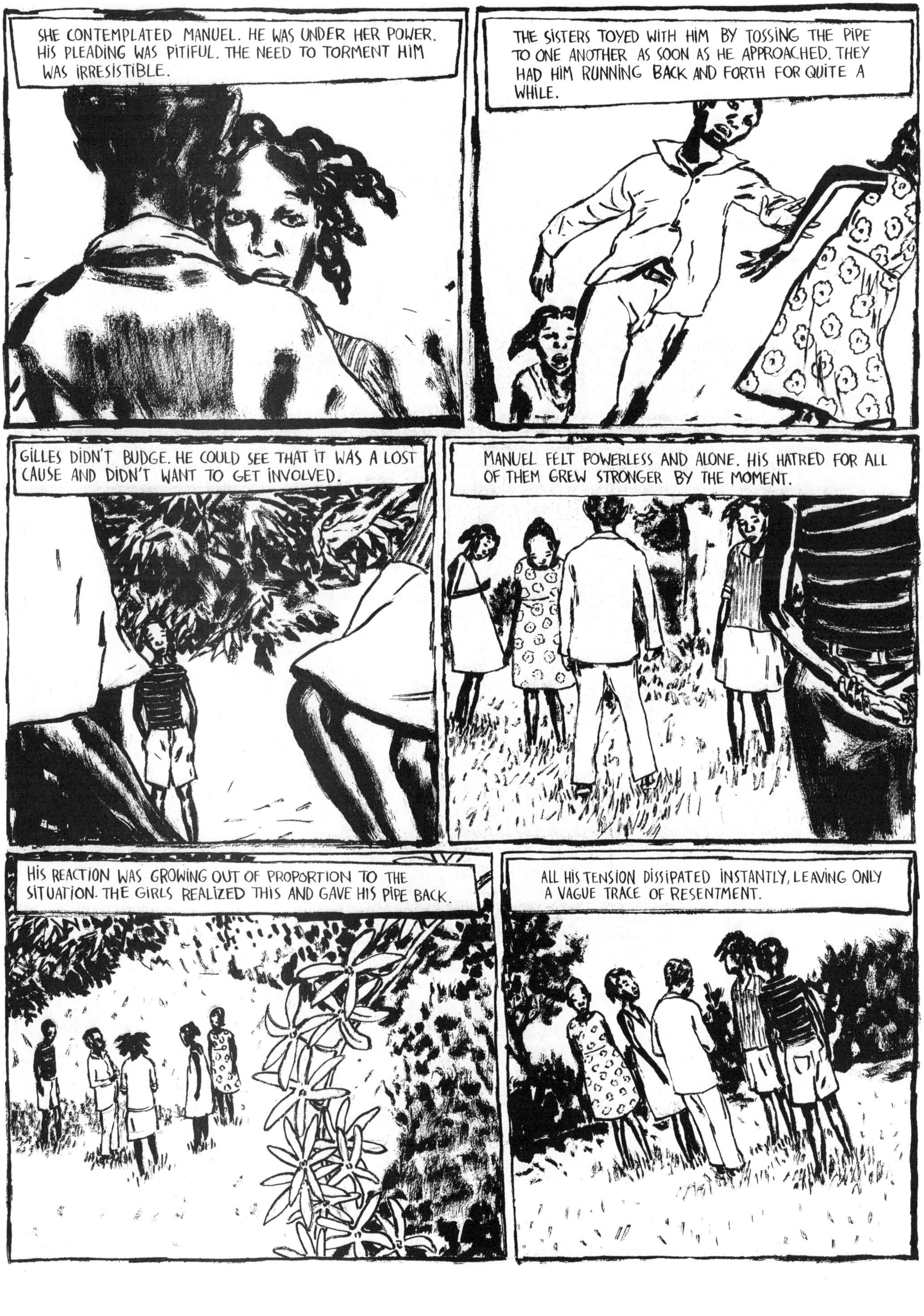
SHE CONTEMPLATED MANUEL. HE WAS UNDER HER POWER. HIS PLEADING WAS PITIFUL. THE NEED TO TORMENT HIM WAS IRRESISTIBLE.
THE SISTERS TOYED WITH HIM BY TOSSING THE PIPE TO ONE ANOTHER AS SOON AS HE APPROACHED. THEY HAD HIM RUNNING BACK AND FORTH FOR QUITE A WHILE.
GILLES DIDN'T BUDGE. HE COULD SEE THAT IT WAS A LOST CAUSE AND DIDN'T WANT TO GET INVOLVED.
MANUEL FELT POWERLESS AND ALONE. HIS HATRED FOR ALL OF THEM GREW STRONGER BY THE MOMENT.
HIS REACTION WAS GROWING OUT OF PROPORTION TO THE SITUATION. THE GIRLS REALIZED THIS AND GAVE HIS PIPE BACK.
ALL HIS TENSION DISSIPATED INSTANTLY, LEAVING ONLY A VAGUE TRACE OF RESENTMENT.

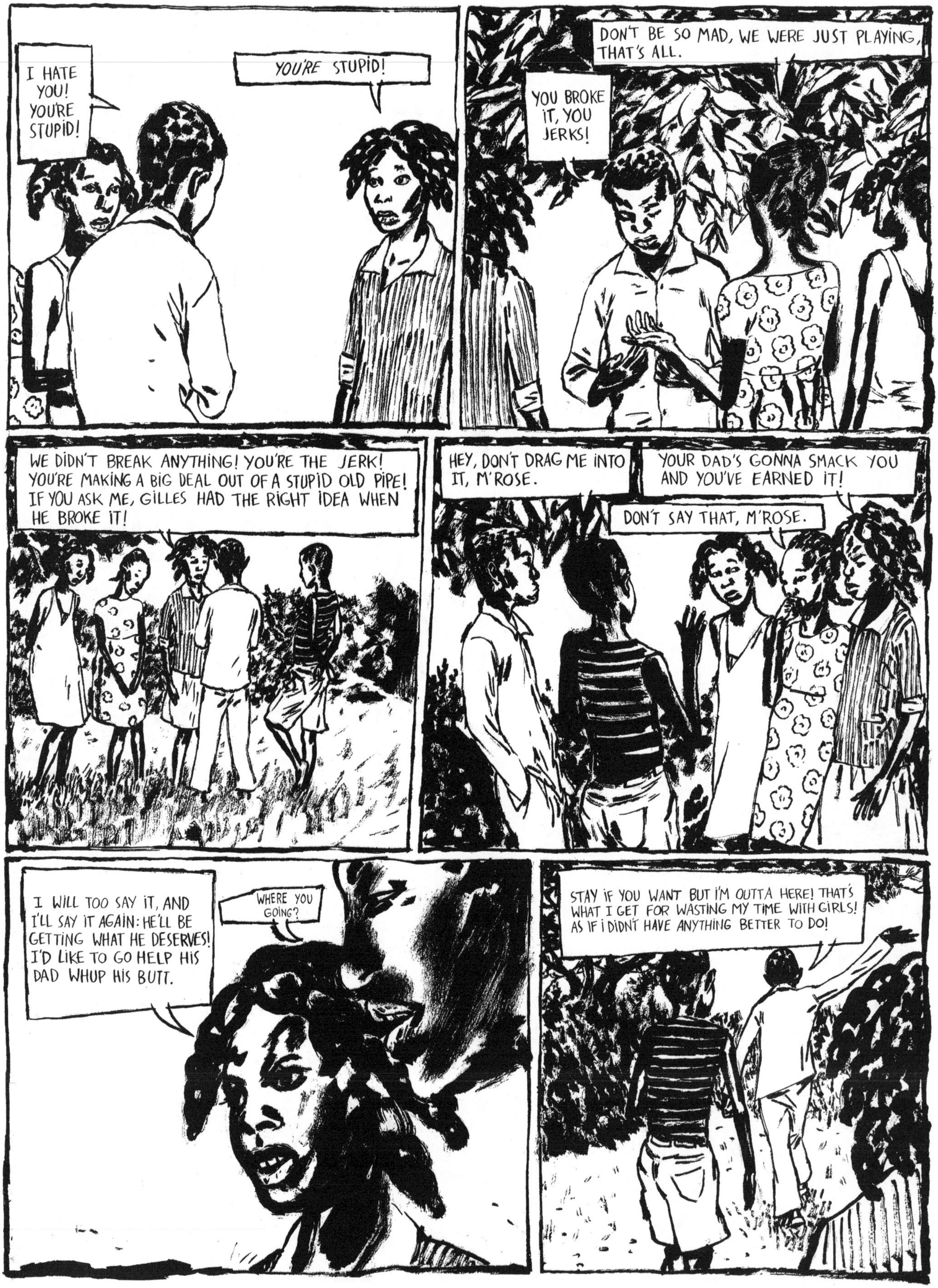

I HATE YOU! YOU'RE STUPID!
YOU'RE STUPID!
DON'T BE SO MAD, WE WERE JUST PLAYING, THAT'S ALL.
YOU BROKE IT, YOU JERKS!
WE DIDN'T BREAK ANYTHING! YOU'RE THE JERK! YOU'RE MAKING A BIG DEAL OUT OF A STUPID OLD PIPE! IF YOU ASK ME, GILLES HAD THE RIGHT IDEA WHEN HE BROKE IT!
HEY, DON'T DRAG ME INTO IT, M'ROSE.
YOUR DAD'S GONNA SMACK YOU AND YOU'VE EARNED IT!
DON'T SAY THAT, M'ROSE.
I WILL TOO SAY IT, AND I'LL SAY IT AGAIN: HE'LL BE GETTING WHAT HE DESERVES! I'D LIKE TO GO HELP HIS DAD WHUP HIS BUTT.
WHERE YOU GOING?
STAY IF YOU WANT BUT I'M OUTTA HERE! THAT'S WHAT I GET FOR WASTING MY TIME WITH GIRLS! AS IF I DIDN'T HAVE ANYTHING BETTER TO DO!

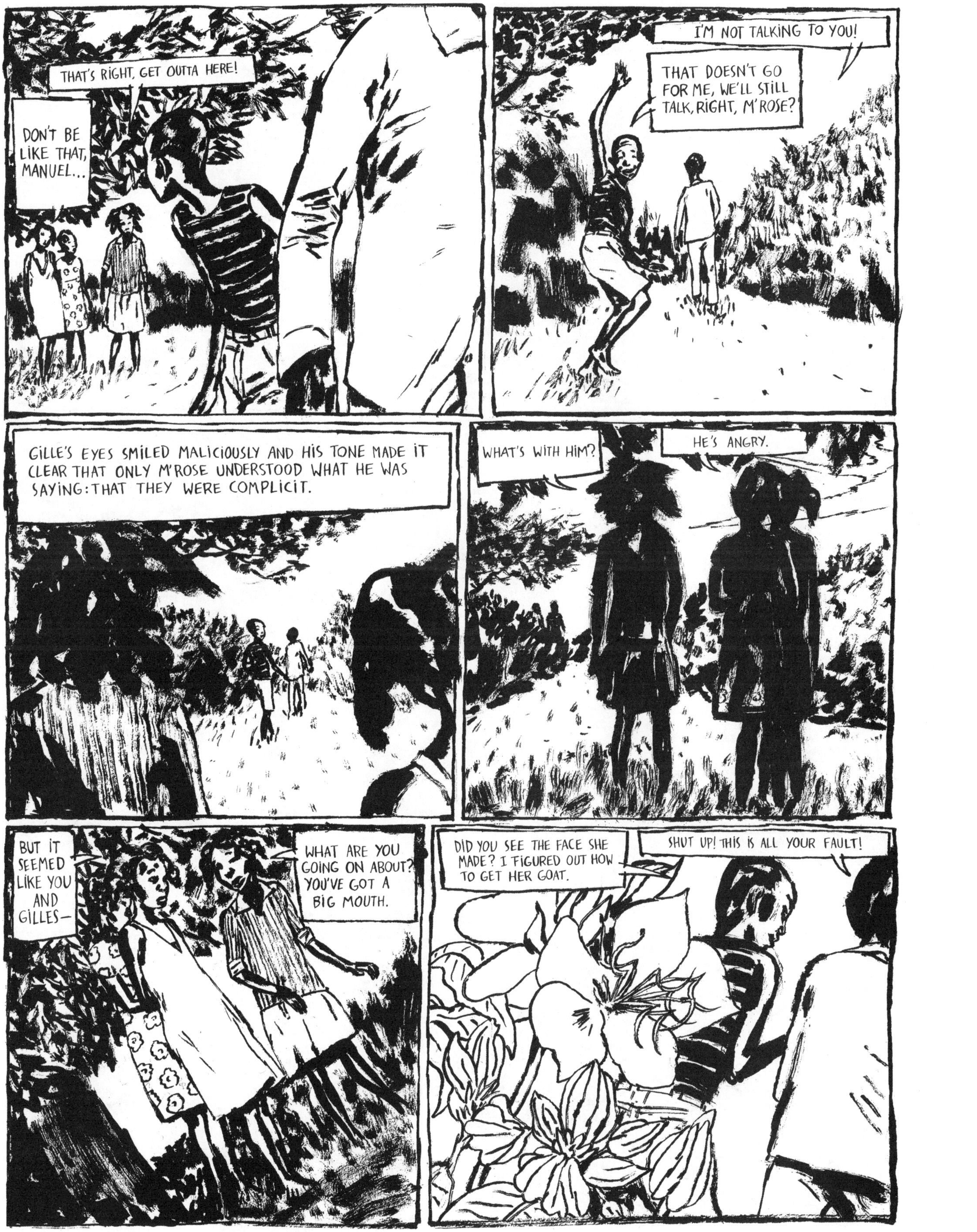
THAT'S RIGHT, GET OUTTA HERE!
DON'T BE LIKE THAT, MANUEL...
I'M NOT TALKING TO YOU!
THAT DOESN'T GO FOR ME, WE'LL STILL TALK, RIGHT, M'ROSE?
GILLE'S EYES SMILED MALICIOUSLY AND HIS TONE MADE IT CLEAR THAT ONLY M'ROSE UNDERSTOOD WHAT HE WAS SAYING: THAT THEY WERE COMPLICIT.
WHAT'S WITH HIM?
HE'S ANGRY.
BUT IT SEEMED LIKE YOU AND GILLES—
WHAT ARE YOU GOING ON ABOUT? YOU'VE GOT A BIG MOUTH.
DID YOU SEE THE FACE SHE MADE? I FIGURED OUT HOW TO GET HER GOAT.
SHUT UP! THIS IS ALL YOUR FAULT!

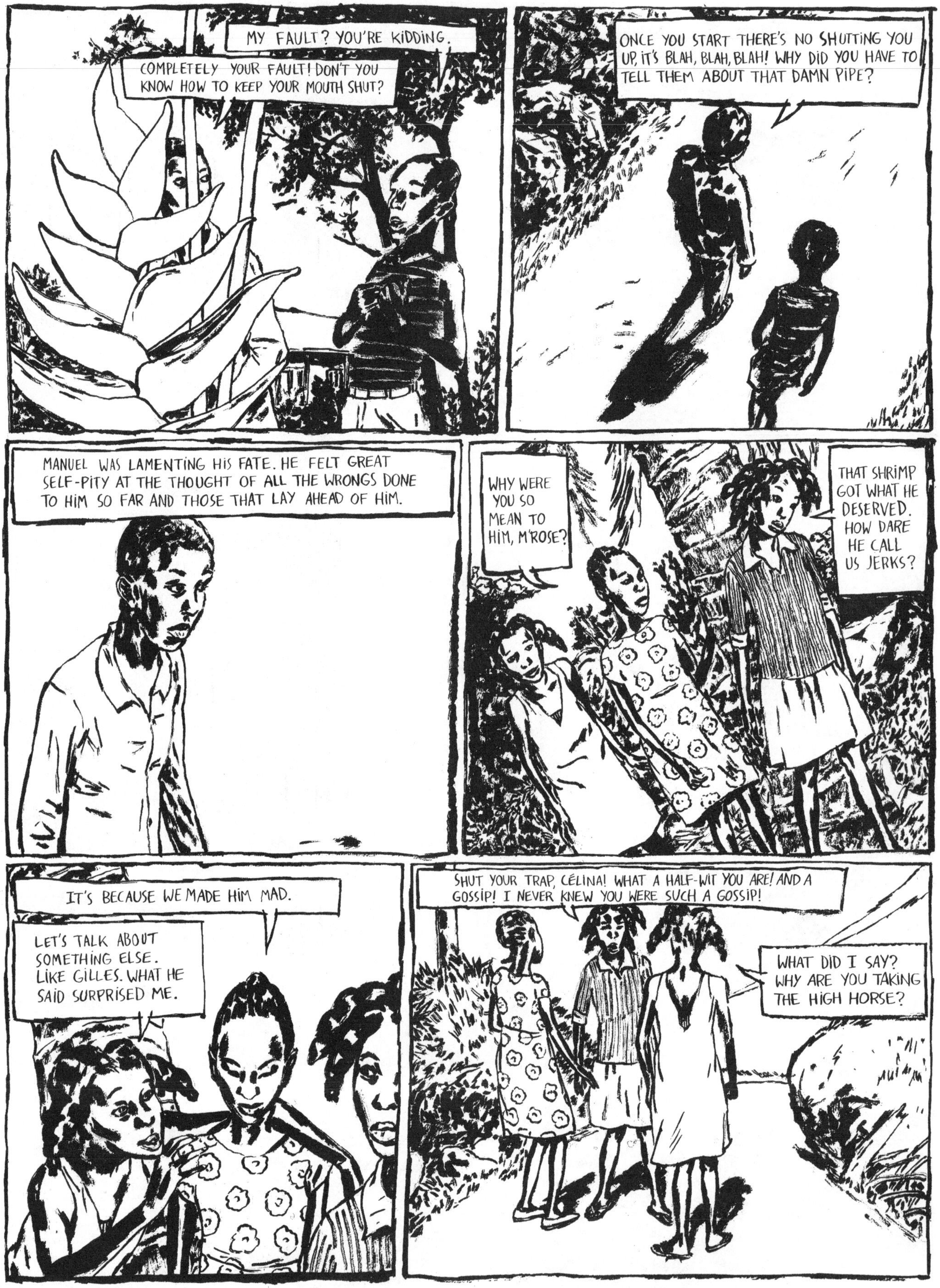
MY FAULT? YOU'RE KIDDING.
COMPLETELY YOUR FAULT! DON'T YOU KNOW HOW TO KEEP YOUR MOUTH SHUT?
ONCE YOU START THERE'S NO SHUTTING YOU UP, IT'S BLAH, BLAH, BLAH! WHY DID YOU HAVE TO TELL THEM ABOUT THAT DAMN PIPE?
MANUEL WAS LAMENTING HIS FATE. HE FELT GREAT SELF-PITY AT THE THOUGHT OF ALL THE WRONGS DONE TO HIM SO FAR AND THOSE THAT LAY AHEAD OF HIM.
WHY WERE YOU SO MEAN TO HIM, M'ROSE?
THAT SHRIMP GOT WHAT HE DESERVED. HOW DARE HE CALL US JERKS?
IT'S BECAUSE WE MADE HIM MAD.
LET'S TALK ABOUT SOMETHING ELSE. LIKE GILLES. WHAT HE SAID SURPRISED ME.
SHUT YOUR TRAP, CÉLINA! WHAT A HALF-WIT YOU ARE! AND A GOSSIP! I NEVER KNEW YOU WERE SUCH A GOSSIP!
WHAT DID I SAY? WHY ARE YOU TAKING THE HIGH HORSE?

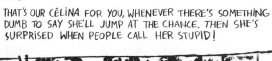

GETTING ON YOUR HIGH HORSE!

YOU SAY "GETTING ON YOUR HIGH HORSE"! AND DON'T SAY "WHAT"! LEARN SOME MANNERS!

WHAT?

THAT'S OUR CÉLINA FOR YOU, WHENEVER THERE'S SOMETHING DUMB TO SAY SHE'LL JUMP AT THE CHANCE. THEN SHE'S SURPRISED WHEN PEOPLE CALL HER STUPID!

YOU SURE ARE MEAN ALL OF A SUDDEN.

WELL, IF YOU DIDN'T JUST SAY ANY OLD THING, I WOULDN'T BE MEAN. YOU'RE GONNA GET WARTS ON YOUR TONGUE IF YOU GO ON LIKE THAT, YOU'LL SEE!

BUT WHAT DID I SAY?

DON'T ACT ALL INNOCENT!

CÉLINA WAS PEEVED AGAIN. SHE FELL SILENT AND STARED STUBBORNLY AT AN OLD TREE OFF TO HER RIGHT.

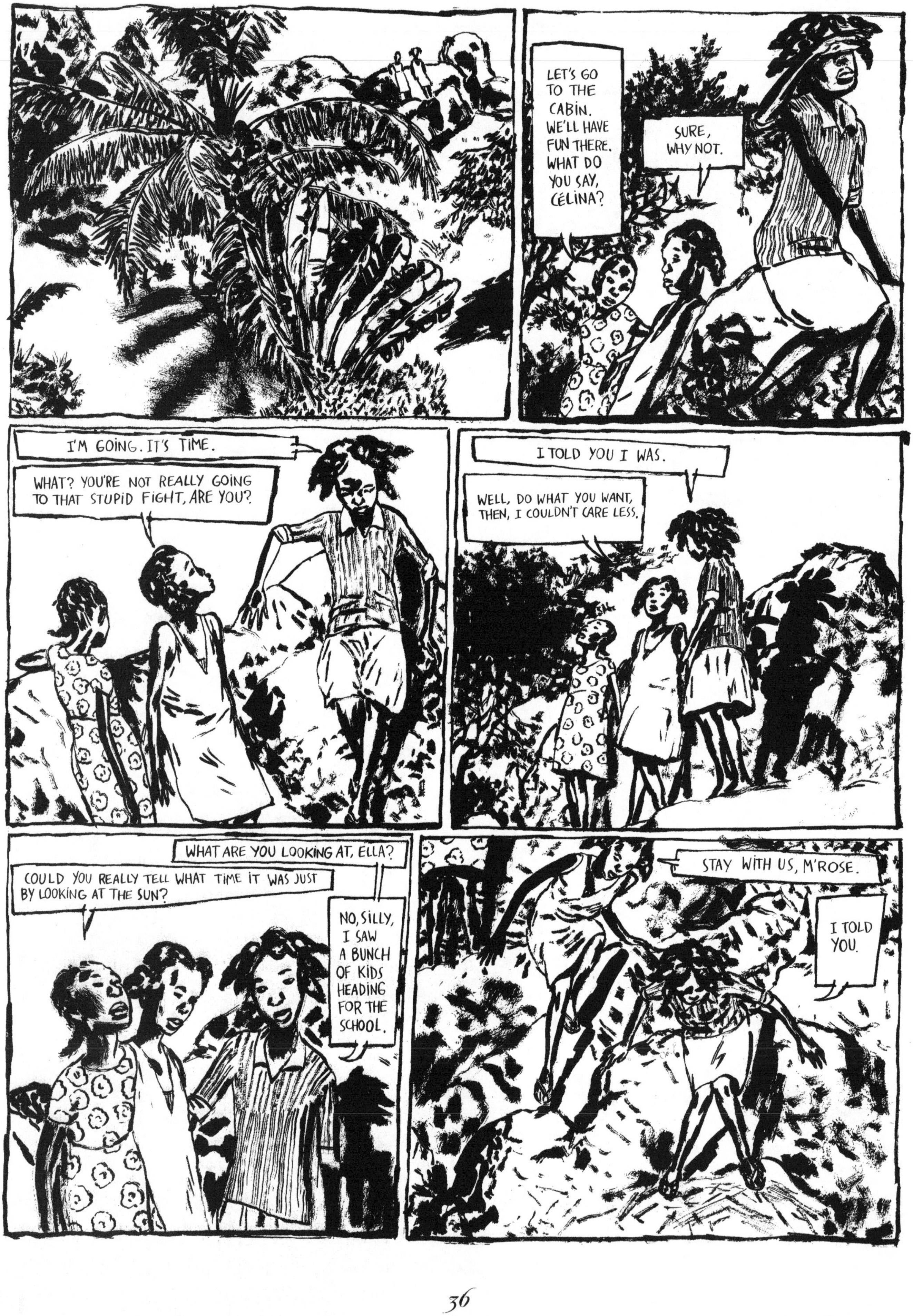
LET'S GO TO THE CABIN. WE'LL HAVE FUN THERE. WHAT DO YOU SAY, CÉLINA?
SURE, WHY NOT.
I'M GOING. IT'S TIME.
WHAT? YOU'RE NOT REALLY GOING TO THAT STUPID FIGHT, ARE YOU?
I TOLD YOU I WAS.
WELL, DO WHAT YOU WANT, THEN, I COULDN'T CARE LESS.
WHAT ARE YOU LOOKING AT, ELLA?
COULD YOU REALLY TELL WHAT TIME IT WAS JUST BY LOOKING AT THE SUN?
NO, SILLY, I SAW A BUNCH OF KIDS HEADING FOR THE SCHOOL.
STAY WITH US, M'ROSE.
I TOLD YOU.

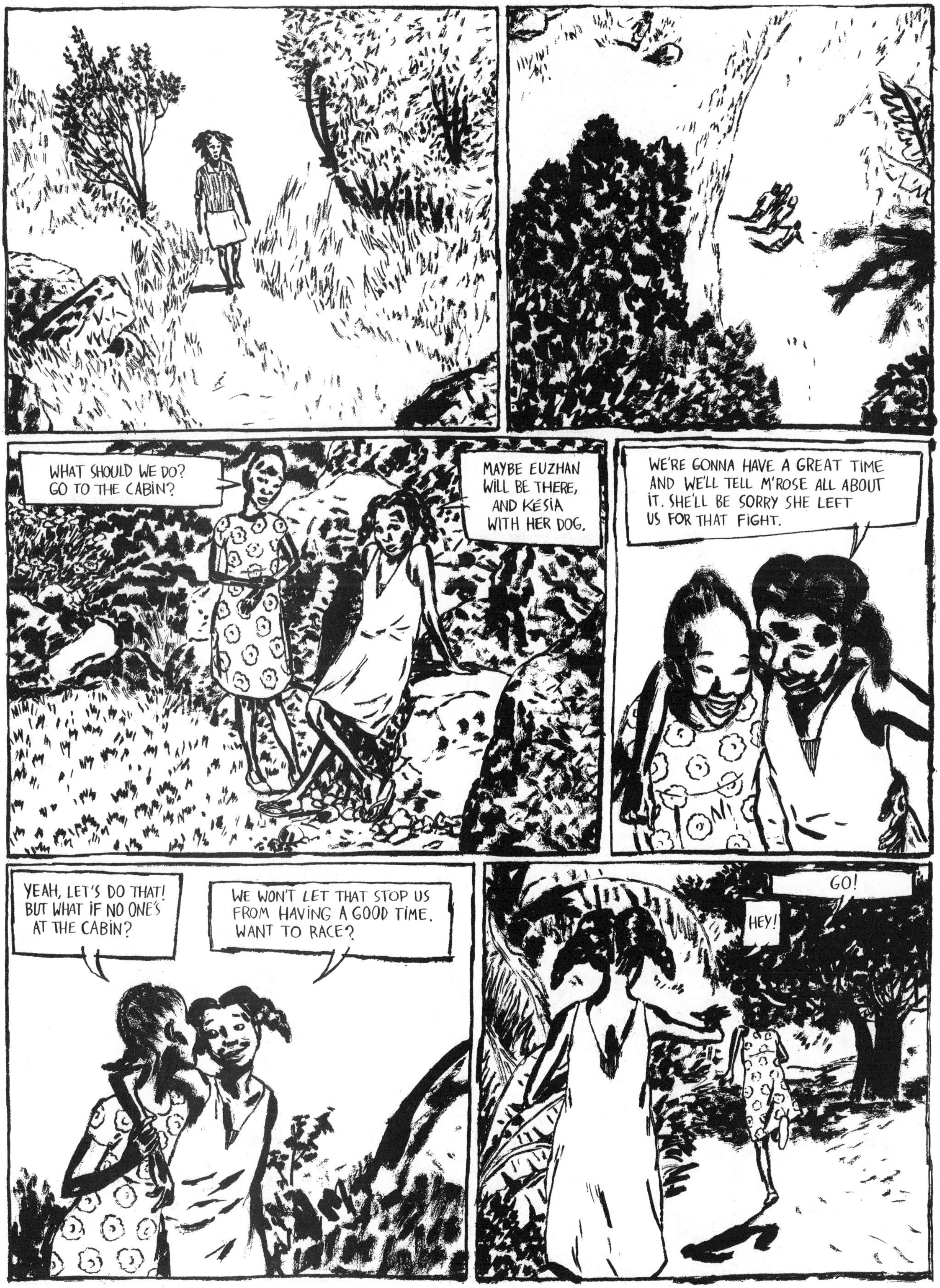
WHAT SHOULD WE DO? GO TO THE CABIN?
MAYBE EUZHAN WILL BE THERE, AND KÉSIA WITH HER DOG.
WE'RE GONNA HAVE A GREAT TIME AND WE'LL TELL M'ROSE ALL ABOUT IT. SHE'LL BE SORRY SHE LEFT US FOR THAT FIGHT.
YEAH, LET'S DO THAT! BUT WHAT IF NO ONE'S AT THE CABIN?
WE WON'T LET THAT STOP US FROM HAVING A GOOD TIME. WANT TO RACE?
GO!
HEY!

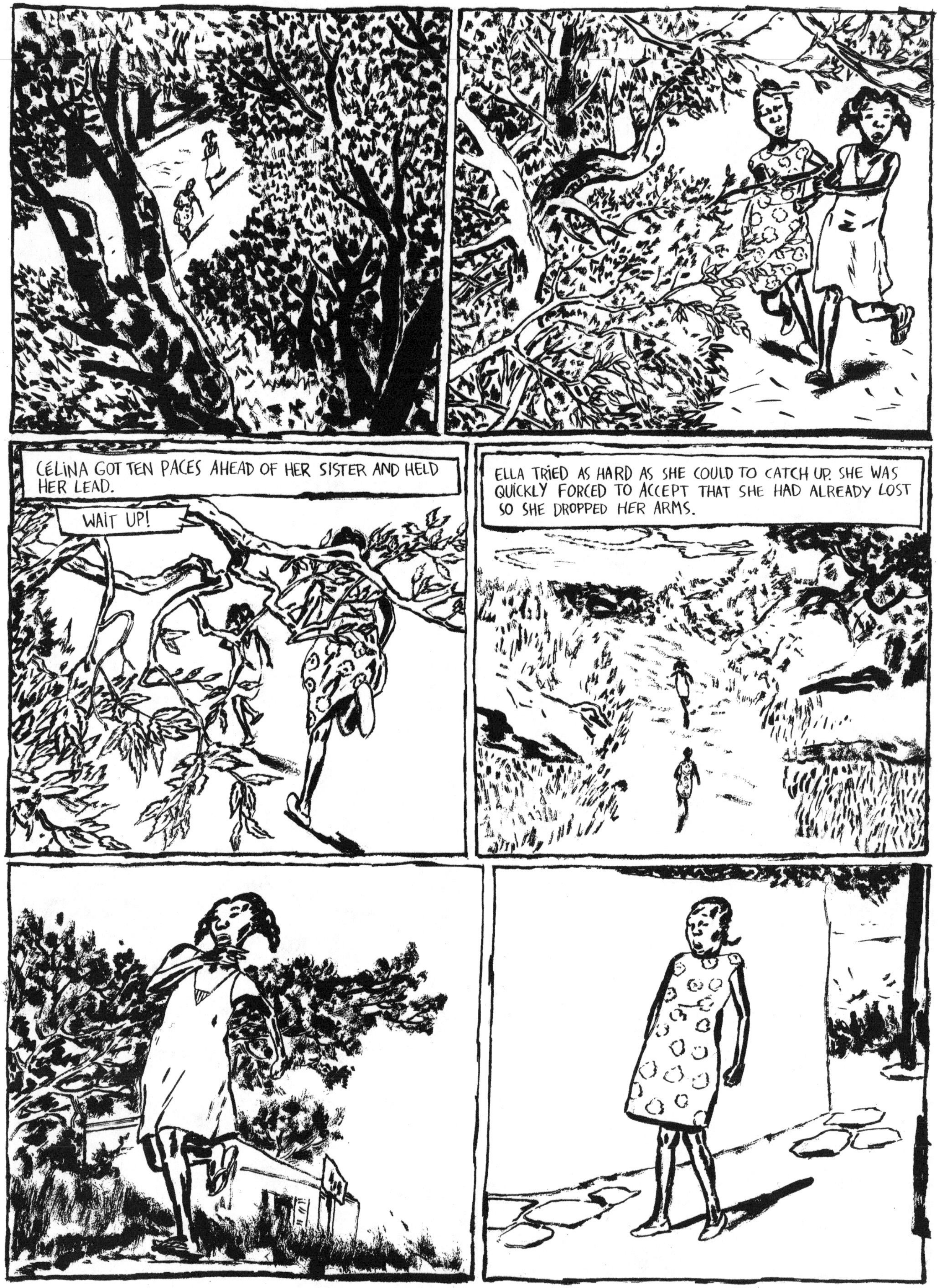

CÉLINA GOT TEN PACES AHEAD OF HER SISTER AND HELD HER LEAD.
WAIT UP!
ELLA TRIED AS HARD AS SHE COULD TO CATCH UP. SHE WAS QUICKLY FORCED TO ACCEPT THAT SHE HAD ALREADY LOST SO SHE DROPPED HER ARMS.

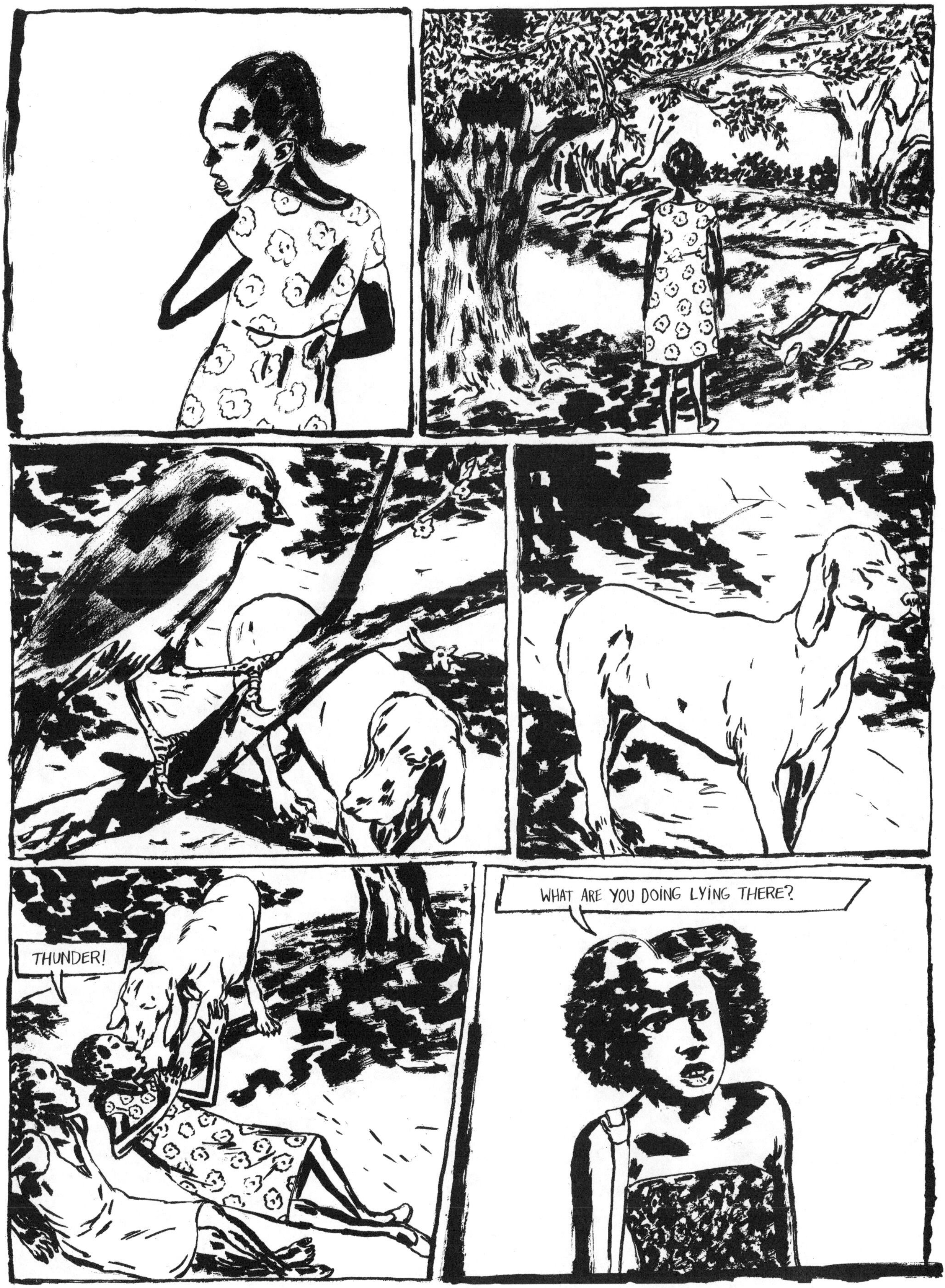
THUNDER!
WHAT ARE YOU DOING LYING THERE?

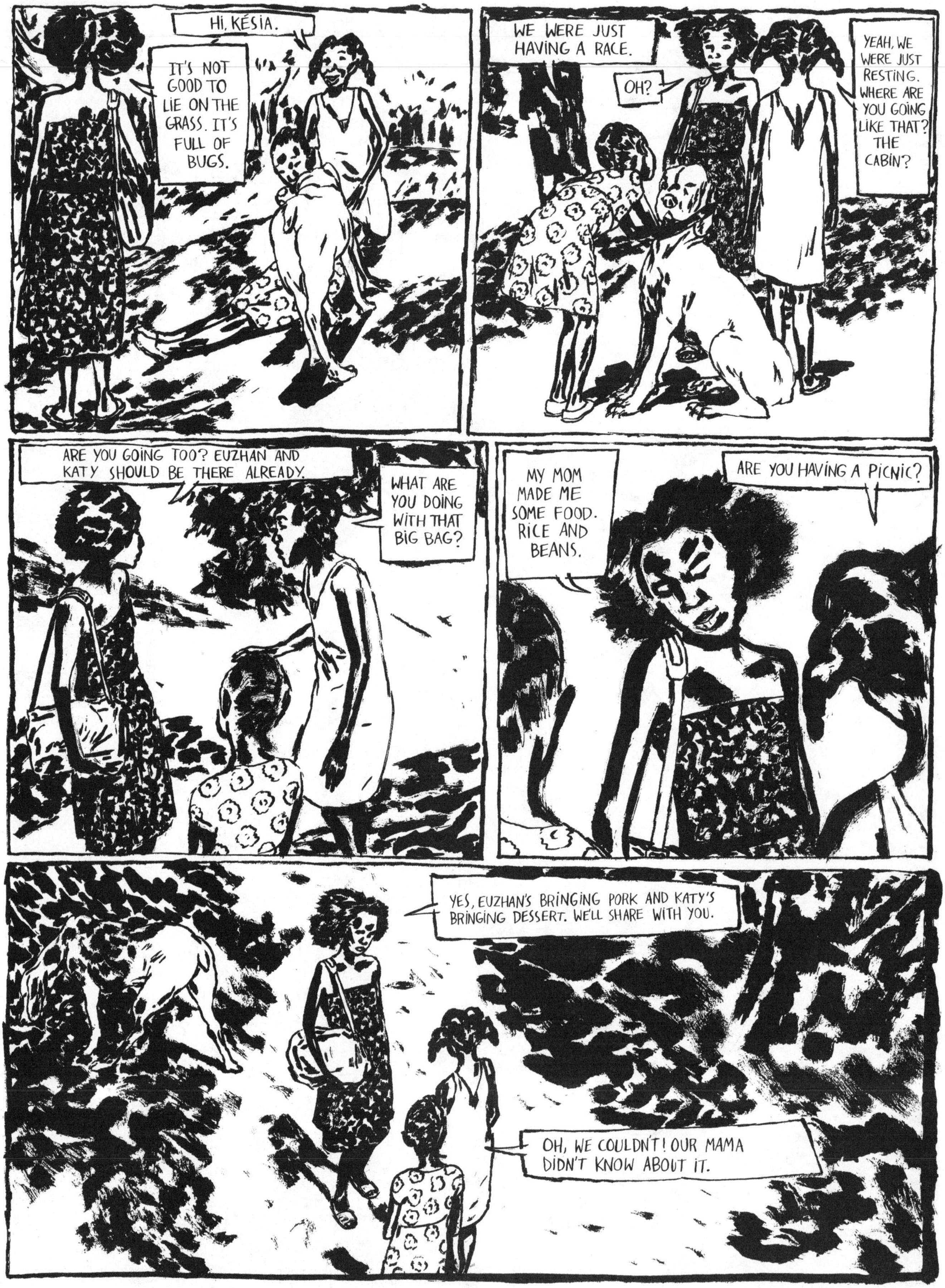

Hi, KÉSIA.
IT'S NOT GOOD TO LIE ON THE GRASS. IT'S FULL OF BUGS.
WE WERE JUST HAVING A RACE.
OH?
YEAH, WE WERE JUST RESTING. WHERE ARE YOU GOING LIKE THAT? THE CABIN?
ARE YOU GOING TOO? EUZHAN AND KATY SHOULD BE THERE ALREADY.
WHAT ARE YOU DOING WITH THAT BIG BAG?
MY MOM MADE ME SOME FOOD. RICE AND BEANS.
ARE YOU HAVING A PICNIC?
YES, EUZHAN'S BRINGING PORK AND KATY'S BRINGING DESSERT. WE'LL SHARE WITH YOU.
OH, WE COULDN'T! OUR MAMA DIDN'T KNOW ABOUT IT.

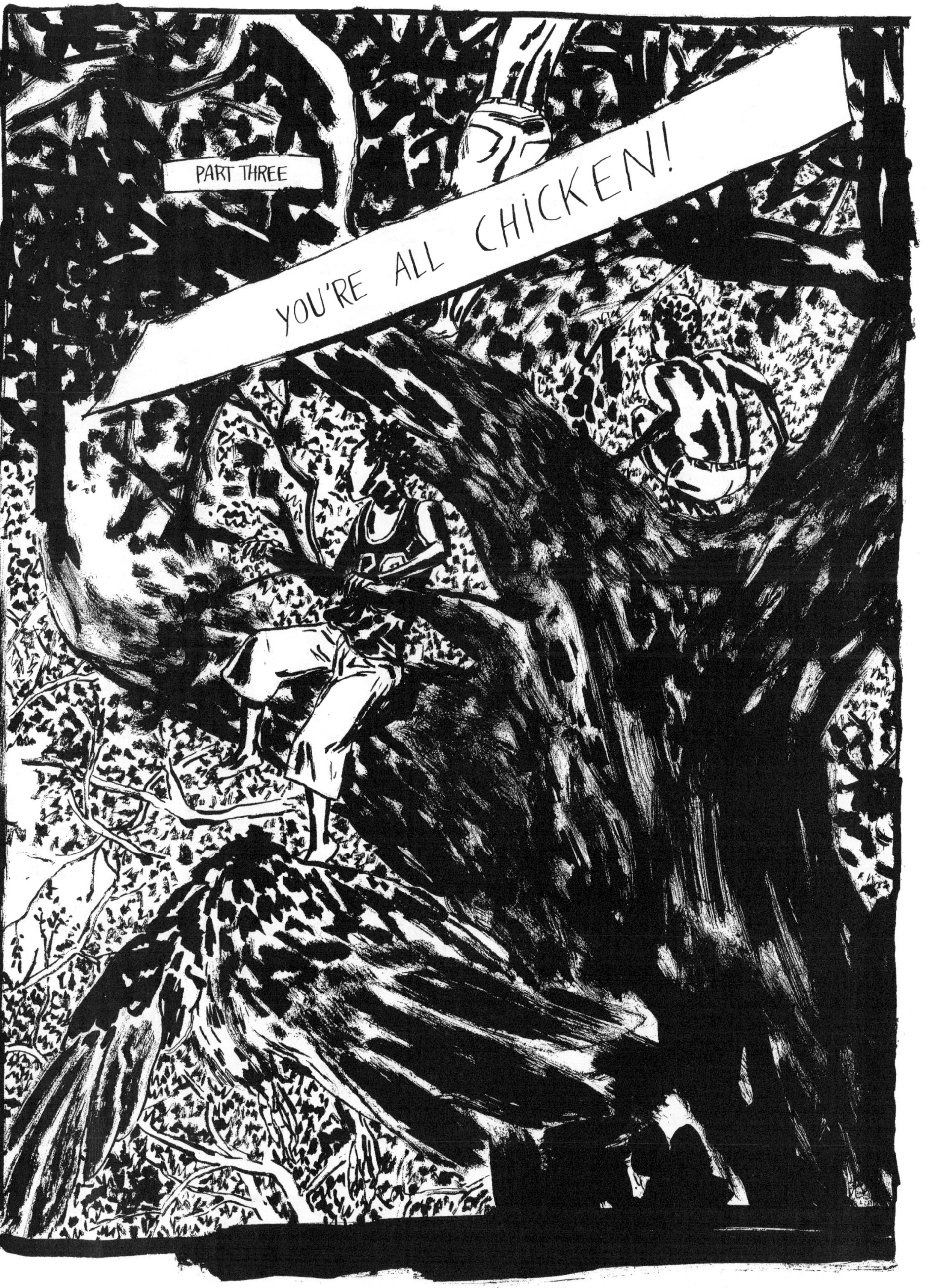
PART THREE
YOU'RE ALL CHICKEN!

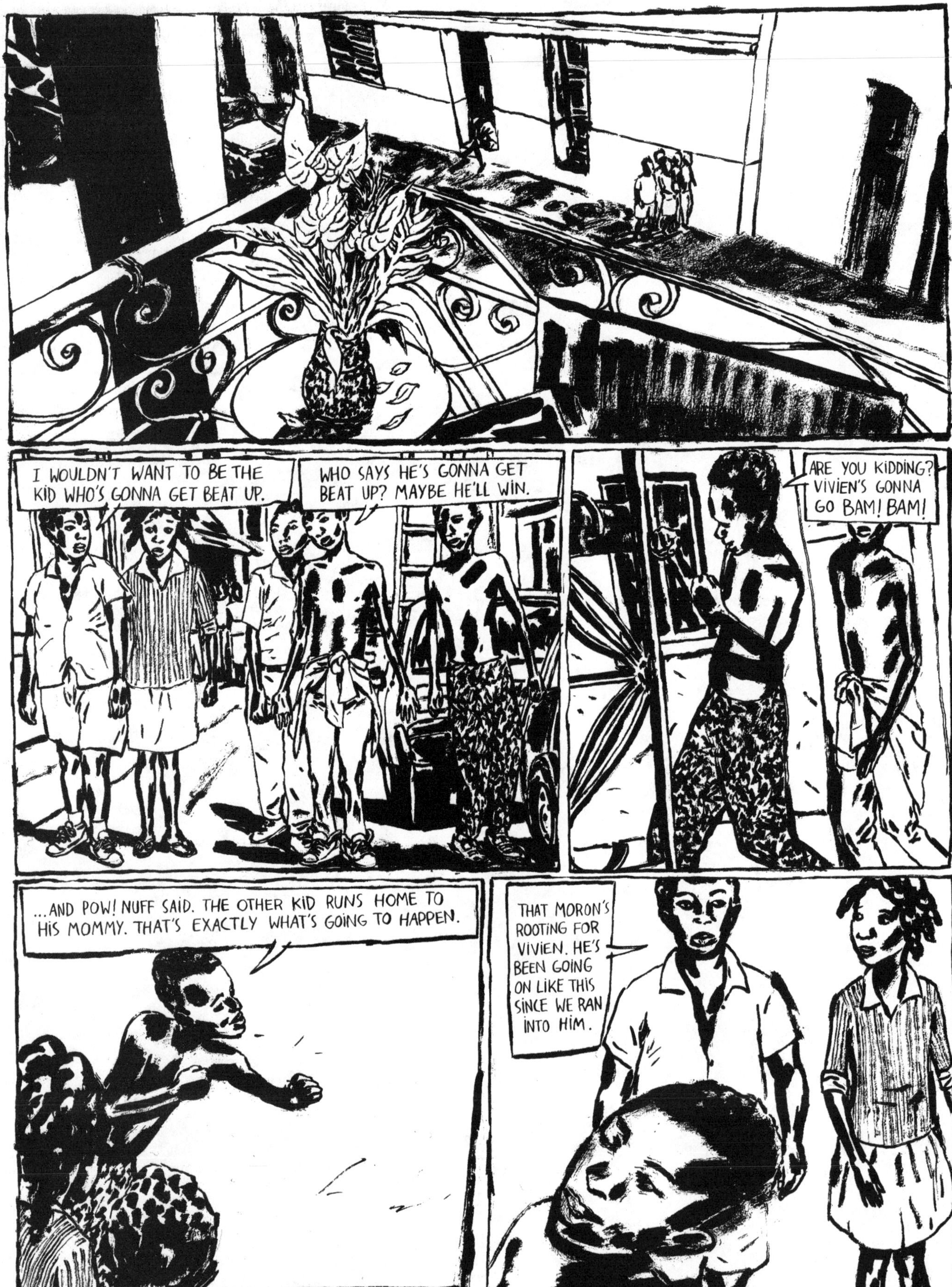
I WOULDN'T WANT TO BE THE KID WHO'S GONNA GET BEAT UP.
WHO SAYS HE'S GONNA GET BEAT UP? MAYBE HE'LL WIN.
ARE YOU KIDDING? VIVIEN'S GONNA GO BAM! BAM!
...AND POW! NUFF SAID. THE OTHER KID RUNS HOME TO HIS MOMMY. THAT'S EXACTLY WHAT'S GOING TO HAPPEN.
THAT MORON'S ROOTING FOR VIVIEN. HE'S BEEN GOING ON LIKE THIS SINCE WE RAN INTO HIM.

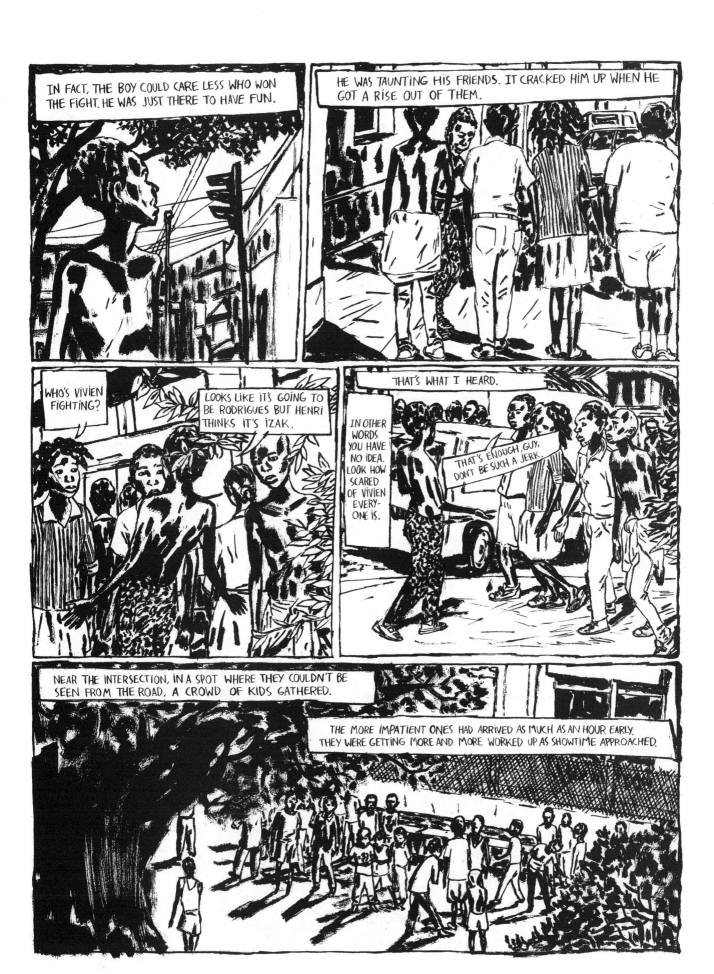

IN FACT, THE BOY COULD CARE LESS WHO WON THE FIGHT. HE WAS JUST THERE TO HAVE FUN.

HE WAS TAUNTING HIS FRIENDS. IT CRACKED HIM UP WHEN HE GOT A RISE OUT OF THEM.

WHO'S VIVIEN FIGHTING?

LOOKS LIKE IT'S GOING TO BE RODRIGUES BUT HENRI THINKS IT'S IZAK.

THAT'S WHAT I HEARD.

IN OTHER WORDS YOU HAVE NO IDEA. LOOK HOW SCARED OF VIVIEN EVERY-ONE IS.

THAT'S ENOUGH, GUY, DON'T BE SUCH A JERK.

NEAR THE INTERSECTION, IN A SPOT WHERE THEY COULDN'T BE SEEN FROM THE ROAD, A CROWD OF KIDS GATHERED.

THE MORE IMPATIENT ONES HAD ARRIVED AS MUCH AS AN HOUR EARLY. THEY WERE GETTING MORE AND MORE WORKED UP AS SHOWTIME APPROACHED.

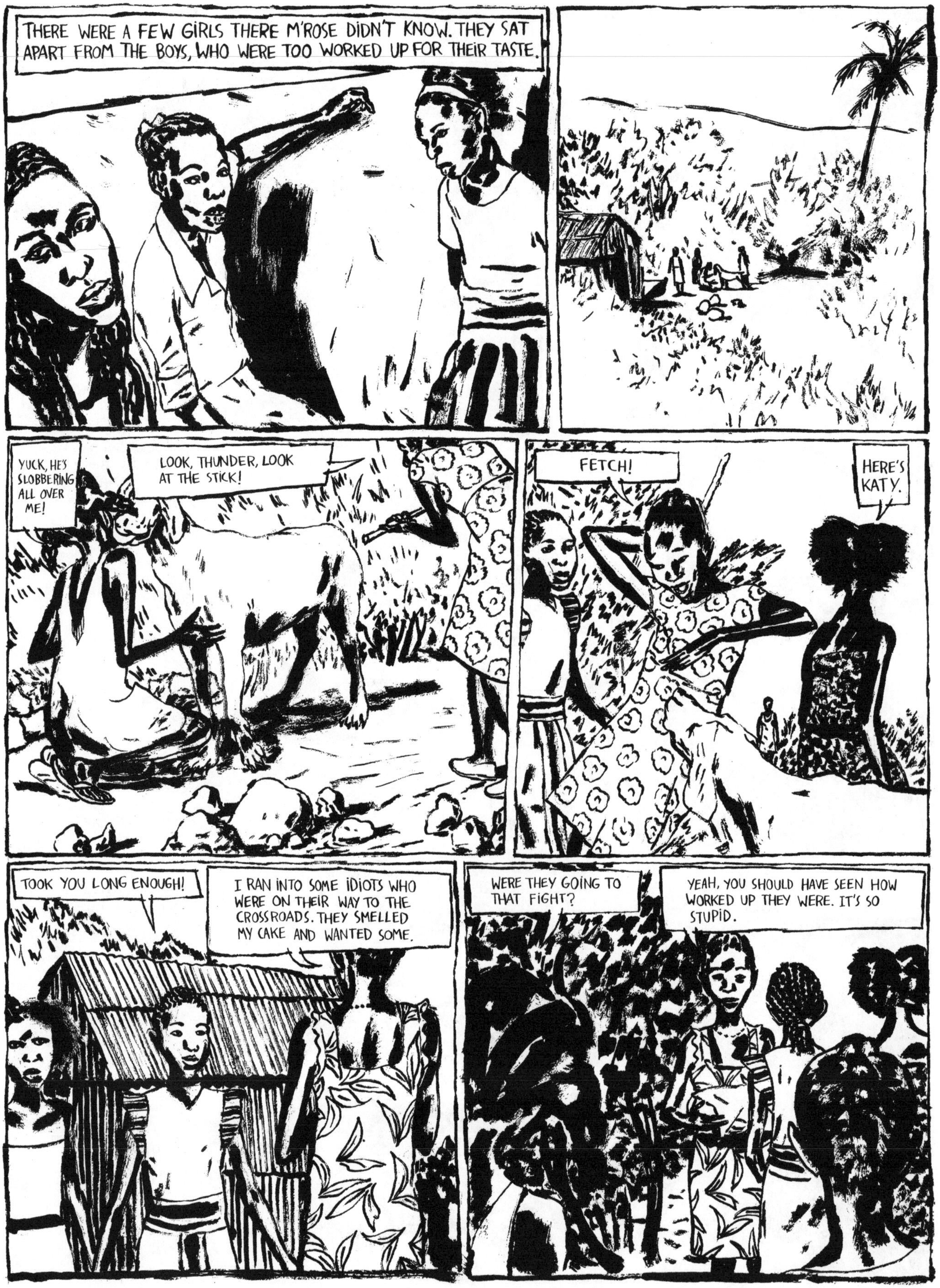

THERE WERE A FEW GIRLS THERE M'ROSE DIDN'T KNOW. THEY SAT APART FROM THE BOYS, WHO WERE TOO WORKED UP FOR THEIR TASTE.
YUCK, HE'S SLOBBERING ALL OVER ME!
LOOK, THUNDER, LOOK AT THE STICK!
FETCH!
HERE'S KATY.
TOOK YOU LONG ENOUGH!
I RAN INTO SOME IDIOTS WHO WERE ON THEIR WAY TO THE CROSSROADS. THEY SMELLED MY CAKE AND WANTED SOME.
WERE THEY GOING TO THAT FIGHT?
YEAH, YOU SHOULD HAVE SEEN HOW WORKED UP THEY WERE. IT'S SO STUPID.

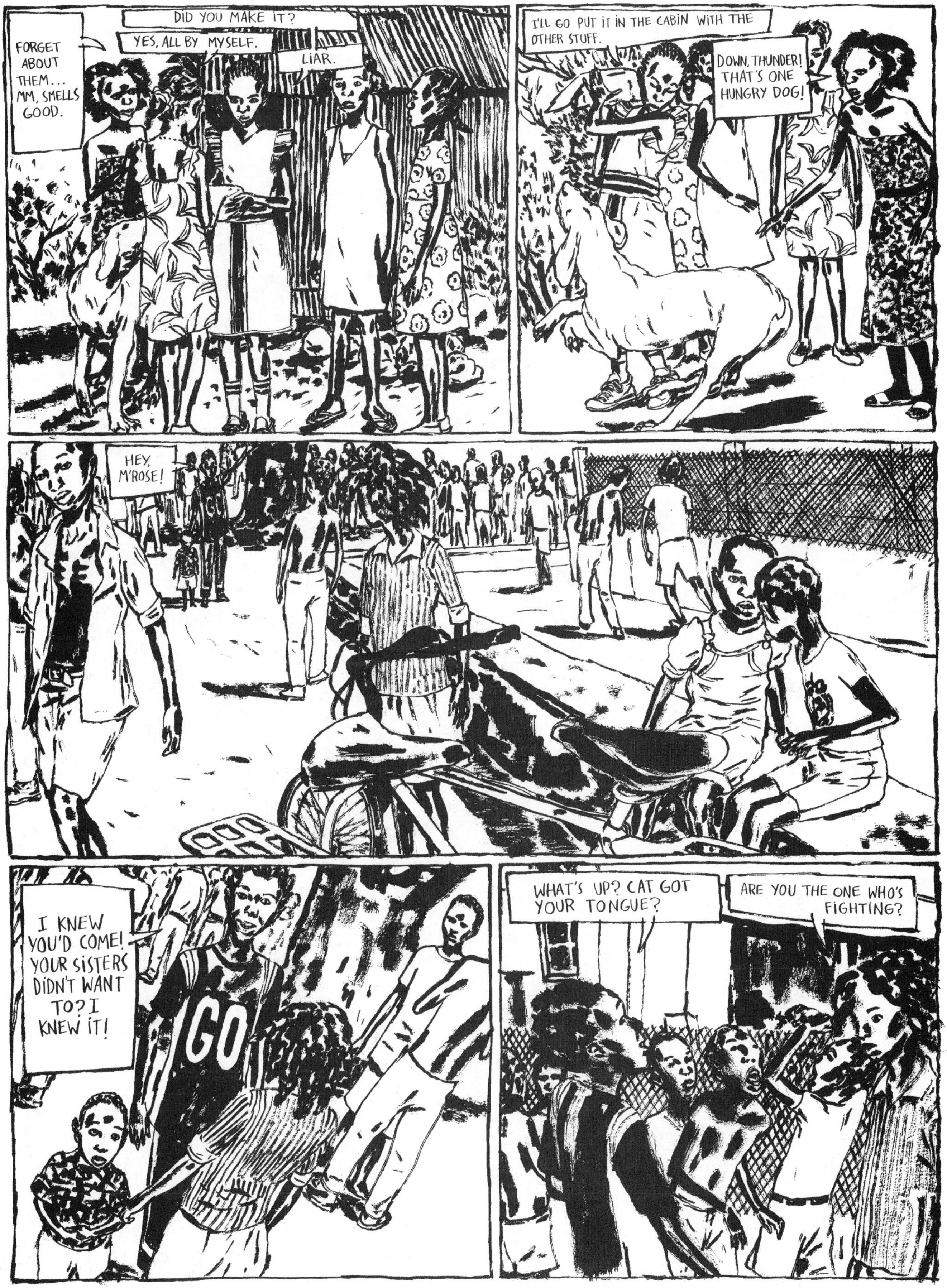
DID YOU MAKE IT?
YES, ALL BY MYSELF.
LIAR.
FORGET ABOUT THEM... MM, SMELLS GOOD.
I'LL GO PUT IT IN THE CABIN WITH THE OTHER STUFF.
DOWN, THUNDER! THAT'S ONE HUNGRY DOG!
HEY, M'ROSE!
GO
I KNEW YOU'D COME! YOUR SISTERS DIDN'T WANT TO? I KNEW IT!
GO
WHAT'S UP? CAT GOT YOUR TONGUE?
ARE YOU THE ONE WHO'S FIGHTING?

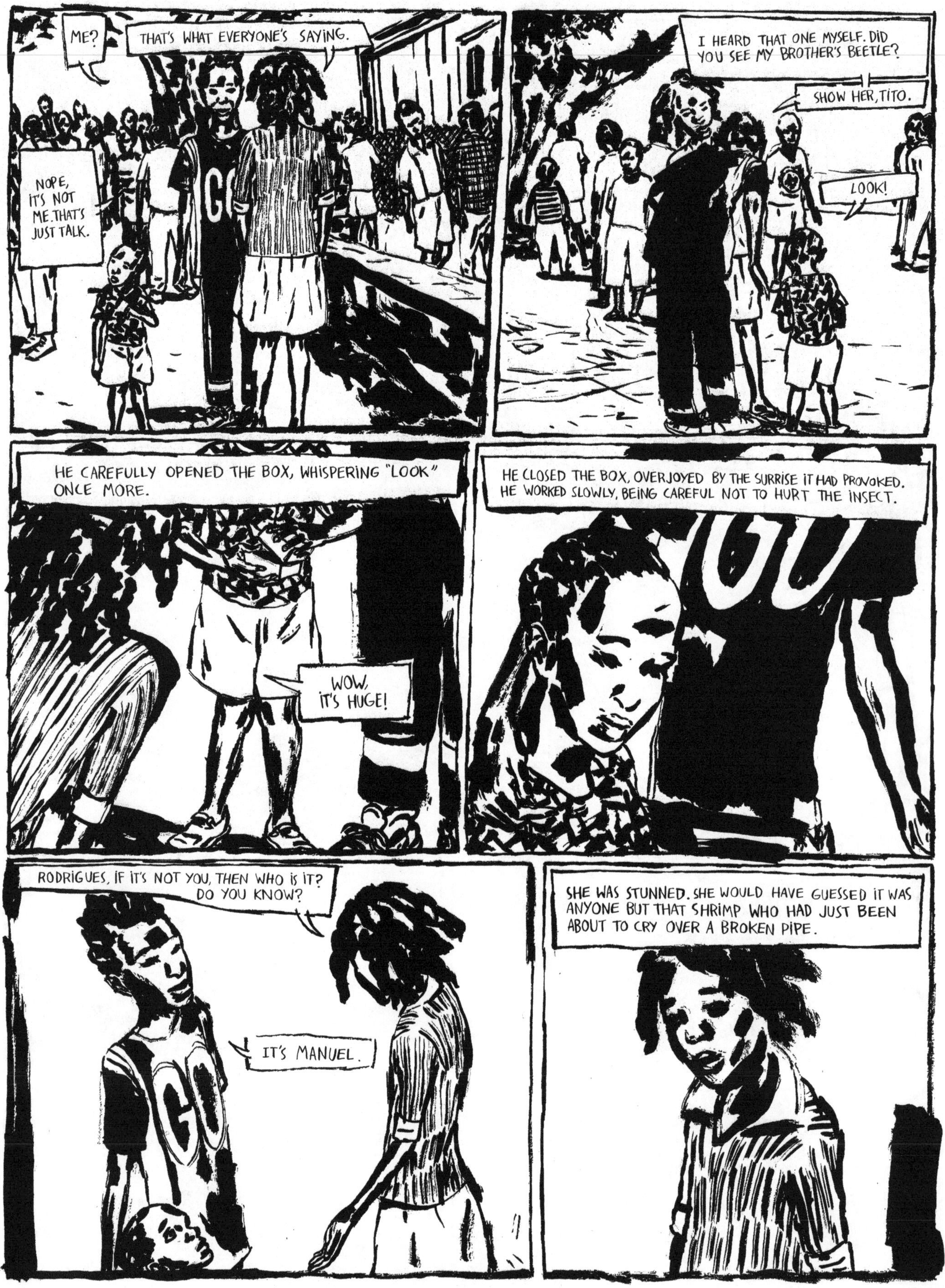
ME?
THAT'S WHAT EVERYONE'S SAYING.
NOPE, IT'S NOT ME. THAT'S JUST TALK.
I HEARD THAT ONE MYSELF. DID YOU SEE MY BROTHER'S BEETLE?
SHOW HER, TITO.
LOOK!
HE CAREFULLY OPENED THE BOX, WHISPERING "LOOK" ONCE MORE.
WOW, IT'S HUGE!
HE CLOSED THE BOX, OVERJOYED BY THE SURRISE IT HAD PROVOKED. HE WORKED SLOWLY, BEING CAREFUL NOT TO HURT THE INSECT.
RODRIGUES, IF IT'S NOT YOU, THEN WHO IS IT? DO YOU KNOW?
IT'S MANUEL.
SHE WAS STUNNED. SHE WOULD HAVE GUESSED IT WAS ANYONE BUT THAT SHRIMP WHO HAD JUST BEEN ABOUT TO CRY OVER A BROKEN PIPE.

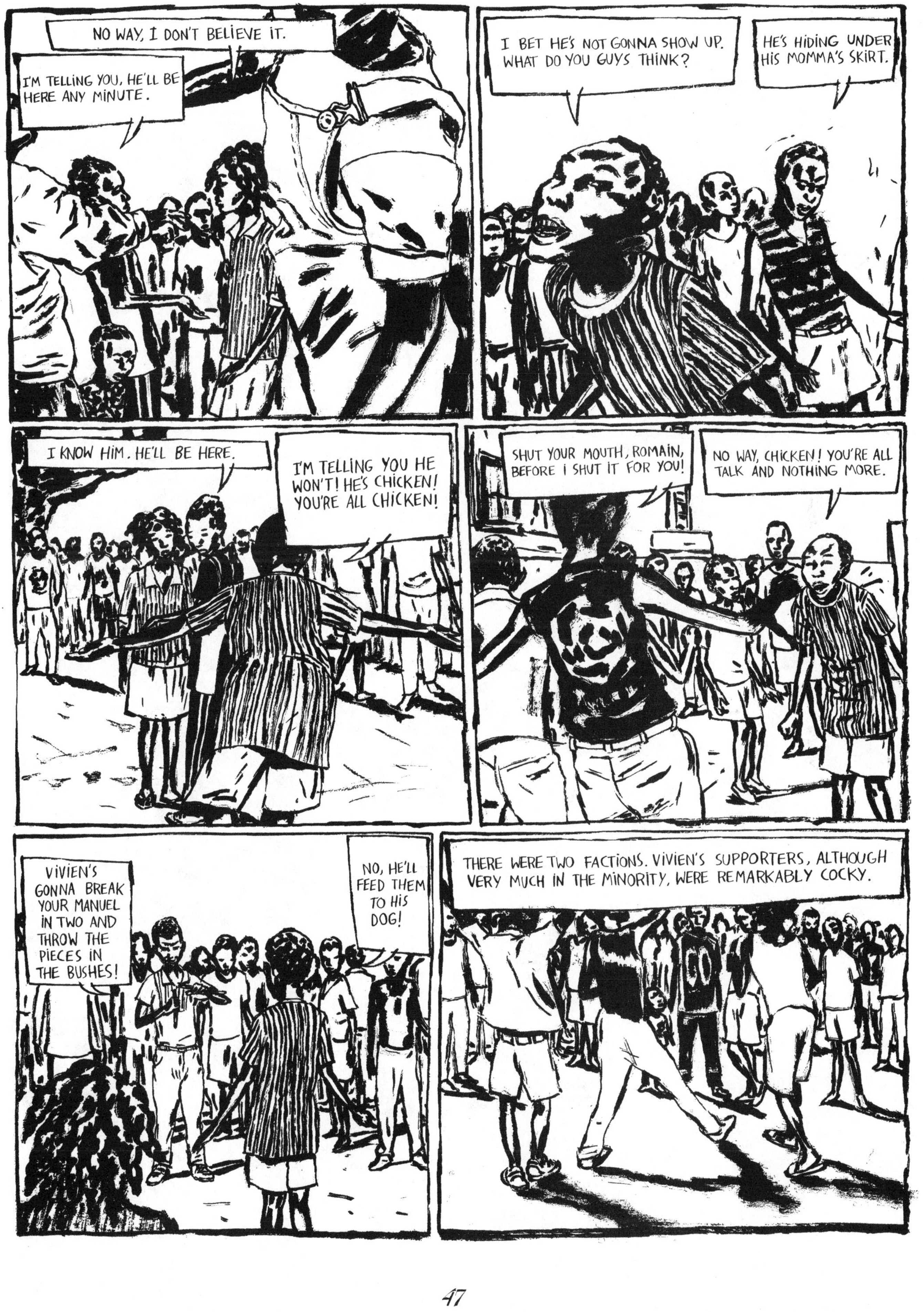
NO WAY, I DON'T BELIEVE IT.
I'M TELLING YOU, HE'LL BE HERE ANY MINUTE.
I BET HE'S NOT GONNA SHOW UP. WHAT DO YOU GUYS THINK?
HE'S HIDING UNDER HIS MOMMA'S SKIRT.
I KNOW HIM. HE'LL BE HERE.
I'M TELLING YOU HE WON'T! HE'S CHICKEN! YOU'RE ALL CHICKEN!
SHUT YOUR MOUTH, ROMAIN, BEFORE I SHUT IT FOR YOU!
NO WAY, CHICKEN! YOU'RE ALL TALK AND NOTHING MORE.
VIVIEN'S GONNA BREAK YOUR MANUEL IN TWO AND THROW THE PIECES IN THE BUSHES!
NO, HE'LL FEED THEM TO HIS DOG!
THERE WERE TWO FACTIONS. VIVIEN'S SUPPORTERS, ALTHOUGH VERY MUCH IN THE MINORITY, WERE REMARKABLY COCKY.

THIS HANDFUL OF BOYS, FEARED AND RESPECTED BY THE REST, GAVE THE IMPRESSION THEY COULD DO ANYTHING.

THE TARGETS OF THEIR BULLYING UNDERSTOOD THEIR RIDICULE PERFECTLY WELL. IN THEIR HEARTS, ANIMOSITY MIXED WITH SHAME.

M'ROSE SHARED THEIR FEELINGS, SHE WAS WITH THEM TO THE CORE OF HER BEING.

SO, M'ROSE-THAT'S YOUR NAME, RIGHT? WHAT DO YOU THINK OF THE SHOW?

THE SHOW?

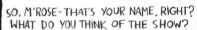

YEAH, THESE CLOWNS WITH ALL THEIR CARRYING ON. DON'T THEY MAKE YOU LAUGH? ALL THEY'RE MISSING IS THE RED NOSES.

AH, I SEE, YOU'RE PLAYING ALONG TOO, AND YOU'RE ON MANUEL'S SIDE!

ME? ON MANUEL'S SIDE?

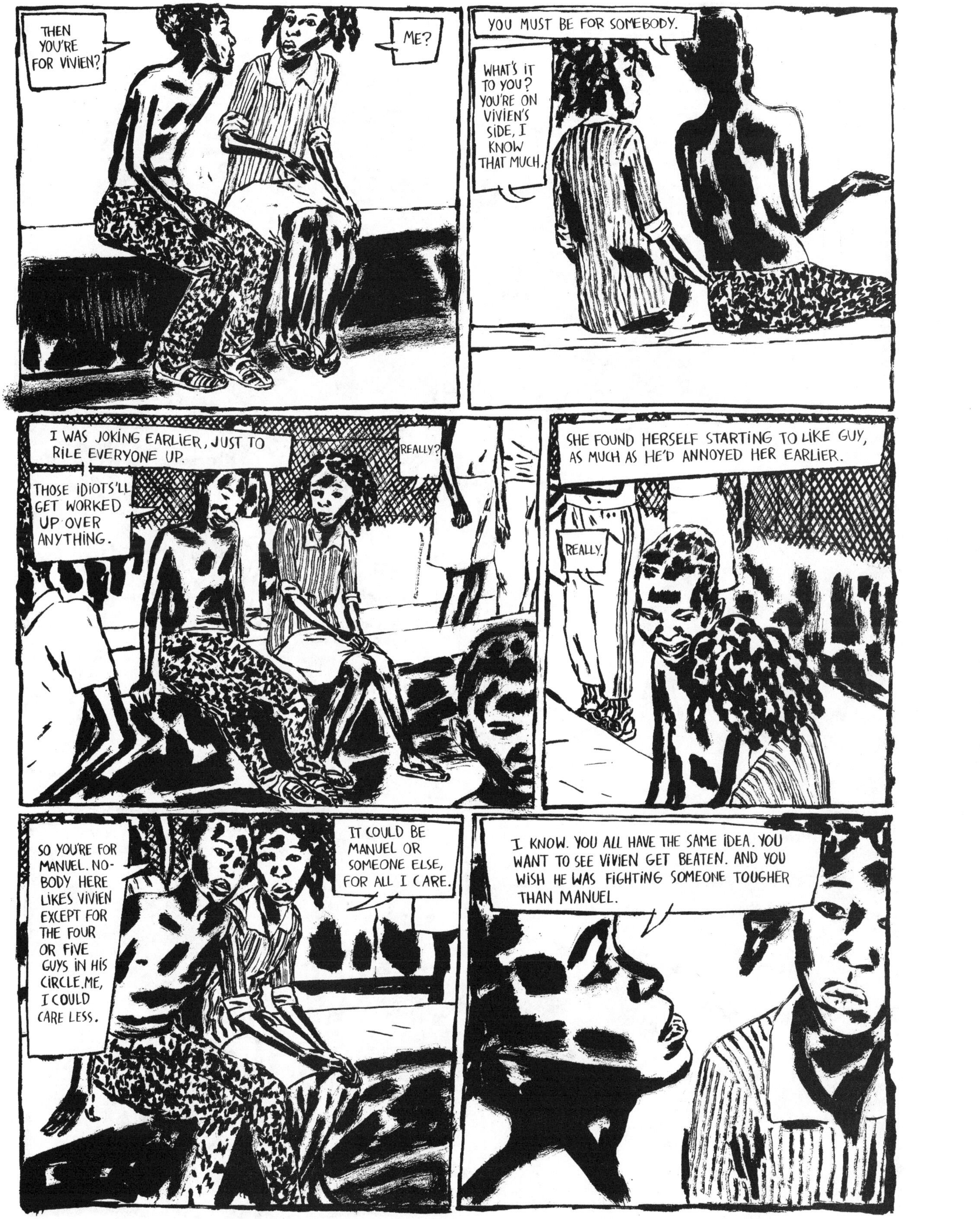
THEN YOU'RE FOR VIVIEN?
ME?
YOU MUST BE FOR SOMEBODY.
WHAT'S IT TO YOU? YOU'RE ON VIVIEN'S SIDE, I KNOW THAT MUCH.
I WAS JOKING EARLIER, JUST TO RILE EVERYONE UP.
THOSE IDIOTS'LL GET WORKED UP OVER ANYTHING.
REALLY?
SHE FOUND HERSELF STARTING TO LIKE GUY, AS MUCH AS HE'D ANNOYED HER EARLIER.
REALLY.
SO YOU'RE FOR MANUEL. NOBODY HERE LIKES VIVIEN EXCEPT FOR THE FOUR OR FIVE GUYS IN HIS CIRCLE. ME, I COULD CARE LESS.
IT COULD BE MANUEL OR SOMEONE ELSE, FOR ALL I CARE.
I KNOW. YOU ALL HAVE THE SAME IDEA. YOU WANT TO SEE VIVIEN GET BEATEN. AND YOU WISH HE WAS FIGHTING SOMEONE TOUGHER THAN MANUEL.

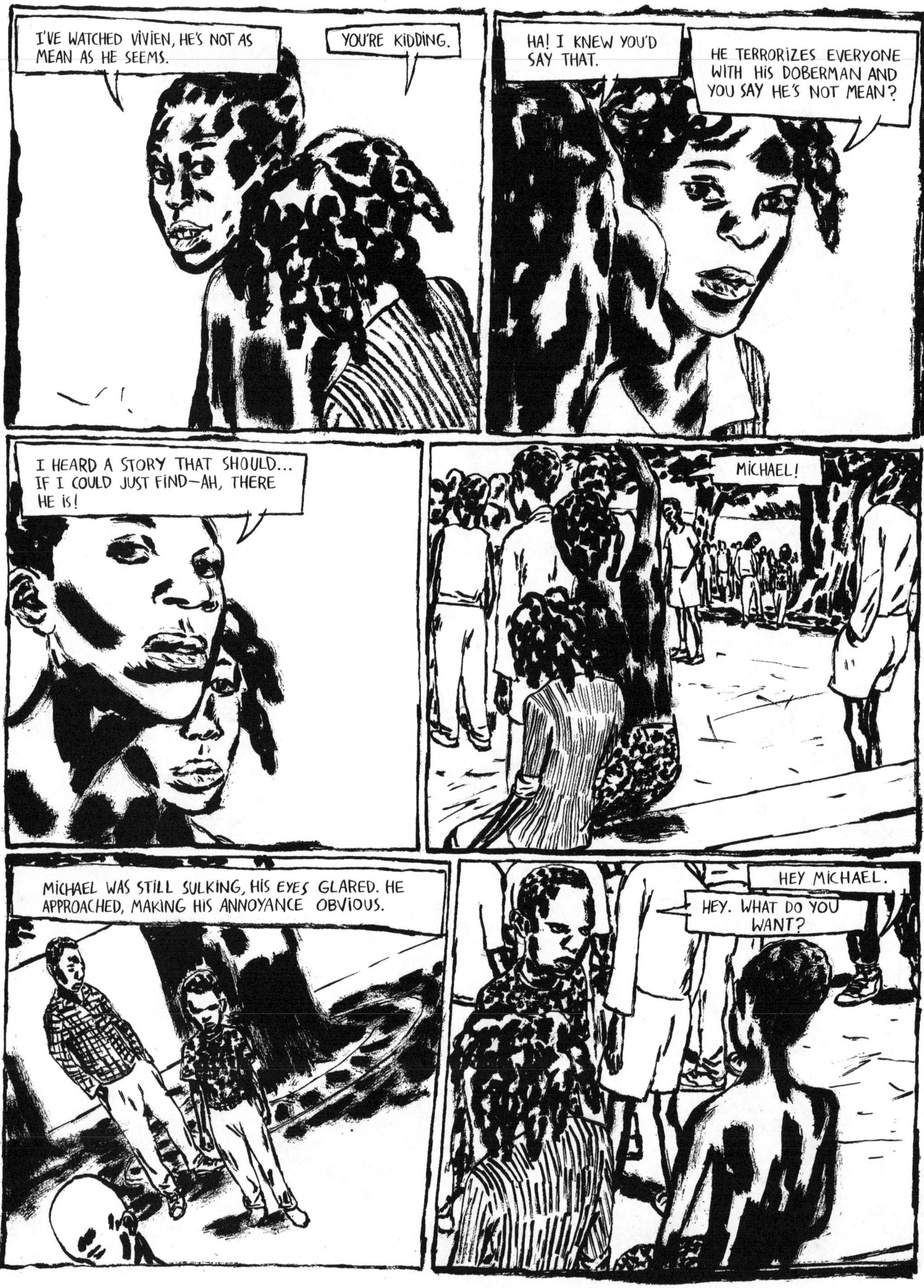
I'VE WATCHED VIVIEN, HE'S NOT AS MEAN AS HE SEEMS.
YOU'RE KIDDING.
HA! I KNEW YOU'D SAY THAT.
HE TERRORIZES EVERYONE WITH HIS DOBERMAN AND YOU SAY HE'S NOT MEAN?
I HEARD A STORY THAT SHOULD... IF I COULD JUST FIND—AH, THERE HE IS!
MICHAEL!
MICHAEL WAS STILL SULKING, HIS EYES GLARED. HE APPROACHED, MAKING HIS ANNOYANCE OBVIOUS.
HEY MICHAEL.
HEY. WHAT DO YOU WANT?

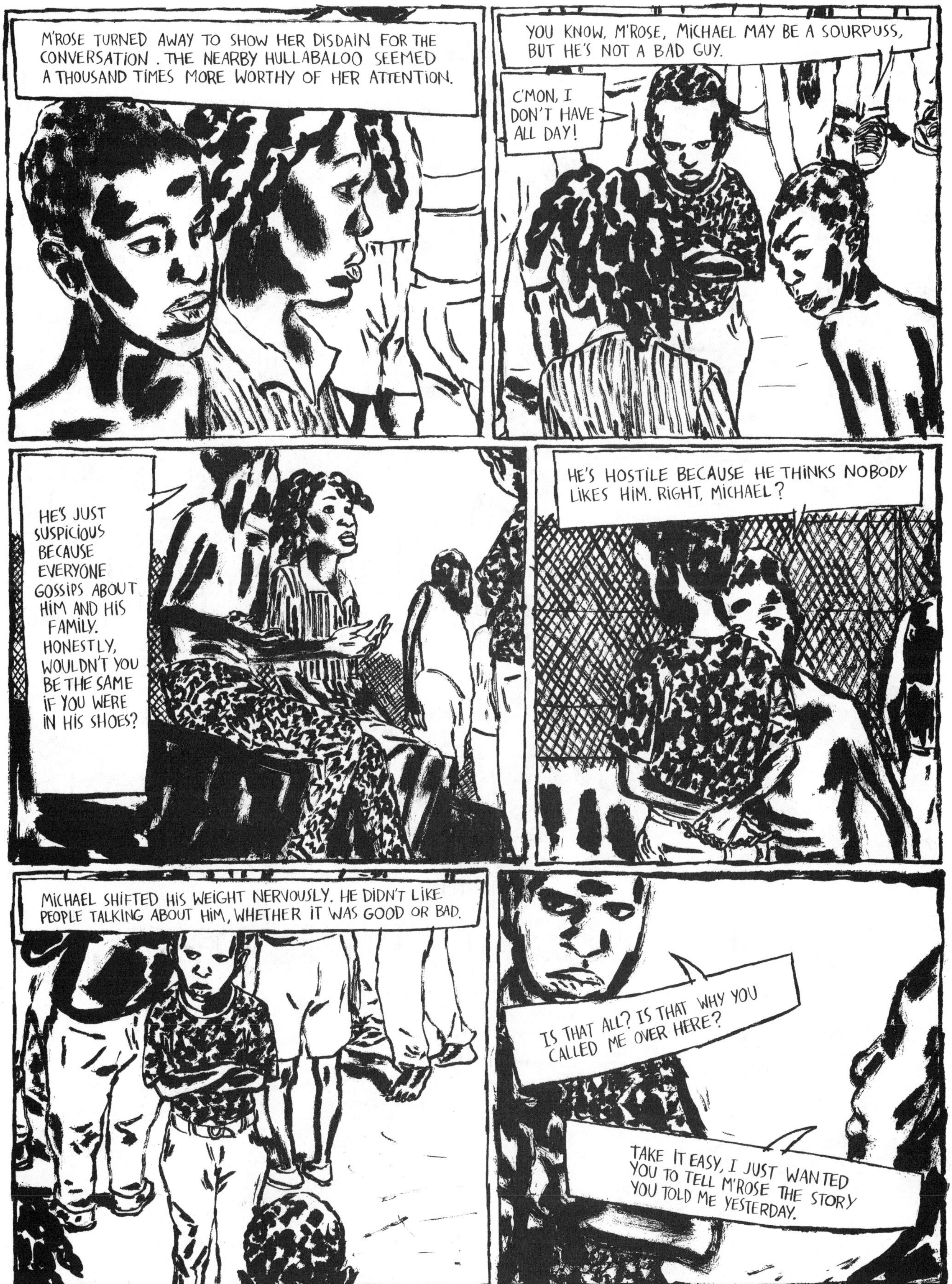
M'ROSE TURNED AWAY TO SHOW HER DISDAIN FOR THE CONVERSATION . THE NEARBY HULLABALOO SEEMED A THOUSAND TIMES MORE WORTHY OF HER ATTENTION.
YOU KNOW, M'ROSE, MICHAEL MAY BE A SOURPUSS, BUT HE'S NOT A BAD GUY.
C'MON, I DON'T HAVE ALL DAY!
HE'S JUST SUSPICIOUS BECAUSE EVERYONE GOSSIPS ABOUT HIM AND HIS FAMILY. HONESTLY, WOULDN'T YOU BE THE SAME IF YOU WERE IN HIS SHOES?
HE'S HOSTILE BECAUSE HE THINKS NOBODY LIKES HIM. RIGHT, MICHAEL?
MICHAEL SHIFTED HIS WEIGHT NERVOUSLY. HE DIDN'T LIKE PEOPLE TALKING ABOUT HIM, WHETHER IT WAS GOOD OR BAD.
IS THAT ALL? IS THAT WHY YOU CALLED ME OVER HERE?
TAKE IT EASY, I JUST WANTED YOU TO TELL M'ROSE THE STORY YOU TOLD ME YESTERDAY.

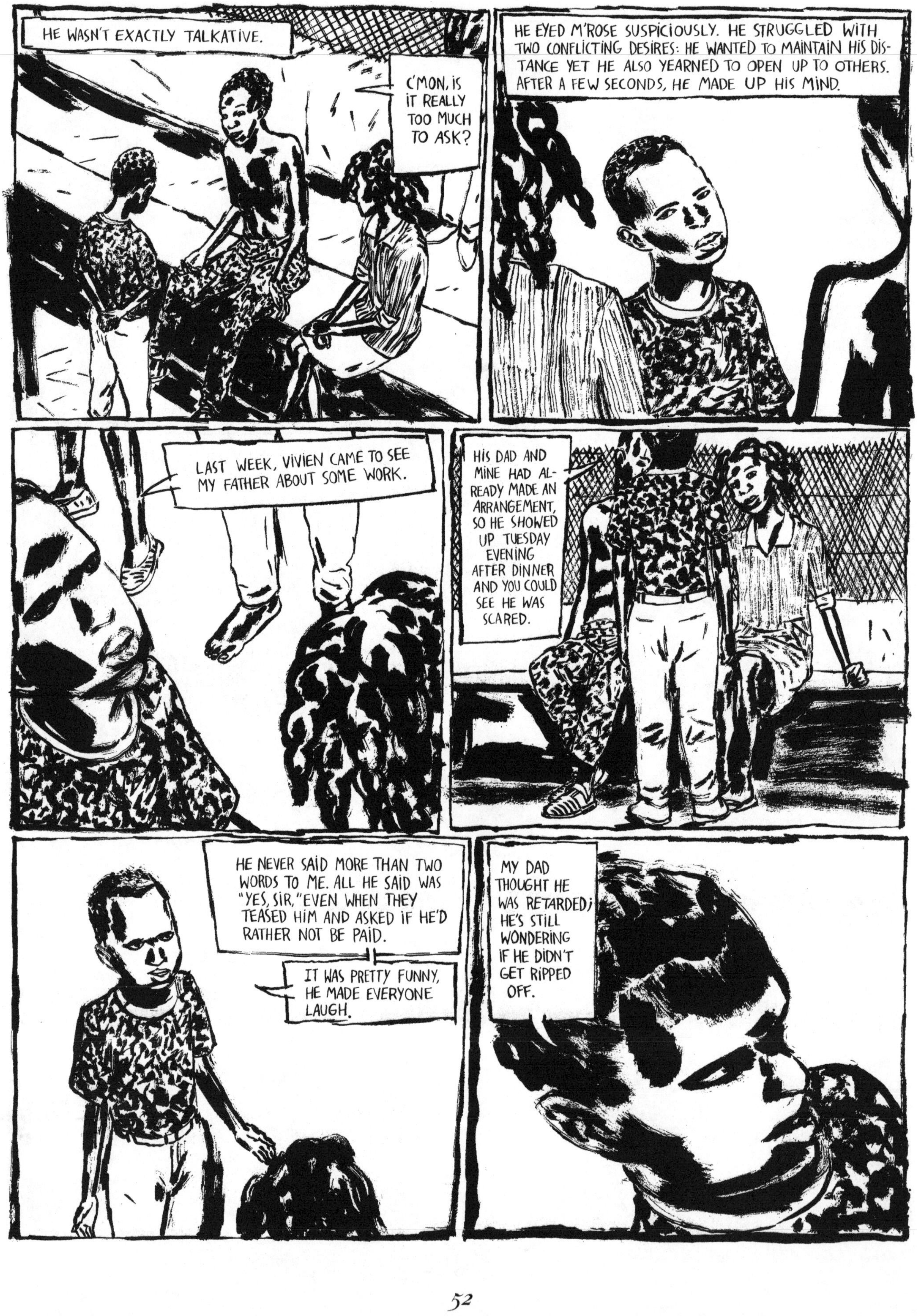
HE WASN'T EXACTLY TALKATIVE.
C'MON, IS IT REALLY TOO MUCH TO ASK?
HE EYED M'ROSE SUSPICIOUSLY. HE STRUGGLED WITH TWO CONFLICTING DESIRES: HE WANTED TO MAINTAIN HIS DISTANCE YET HE ALSO YEARNED TO OPEN UP TO OTHERS. AFTER A FEW SECONDS, HE MADE UP HIS MIND.
LAST WEEK, VIVIEN CAME TO SEE MY FATHER ABOUT SOME WORK.
HIS DAD AND MINE HAD ALREADY MADE AN ARRANGEMENT, SO HE SHOWED UP TUESDAY EVENING AFTER DINNER AND YOU COULD SEE HE WAS SCARED.
HE NEVER SAID MORE THAN TWO WORDS TO ME. ALL HE SAID WAS "YES, SIR," EVEN WHEN THEY TEASED HIM AND ASKED IF HE'D RATHER NOT BE PAID.
IT WAS PRETTY FUNNY, HE MADE EVERYONE LAUGH.
MY DAD THOUGHT HE WAS RETARDED; HE'S STILL WONDERING IF HE DIDN'T GET RIPPED OFF.

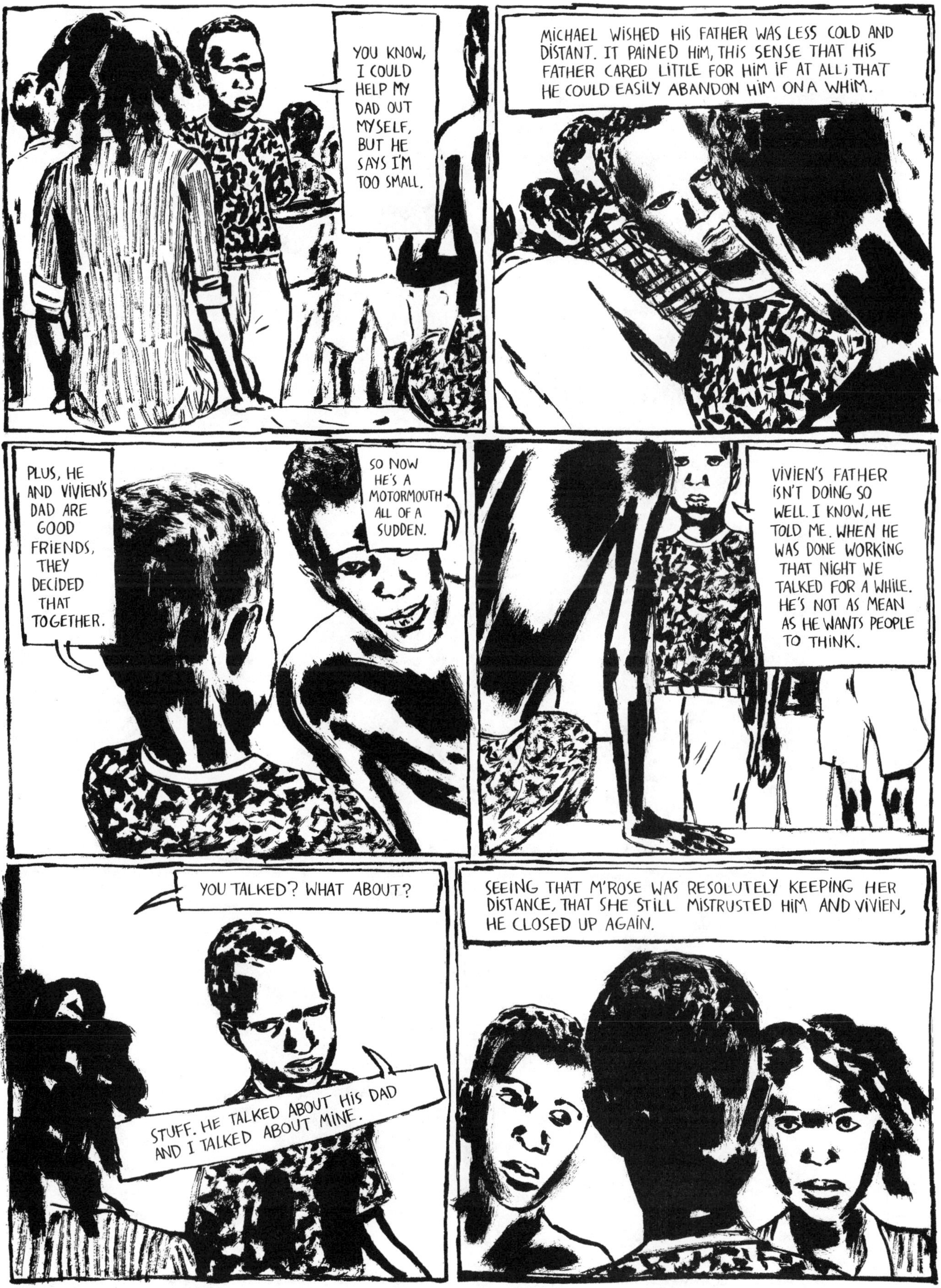
YOU KNOW, I COULD HELP MY DAD OUT MYSELF, BUT HE SAYS I'M TOO SMALL.
MICHAEL WISHED HIS FATHER WAS LESS COLD AND DISTANT. IT PAINED HIM, THIS SENSE THAT HIS FATHER CARED LITTLE FOR HIM IF AT ALL; THAT HE COULD EASILY ABANDON HIM ON A WHIM.
PLUS, HE AND VIVIEN'S DAD ARE GOOD FRIENDS, THEY DECIDED THAT TOGETHER.
SO NOW HE'S A MOTORMOUTH ALL OF A SUDDEN.
VIVIEN'S FATHER ISN'T DOING SO WELL. I KNOW, HE TOLD ME. WHEN HE WAS DONE WORKING THAT NIGHT WE TALKED FOR A WHILE. HE'S NOT AS MEAN AS HE WANTS PEOPLE TO THINK.
YOU TALKED? WHAT ABOUT?
STUFF. HE TALKED ABOUT HIS DAD AND I TALKED ABOUT MINE.
SEEING THAT M'ROSE WAS RESOLUTELY KEEPING HER DISTANCE, THAT SHE STILL MISTRUSTED HIM AND VIVIEN, HE CLOSED UP AGAIN.

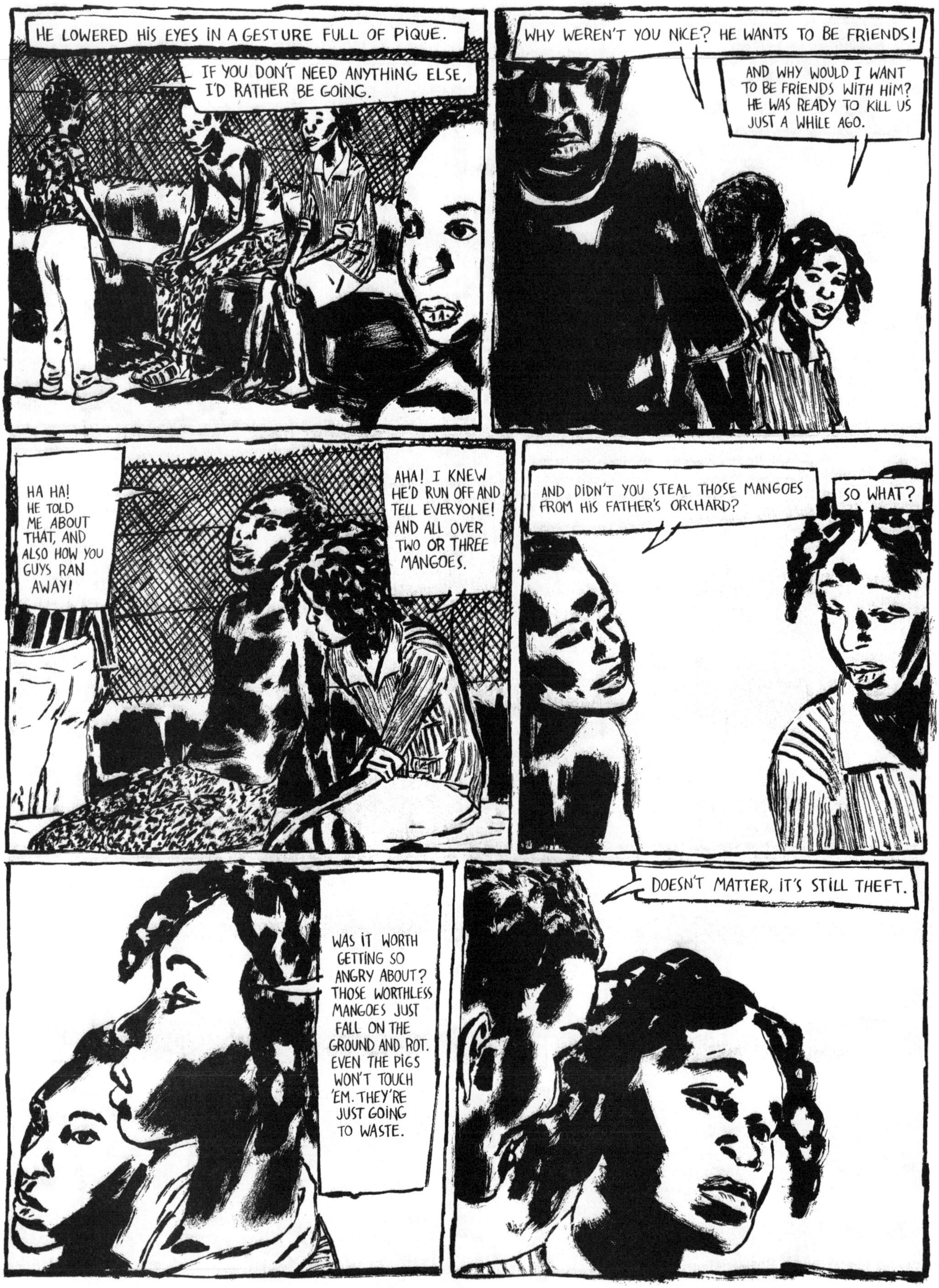
HE LOWERED HIS EYES IN A GESTURE FULL OF PIQUE.
IF YOU DON'T NEED ANYTHING ELSE, I'D RATHER BE GOING.
WHY WEREN'T YOU NICE? HE WANTS TO BE FRIENDS!
AND WHY WOULD I WANT TO BE FRIENDS WITH HIM? HE WAS READY TO KILL US JUST A WHILE AGO.
HA HA! HE TOLD ME ABOUT THAT, AND ALSO HOW YOU GUYS RAN AWAY!
AHA! I KNEW HE'D RUN OFF AND TELL EVERYONE! AND ALL OVER TWO OR THREE MANGOES.
AND DIDN'T YOU STEAL THOSE MANGOES FROM HIS FATHER'S ORCHARD?
SO WHAT?
WAS IT WORTH GETTING SO ANGRY ABOUT? THOSE WORTHLESS MANGOES JUST FALL ON THE GROUND AND ROT. EVEN THE PIGS WON'T TOUCH 'EM. THEY'RE JUST GOING TO WASTE.
DOESN'T MATTER, IT'S STILL THEFT.

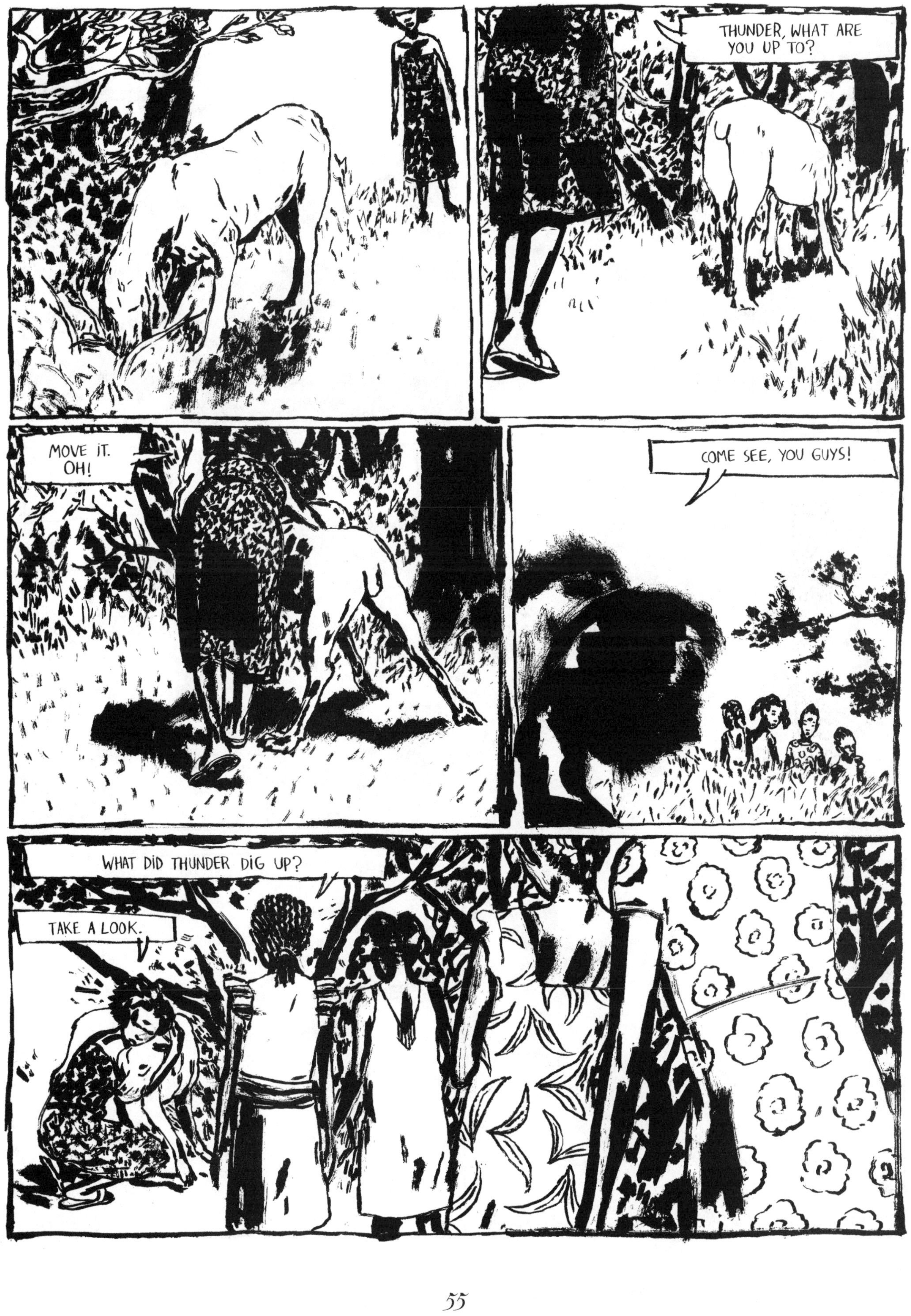
THUNDER, WHAT ARE YOU UP TO?
MOVE IT.
OH!
COME SEE, YOU GUYS!
WHAT DID THUNDER DIG UP?
TAKE A LOOK.

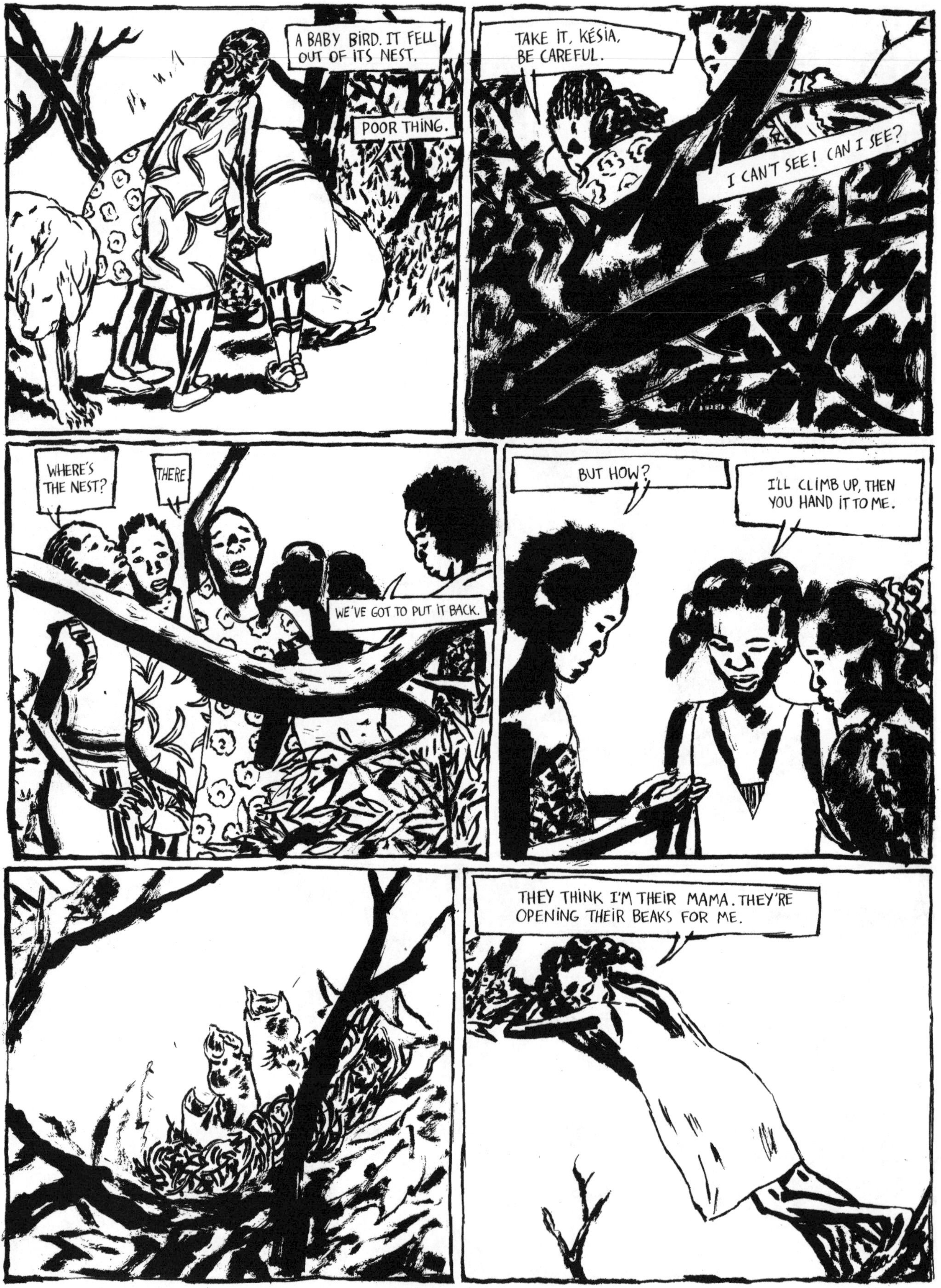
A BABY BIRD. IT FELL OUT OF ITS NEST.
POOR THING.
TAKE IT, KÉSIA, BE CAREFUL.
I CAN'T SEE! CAN I SEE?
WHERE'S THE NEST?
THERE.
WE'VE GOT TO PUT IT BACK.
BUT HOW?
I'LL CLIMB UP, THEN YOU HAND IT TO ME.
THEY THINK I'M THEIR MAMA. THEY'RE OPENING THEIR BEAKS FOR ME.

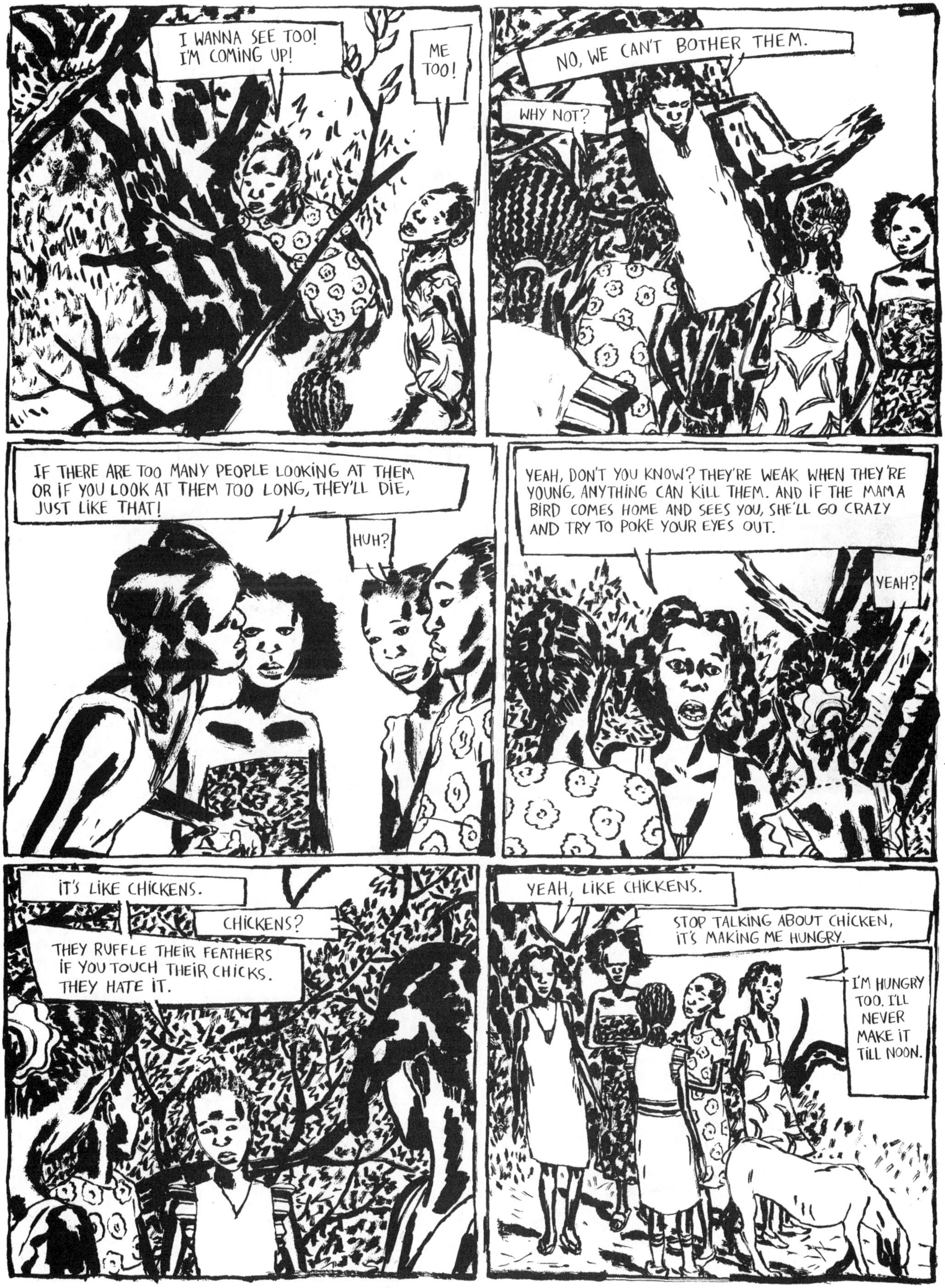
I WANNA SEE TOO! I'M COMING UP!
ME TOO!
NO, WE CAN'T BOTHER THEM.
WHY NOT?
IF THERE ARE TOO MANY PEOPLE LOOKING AT THEM OR IF YOU LOOK AT THEM TOO LONG, THEY'LL DIE, JUST LIKE THAT!
HUH?
YEAH, DON'T YOU KNOW? THEY'RE WEAK WHEN THEY'RE YOUNG, ANYTHING CAN KILL THEM. AND IF THE MAMA BIRD COMES HOME AND SEES YOU, SHE'LL GO CRAZY AND TRY TO POKE YOUR EYES OUT.
YEAH?
IT'S LIKE CHICKENS.
CHICKENS?
THEY RUFFLE THEIR FEATHERS IF YOU TOUCH THEIR CHICKS. THEY HATE IT.
YEAH, LIKE CHICKENS.
STOP TALKING ABOUT CHICKEN, IT'S MAKING ME HUNGRY.
I'M HUNGRY TOO. I'LL NEVER MAKE IT TILL NOON.

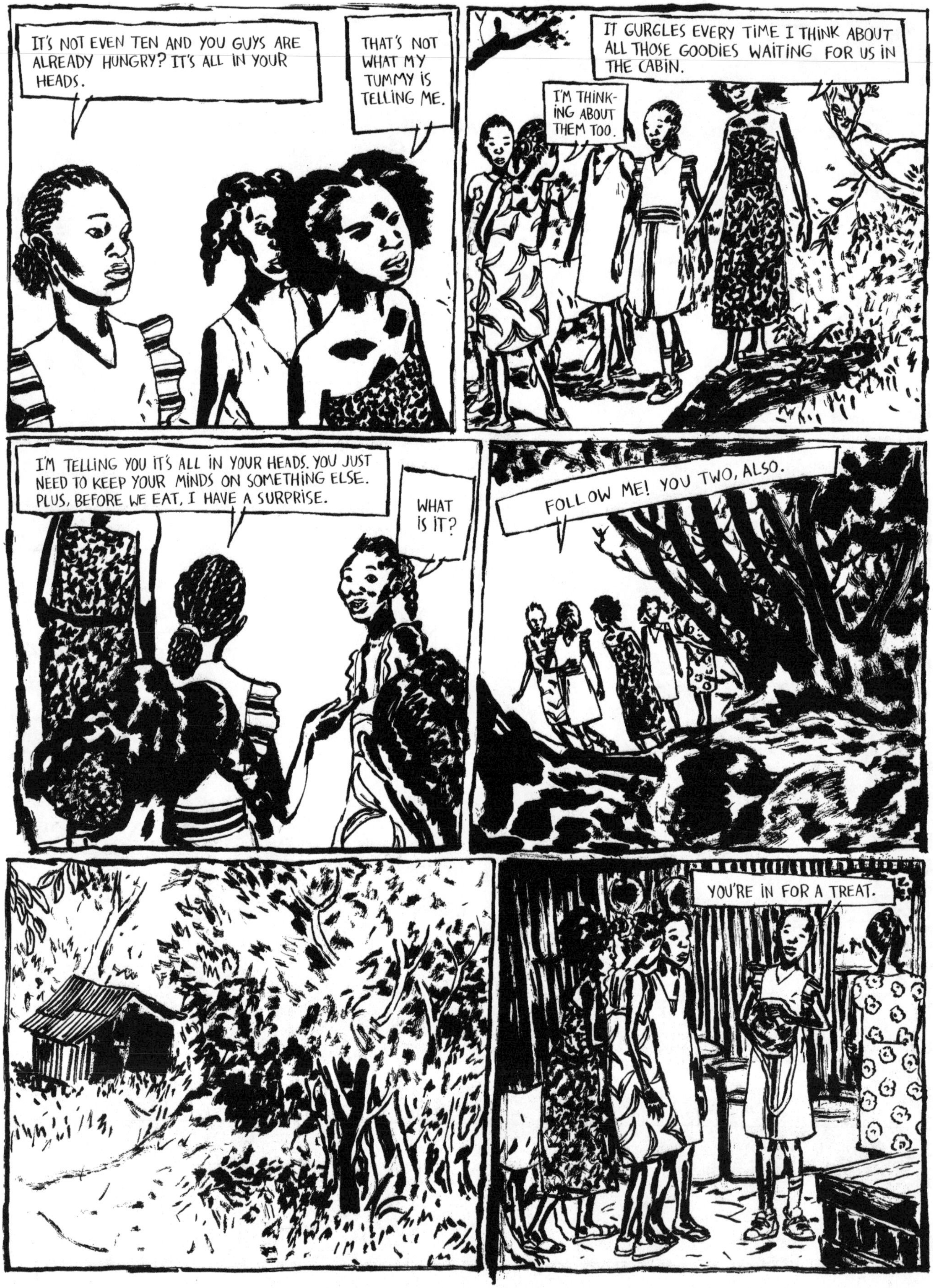
IT'S NOT EVEN TEN AND YOU GUYS ARE ALREADY HUNGRY? IT'S ALL IN YOUR HEADS.
THAT'S NOT WHAT MY TUMMY IS TELLING ME.
IT GURGLES EVERY TIME I THINK ABOUT ALL THOSE GOODIES WAITING FOR US IN THE CABIN.
I'M THINKING ABOUT THEM TOO.
I'M TELLING YOU IT'S ALL IN YOUR HEADS. YOU JUST NEED TO KEEP YOUR MINDS ON SOMETHING ELSE. PLUS, BEFORE WE EAT, I HAVE A SURPRISE.
WHAT IS IT?
FOLLOW ME! YOU TWO, ALSO.
YOU'RE IN FOR A TREAT.

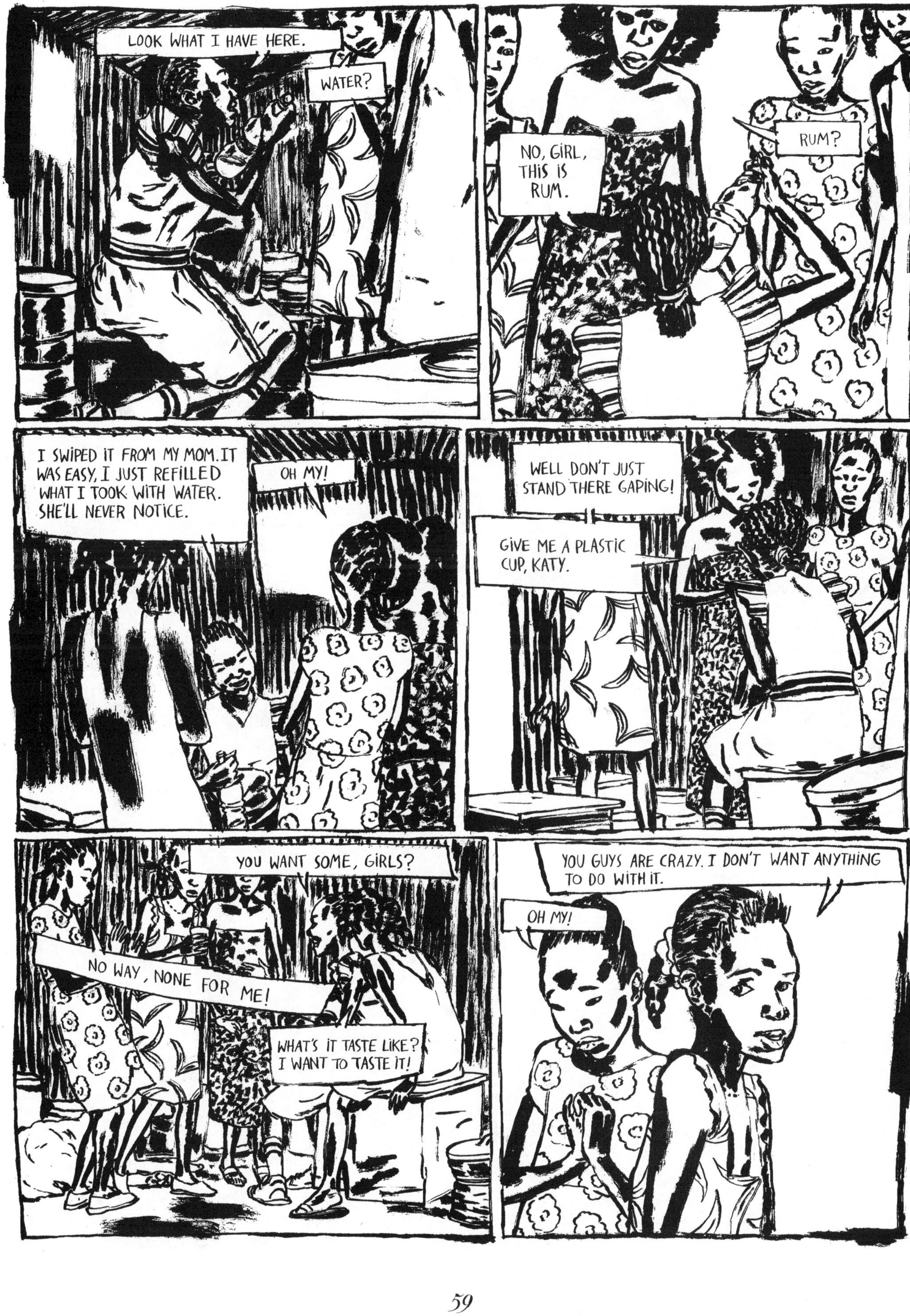
LOOK WHAT I HAVE HERE.
WATER?
NO, GIRL, THIS IS RUM.
RUM?
I SWIPED IT FROM MY MOM. IT WAS EASY, I JUST REFILLED WHAT I TOOK WITH WATER. SHE'LL NEVER NOTICE.
OH MY!
WELL DON'T JUST STAND THERE GAPING!
GIVE ME A PLASTIC CUP, KATY.
YOU WANT SOME, GIRLS?
NO WAY, NONE FOR ME!
WHAT'S IT TASTE LIKE? I WANT TO TASTE IT!
YOU GUYS ARE CRAZY. I DON'T WANT ANYTHING TO DO WITH IT.
OH MY!

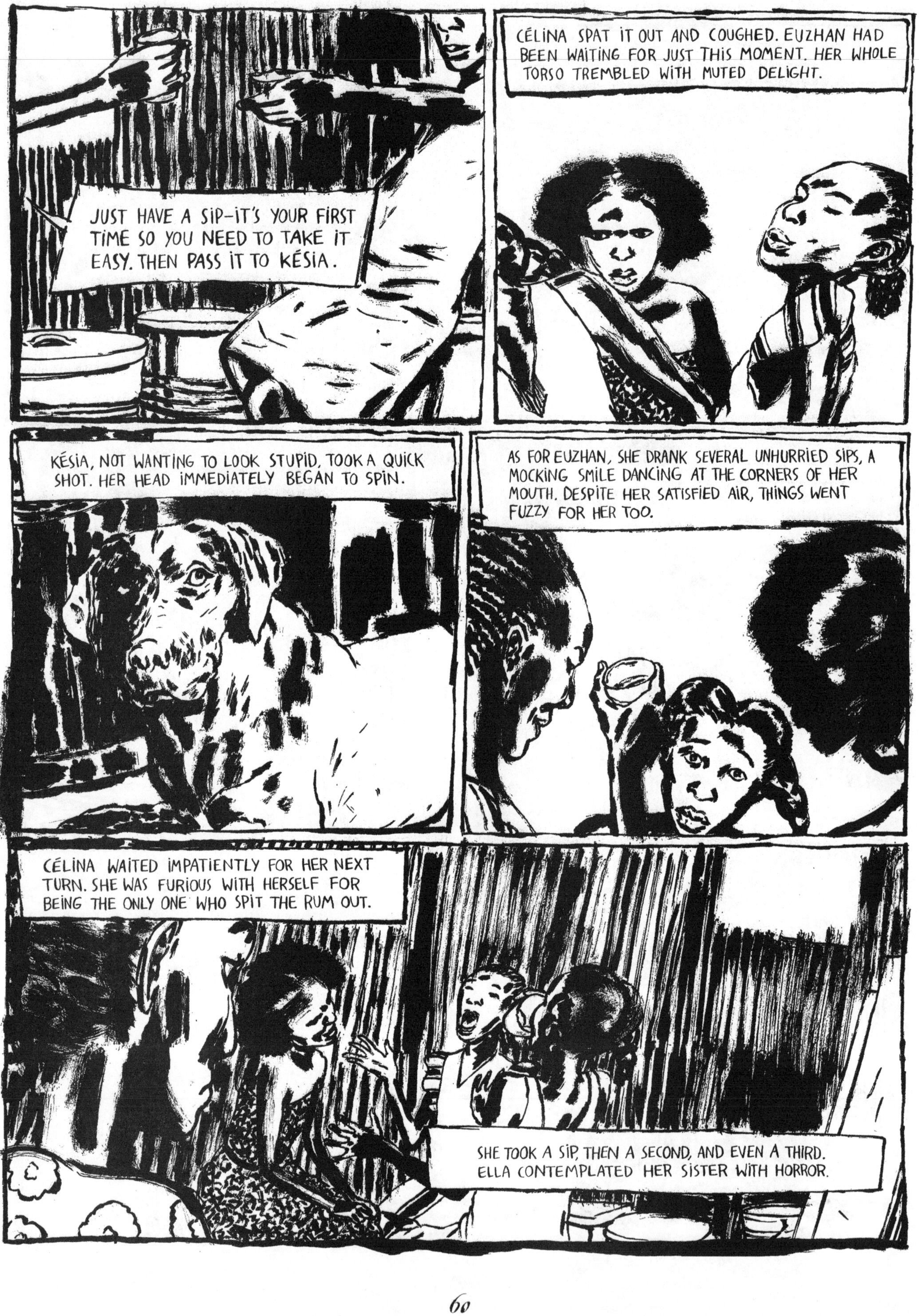
JUST HAVE A SIP–IT'S YOUR FIRST TIME SO YOU NEED TO TAKE IT EASY. THEN PASS IT TO KÉSIA.
CÉLINA SPAT IT OUT AND COUGHED. EUZHAN HAD BEEN WAITING FOR JUST THIS MOMENT. HER WHOLE TORSO TREMBLED WITH MUTED DELIGHT.
KÉSIA, NOT WANTING TO LOOK STUPID, TOOK A QUICK SHOT. HER HEAD IMMEDIATELY BEGAN TO SPIN.
AS FOR EUZHAN, SHE DRANK SEVERAL UNHURRIED SIPS, A MOCKING SMILE DANCING AT THE CORNERS OF HER MOUTH. DESPITE HER SATISFIED AIR, THINGS WENT FUZZY FOR HER TOO.
CÉLINA WAITED IMPATIENTLY FOR HER NEXT TURN. SHE WAS FURIOUS WITH HERSELF FOR BEING THE ONLY ONE WHO SPIT THE RUM OUT.
SHE TOOK A SIP, THEN A SECOND, AND EVEN A THIRD. ELLA CONTEMPLATED HER SISTER WITH HORROR.

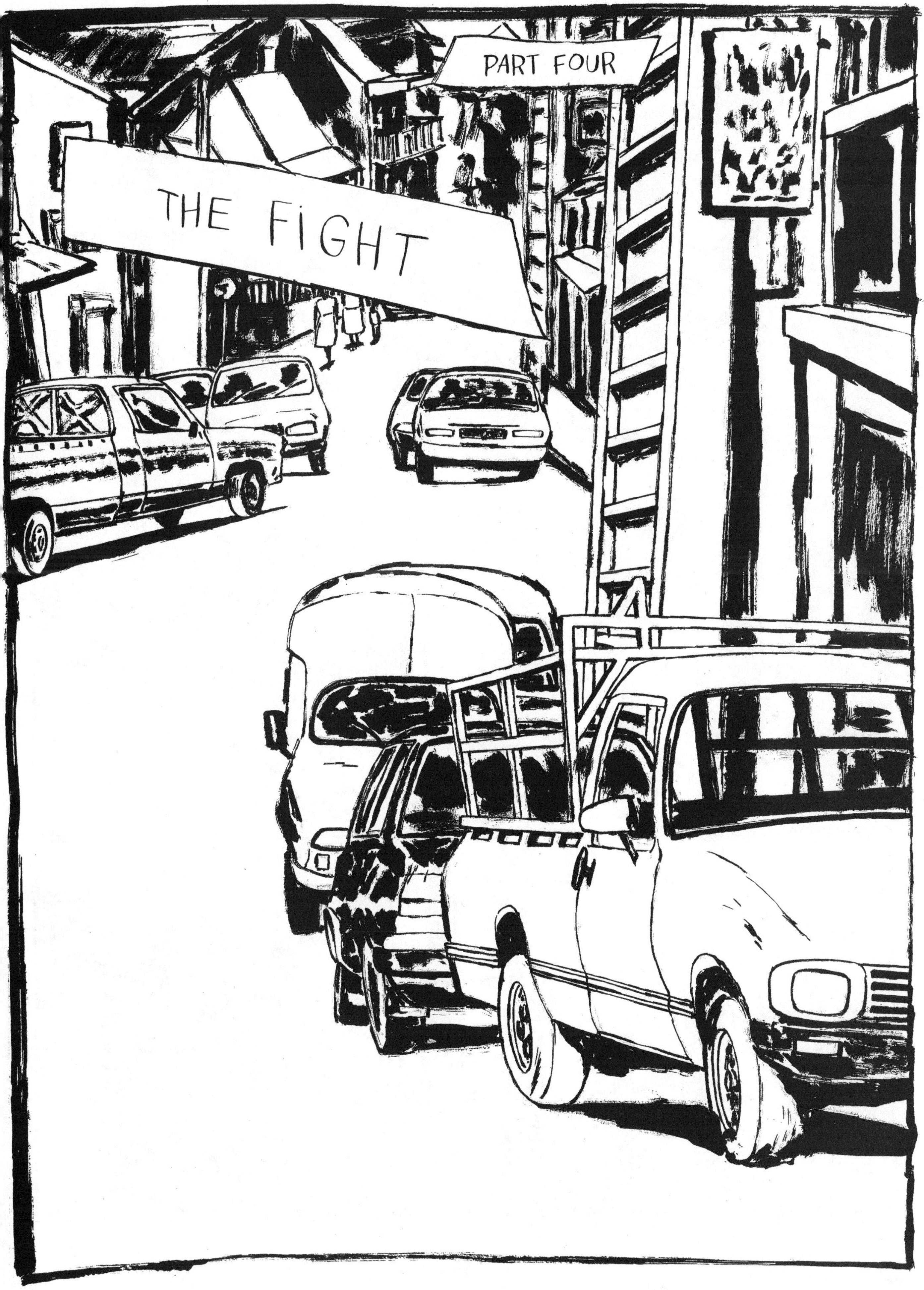
PART FOUR
THE FIGHT

TITO WAS RUNNING LEFT AND RIGHT, DEFYING ANYONE WHO CROSSED HIS PATH, REGARDLESS OF WHICH SIDE THEY WERE ON.

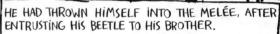

HE HAD THROWN HIMSELF INTO THE MELÉE, AFTER ENTRUSTING HIS BEETLE TO HIS BROTHER.

VIVIEN'S GANG WAS RUNNING OUT OF INSULTS. IT WAS ALMOST TIME. EVERYONE WAS TENSE.

TITO WAS GESTICULATING WILDLY. THE CROWD LAUGHED BUT HE WAS DEADLY SERIOUS.

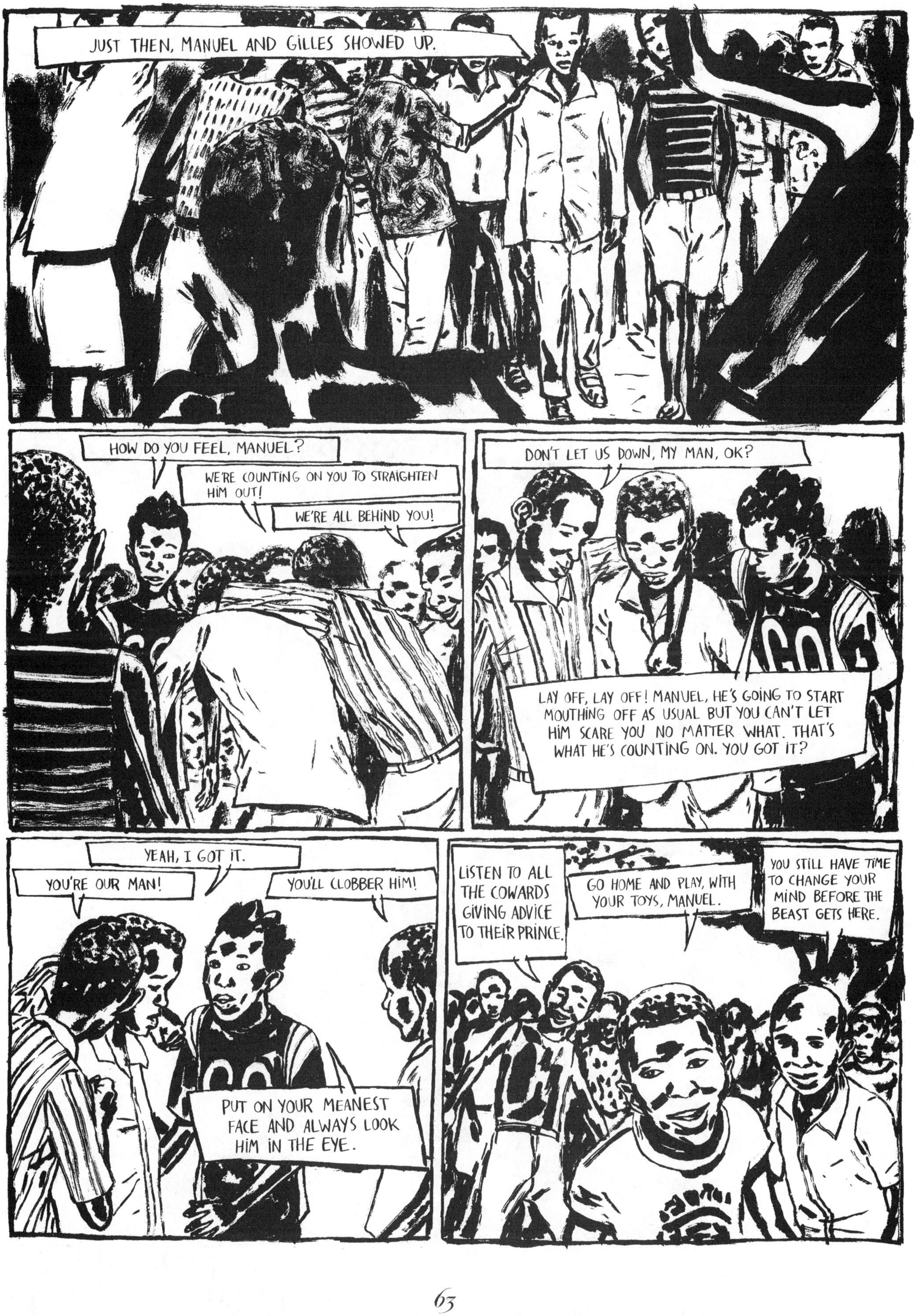
JUST THEN, MANUEL AND GILLES SHOWED UP.
HOW DO YOU FEEL, MANUEL?
WE'RE COUNTING ON YOU TO STRAIGHTEN HIM OUT!
WE'RE ALL BEHIND YOU!
DON'T LET US DOWN, MY MAN, OK?
LAY OFF, LAY OFF! MANUEL, HE'S GOING TO START MOUTHING OFF AS USUAL BUT YOU CAN'T LET HIM SCARE YOU NO MATTER WHAT. THAT'S WHAT HE'S COUNTING ON. YOU GOT IT?
YEAH, I GOT IT.
YOU'RE OUR MAN!
YOU'LL CLOBBER HIM!
PUT ON YOUR MEANEST FACE AND ALWAYS LOOK HIM IN THE EYE.
LISTEN TO ALL THE COWARDS GIVING ADVICE TO THEIR PRINCE.
GO HOME AND PLAY, WITH YOUR TOYS, MANUEL.
YOU STILL HAVE TIME TO CHANGE YOUR MIND BEFORE THE BEAST GETS HERE.

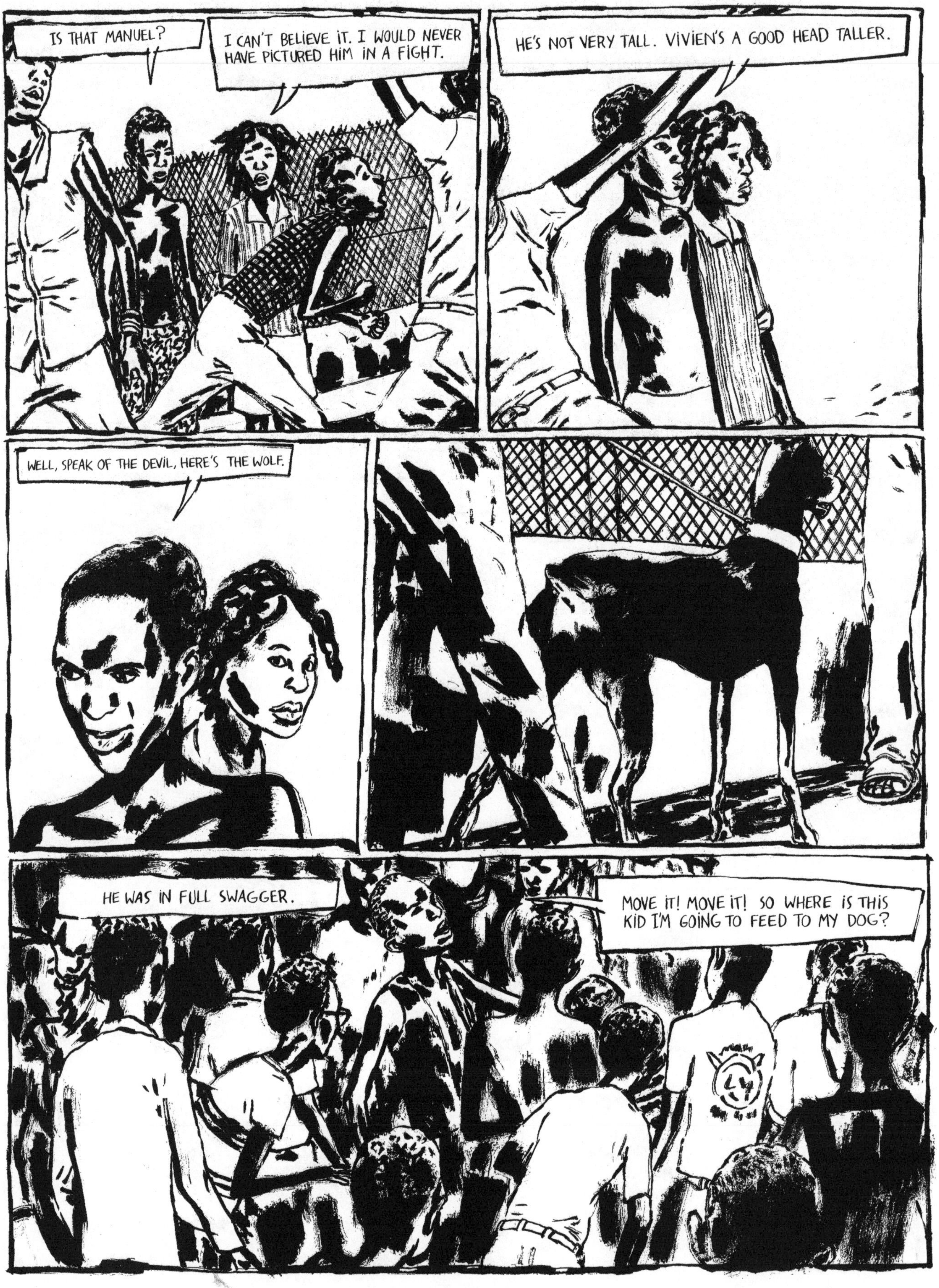
IS THAT MANUEL?
I CAN'T BELIEVE IT. I WOULD NEVER HAVE PICTURED HIM IN A FIGHT.
HE'S NOT VERY TALL. VIVIEN'S A GOOD HEAD TALLER.
WELL, SPEAK OF THE DEVIL, HERE'S THE WOLF.
HE WAS IN FULL SWAGGER.
MOVE IT! MOVE IT! SO WHERE IS THIS KID I'M GOING TO FEED TO MY DOG?

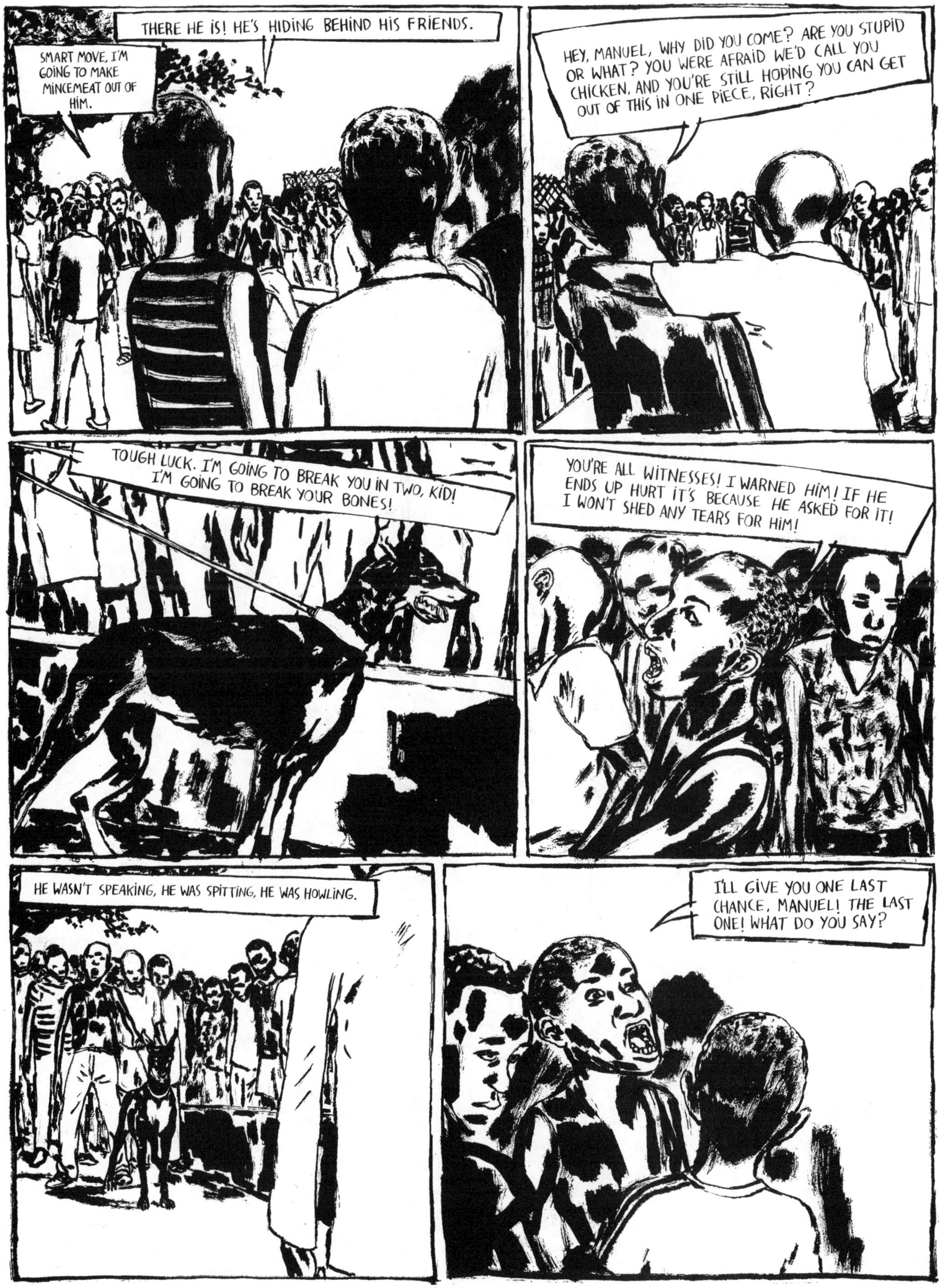
THERE HE IS! HE'S HIDING BEHIND HIS FRIENDS.
SMART MOVE, I'M GOING TO MAKE MINCEMEAT OUT OF HIM.
HEY, MANUEL, WHY DID YOU COME? ARE YOU STUPID OR WHAT? YOU WERE AFRAID WE'D CALL YOU CHICKEN, AND YOU'RE STILL HOPING YOU CAN GET OUT OF THIS IN ONE PIECE, RIGHT?
TOUGH LUCK. I'M GOING TO BREAK YOU IN TWO, KID! I'M GOING TO BREAK YOUR BONES!
YOU'RE ALL WITNESSES! I WARNED HIM! IF HE ENDS UP HURT IT'S BECAUSE HE ASKED FOR IT! I WON'T SHED ANY TEARS FOR HIM!
HE WASN'T SPEAKING, HE WAS SPITTING, HE WAS HOWLING.
I'LL GIVE YOU ONE LAST CHANCE, MANUEL! THE LAST ONE! WHAT DO YOU SAY?

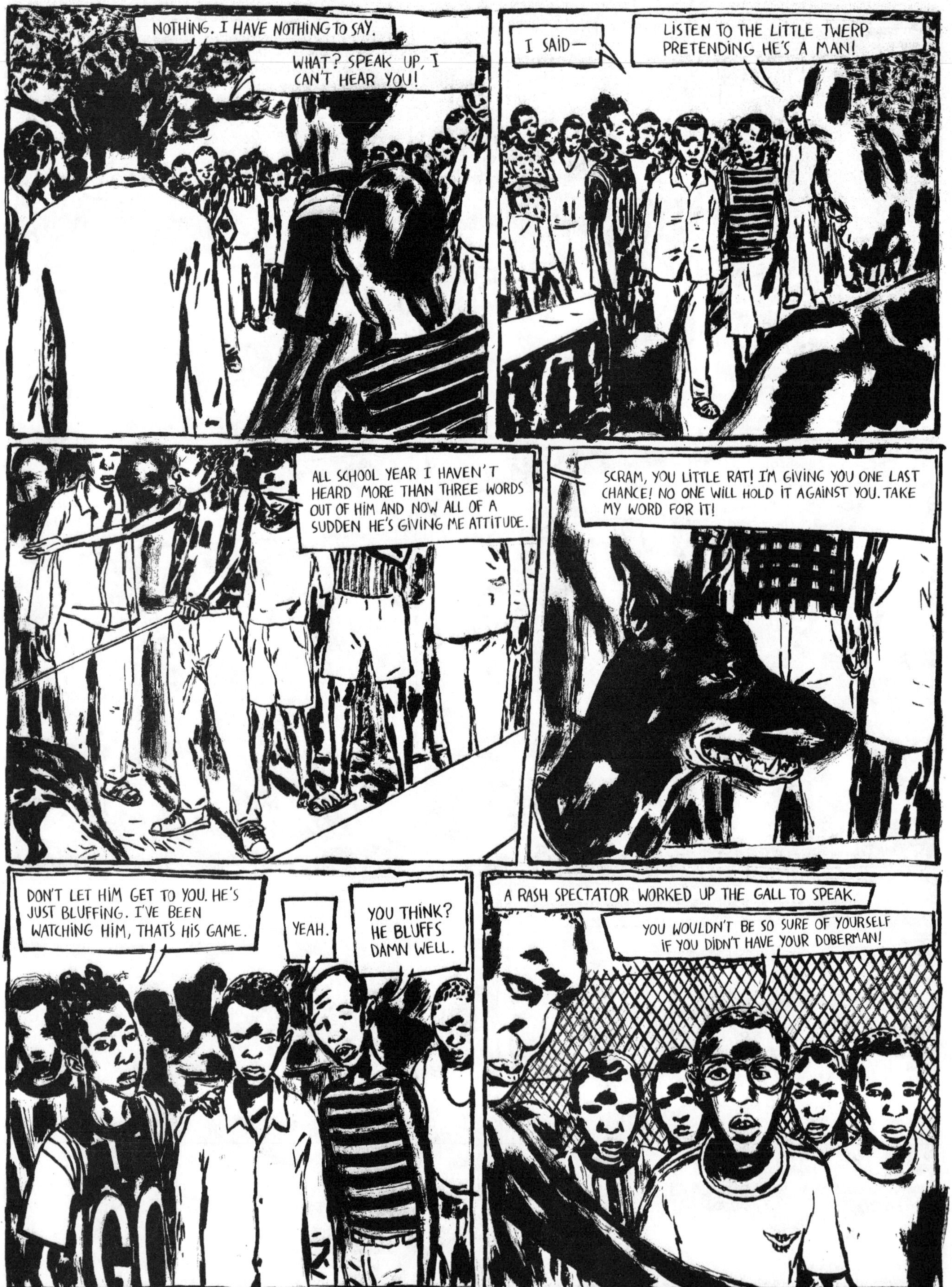

NOTHING. I HAVE NOTHING TO SAY.
WHAT? SPEAK UP, I CAN'T HEAR YOU!
I SAID—
LISTEN TO THE LITTLE TWERP PRETENDING HE'S A MAN!
ALL SCHOOL YEAR I HAVEN'T HEARD MORE THAN THREE WORDS OUT OF HIM AND NOW ALL OF A SUDDEN HE'S GIVING ME ATTITUDE.
SCRAM, YOU LITTLE RAT! I'M GIVING YOU ONE LAST CHANCE! NO ONE WILL HOLD IT AGAINST YOU. TAKE MY WORD FOR IT!
DON'T LET HIM GET TO YOU. HE'S JUST BLUFFING. I'VE BEEN WATCHING HIM, THAT'S HIS GAME.
YEAH.
YOU THINK? HE BLUFFS DAMN WELL.
A RASH SPECTATOR WORKED UP THE GALL TO SPEAK.
YOU WOULDN'T BE SO SURE OF YOURSELF IF YOU DIDN'T HAVE YOUR DOBERMAN!

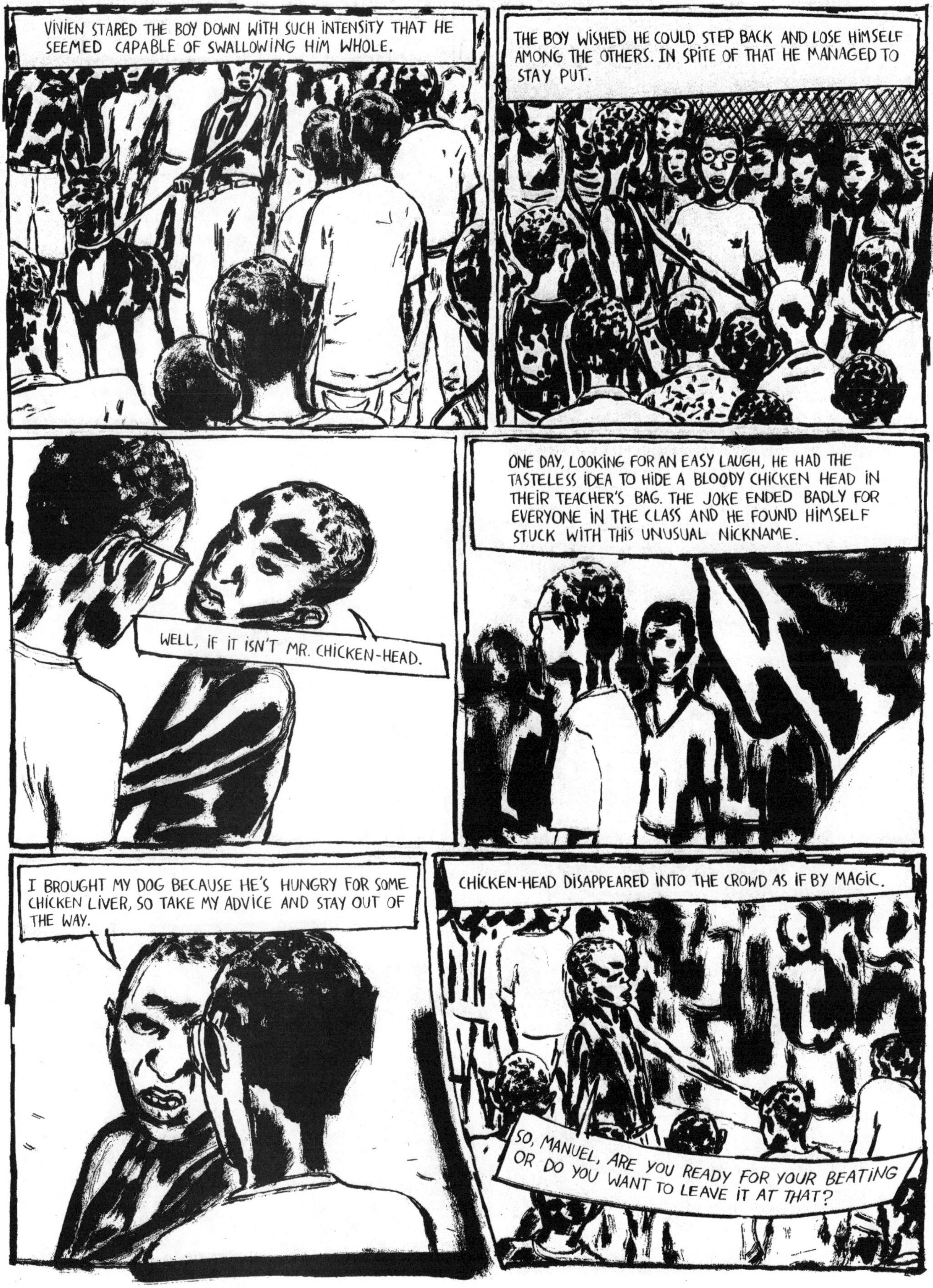
VIVIEN STARED THE BOY DOWN WITH SUCH INTENSITY THAT HE SEEMED CAPABLE OF SWALLOWING HIM WHOLE.
THE BOY WISHED HE COULD STEP BACK AND LOSE HIMSELF AMONG THE OTHERS. IN SPITE OF THAT HE MANAGED TO STAY PUT.
WELL, IF IT ISN'T MR. CHICKEN-HEAD.
ONE DAY, LOOKING FOR AN EASY LAUGH, HE HAD THE TASTELESS IDEA TO HIDE A BLOODY CHICKEN HEAD IN THEIR TEACHER'S BAG. THE JOKE ENDED BADLY FOR EVERYONE IN THE CLASS AND HE FOUND HIMSELF STUCK WITH THIS UNUSUAL NICKNAME.
I BROUGHT MY DOG BECAUSE HE'S HUNGRY FOR SOME CHICKEN LIVER, SO TAKE MY ADVICE AND STAY OUT OF THE WAY.
CHICKEN-HEAD DISAPPEARED INTO THE CROWD AS IF BY MAGIC.
SO, MANUEL, ARE YOU READY FOR YOUR BEATING OR DO YOU WANT TO LEAVE IT AT THAT?

I'M WAITING!

VIVIEN WAS GETTING IMPATIENT. HE HADN'T BEEN EXPECTING TO STICK AROUND LONG.

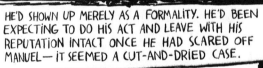

HE'D SHOWN UP MERELY AS A FORMALITY. HE'D BEEN EXPECTING TO DO HIS ACT AND LEAVE WITH HIS REPUTATION INTACT ONCE HE HAD SCARED OFF MANUEL — IT SEEMED A CUT-AND-DRIED CASE.

BUT THE LITTLE RUNT, WHO WAS STARTING TO TROUBLE HIM, WAS STILL THERE, LOOKING HIM STRAIGHT IN THE EYES.

AFTER A FEW MORE INSULTS HE WAS FORCED TO REALIZE THAT A FIGHT WAS INEVITABLE.

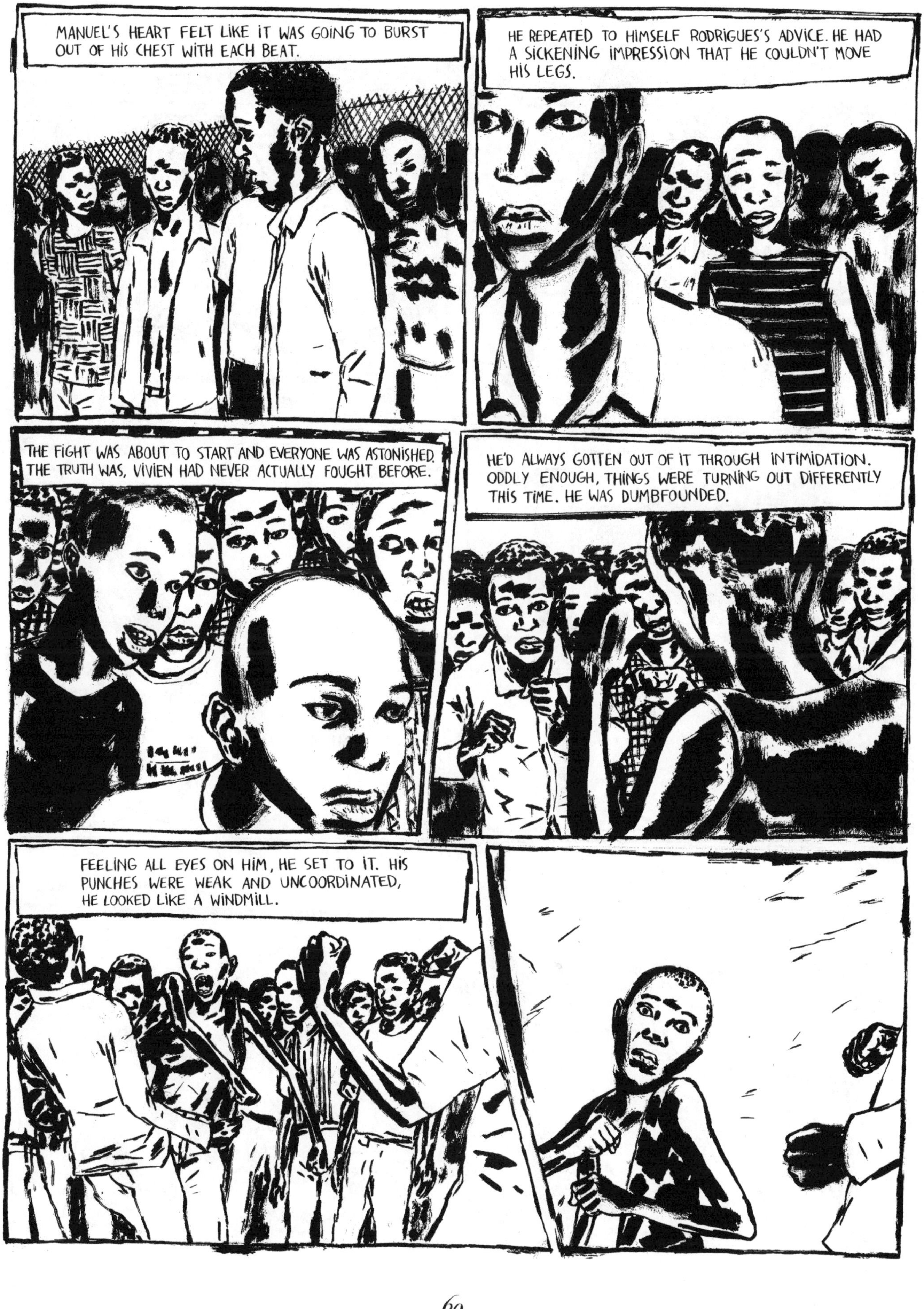
MANUEL'S HEART FELT LIKE IT WAS GOING TO BURST OUT OF HIS CHEST WITH EACH BEAT.
HE REPEATED TO HIMSELF RODRIGUES'S ADVICE. HE HAD A SICKENING IMPRESSION THAT HE COULDN'T MOVE HIS LEGS.
THE FIGHT WAS ABOUT TO START AND EVERYONE WAS ASTONISHED. THE TRUTH WAS, VIVIEN HAD NEVER ACTUALLY FOUGHT BEFORE.
HE'D ALWAYS GOTTEN OUT OF IT THROUGH INTIMIDATION. ODDLY ENOUGH, THINGS WERE TURNING OUT DIFFERENTLY THIS TIME. HE WAS DUMBFOUNDED.
FEELING ALL EYES ON HIM, HE SET TO IT. HIS PUNCHES WERE WEAK AND UNCOORDINATED, HE LOOKED LIKE A WINDMILL.

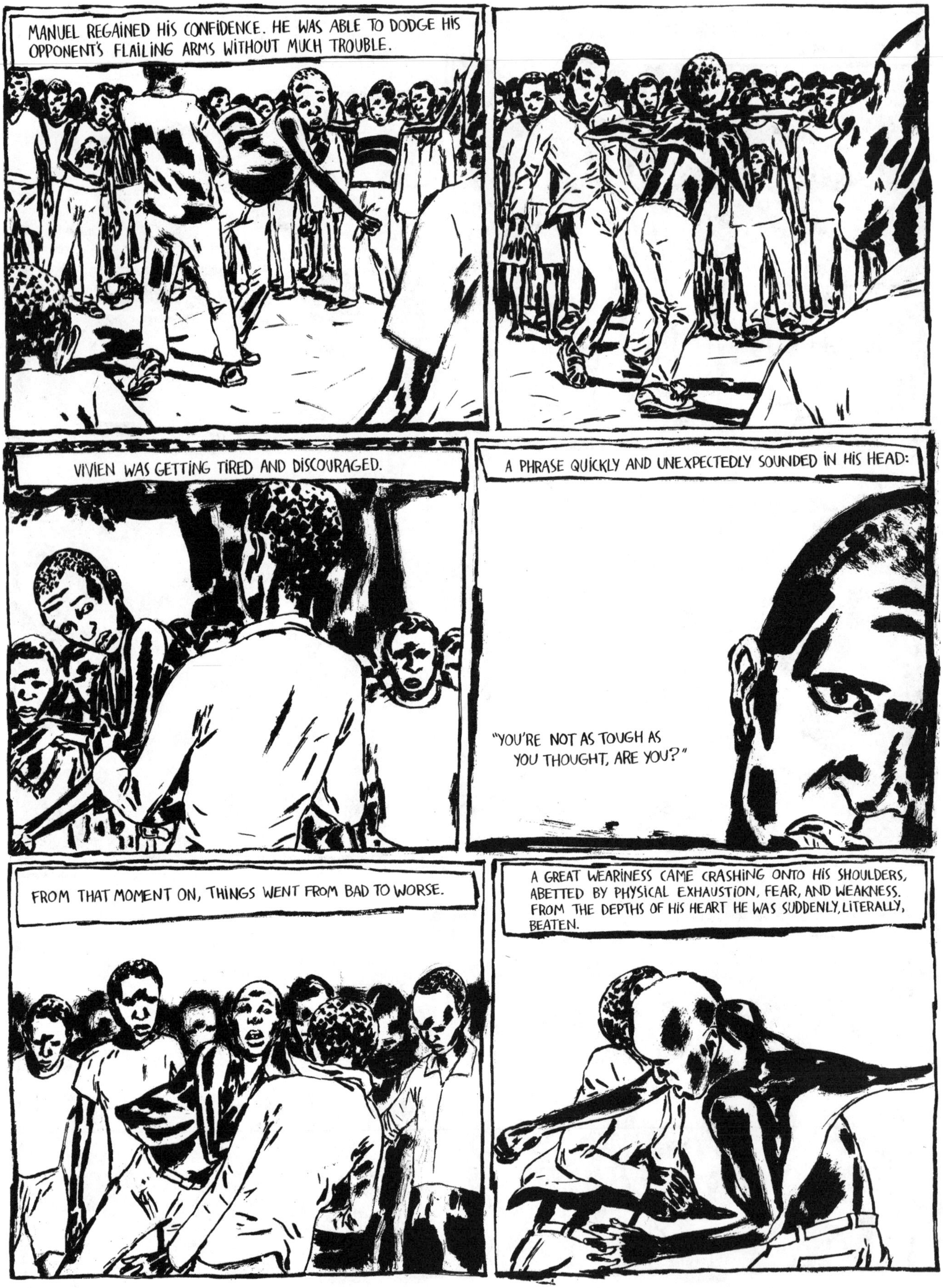
MANUEL REGAINED HIS CONFIDENCE. HE WAS ABLE TO DODGE HIS OPPONENT'S FLAILING ARMS WITHOUT MUCH TROUBLE.
VIVIEN WAS GETTING TIRED AND DISCOURAGED.
A PHRASE QUICKLY AND UNEXPECTEDLY SOUNDED IN HIS HEAD:
"YOU'RE NOT AS TOUGH AS YOU THOUGHT, ARE YOU?"
FROM THAT MOMENT ON, THINGS WENT FROM BAD TO WORSE.
A GREAT WEARINESS CAME CRASHING ONTO HIS SHOULDERS, ABETTED BY PHYSICAL EXHAUSTION, FEAR, AND WEAKNESS. FROM THE DEPTHS OF HIS HEART HE WAS SUDDENLY, LITERALLY, BEATEN.

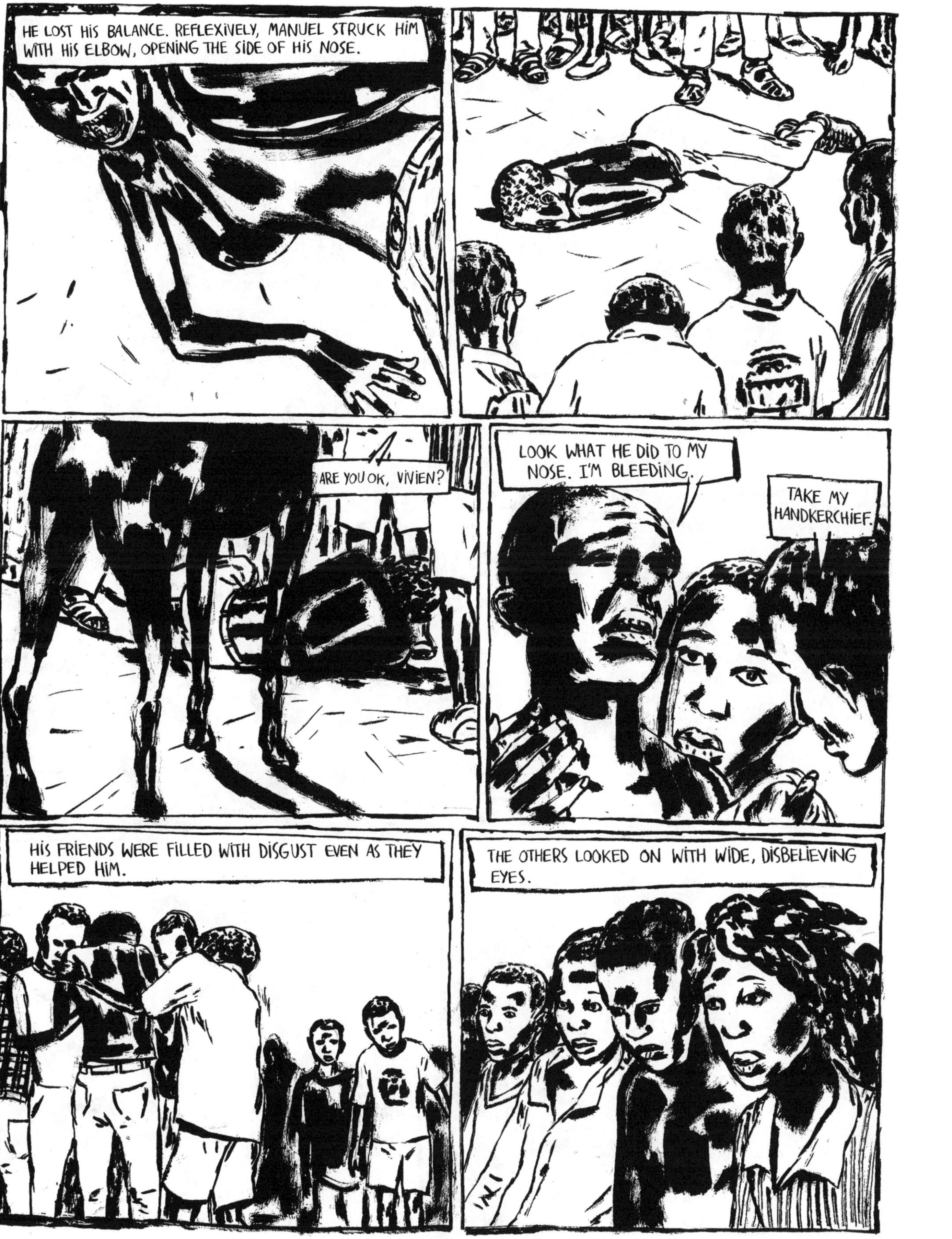
HE LOST HIS BALANCE. REFLEXIVELY, MANUEL STRUCK HIM WITH HIS ELBOW, OPENING THE SIDE OF HIS NOSE.
ARE YOU OK, VIVIEN?
LOOK WHAT HE DID TO MY NOSE. I'M BLEEDING.
TAKE MY HANDKERCHIEF.
HIS FRIENDS WERE FILLED WITH DISGUST EVEN AS THEY HELPED HIM.
THE OTHERS LOOKED ON WITH WIDE, DISBELIEVING EYES.

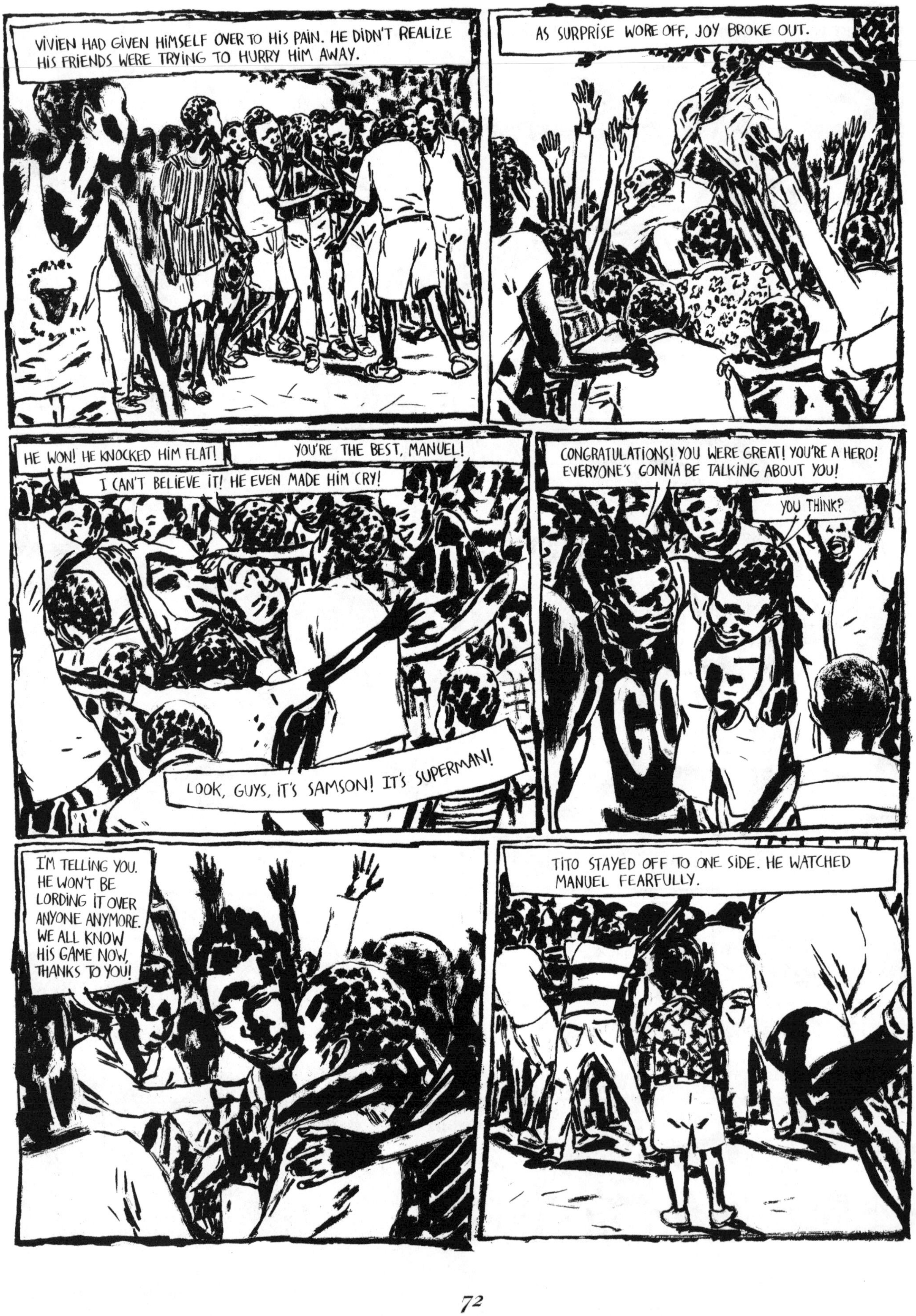
VIVIEN HAD GIVEN HIMSELF OVER TO HIS PAIN. HE DIDN'T REALIZE HIS FRIENDS WERE TRYING TO HURRY HIM AWAY.
AS SURPRISE WORE OFF, JOY BROKE OUT.
HE WON! HE KNOCKED HIM FLAT!
YOU'RE THE BEST, MANUEL!
I CAN'T BELIEVE IT! HE EVEN MADE HIM CRY!
LOOK, GUYS, IT'S SAMSON! IT'S SUPERMAN!
CONGRATULATIONS! YOU WERE GREAT! YOU'RE A HERO! EVERYONE'S GONNA BE TALKING ABOUT YOU!
YOU THINK?
GO
I'M TELLING YOU. HE WON'T BE LORDING IT OVER ANYONE ANYMORE. WE ALL KNOW HIS GAME NOW, THANKS TO YOU!
TITO STAYED OFF TO ONE SIDE. HE WATCHED MANUEL FEARFULLY.

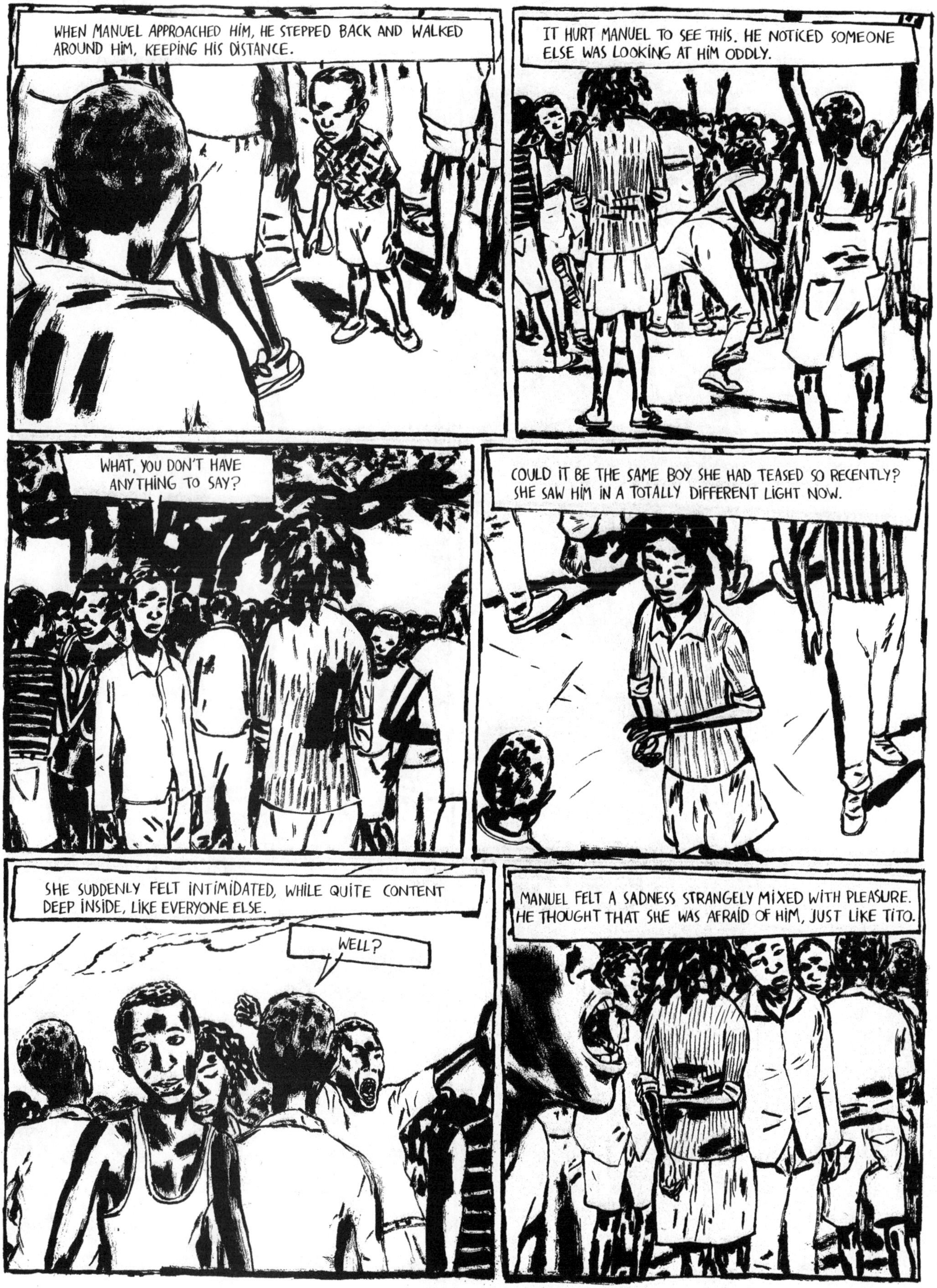
WHEN MANUEL APPROACHED HIM, HE STEPPED BACK AND WALKED AROUND HIM, KEEPING HIS DISTANCE.
IT HURT MANUEL TO SEE THIS. HE NOTICED SOMEONE ELSE WAS LOOKING AT HIM ODDLY.
WHAT, YOU DON'T HAVE ANYTHING TO SAY?
COULD IT BE THE SAME BOY SHE HAD TEASED SO RECENTLY? SHE SAW HIM IN A TOTALLY DIFFERENT LIGHT NOW.
SHE SUDDENLY FELT INTIMIDATED, WHILE QUITE CONTENT DEEP INSIDE, LIKE EVERYONE ELSE.
WELL?
MANUEL FELT A SADNESS STRANGELY MIXED WITH PLEASURE. HE THOUGHT THAT SHE WAS AFRAID OF HIM, JUST LIKE TITO.

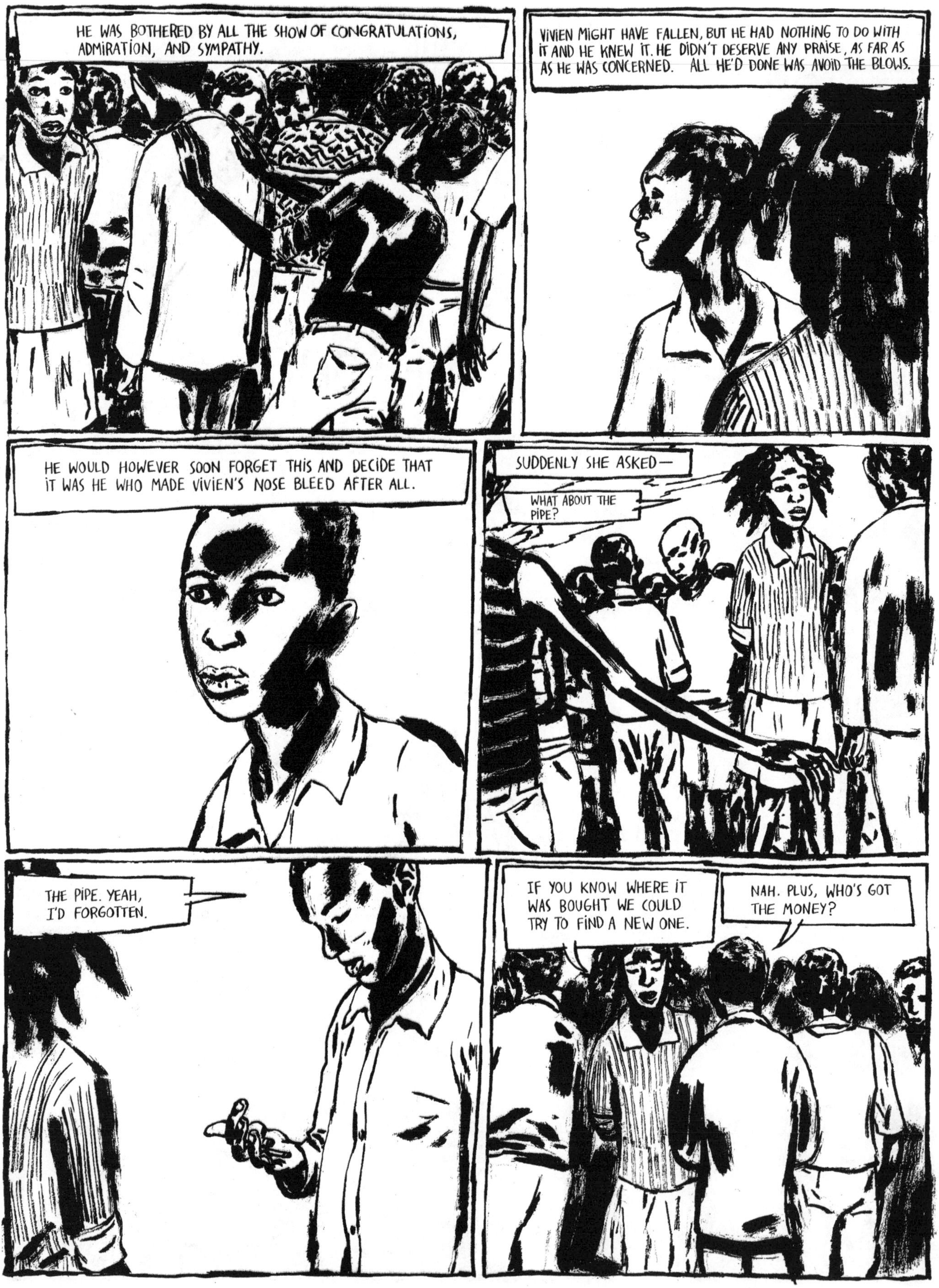
HE WAS BOTHERED BY ALL THE SHOW OF CONGRATULATIONS, ADMIRATION, AND SYMPATHY.
VIVIEN MIGHT HAVE FALLEN, BUT HE HAD NOTHING TO DO WITH IT AND HE KNEW IT. HE DIDN'T DESERVE ANY PRAISE, AS FAR AS AS HE WAS CONCERNED. ALL HE'D DONE WAS AVOID THE BLOWS.
HE WOULD HOWEVER SOON FORGET THIS AND DECIDE THAT IT WAS HE WHO MADE VIVIEN'S NOSE BLEED AFTER ALL.
SUDDENLY SHE ASKED—
WHAT ABOUT THE PIPE?
THE PIPE. YEAH, I'D FORGOTTEN.
IF YOU KNOW WHERE IT WAS BOUGHT WE COULD TRY TO FIND A NEW ONE.
NAH. PLUS, WHO'S GOT THE MONEY?

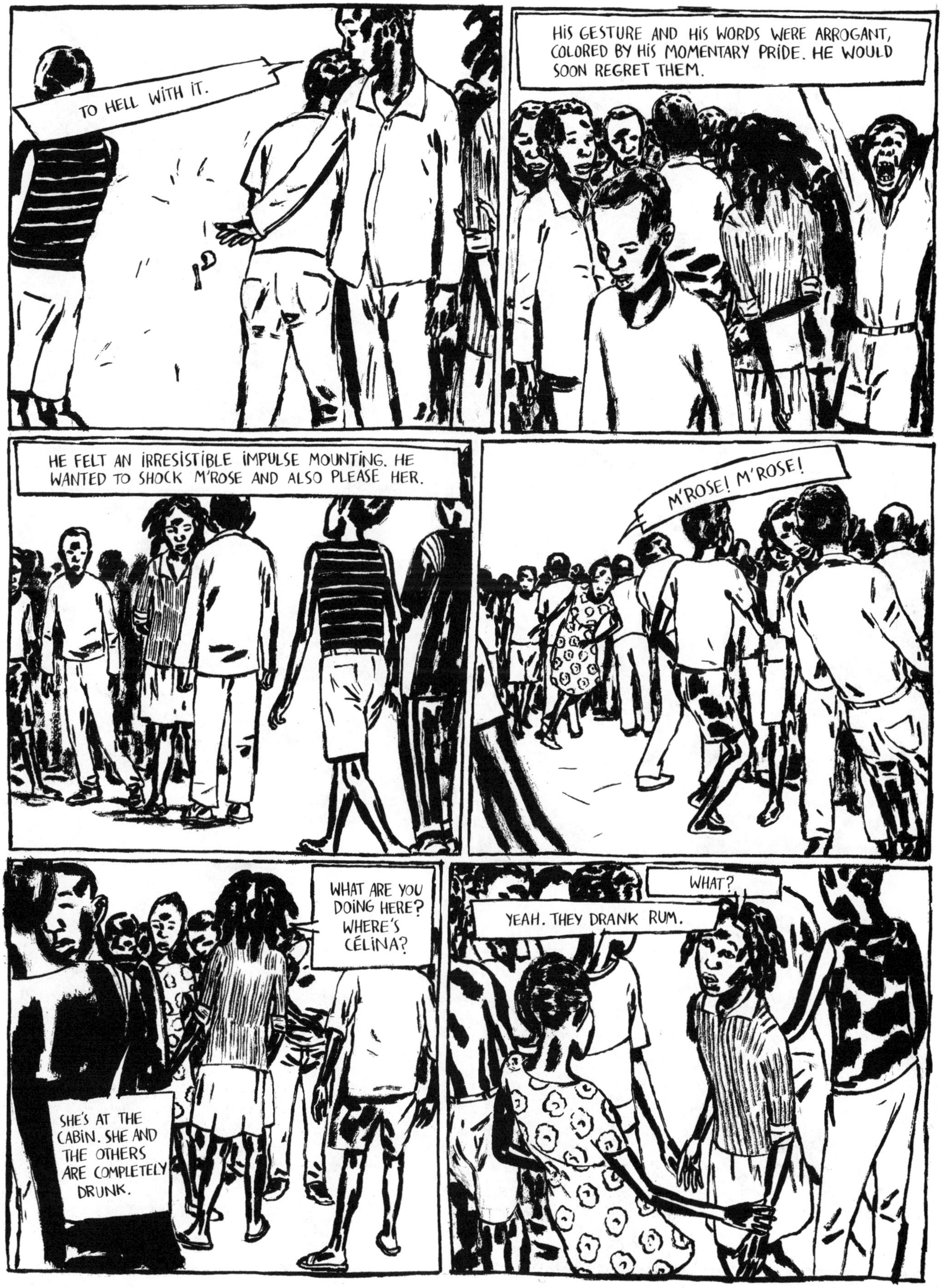
TO HELL WITH IT.
HIS GESTURE AND HIS WORDS WERE ARROGANT, COLORED BY HIS MOMENTARY PRIDE. HE WOULD SOON REGRET THEM.
HE FELT AN IRRESISTIBLE IMPULSE MOUNTING. HE WANTED TO SHOCK M'ROSE AND ALSO PLEASE HER.
M'ROSE! M'ROSE!
WHAT ARE YOU DOING HERE? WHERE'S CÉLINA?
SHE'S AT THE CABIN. SHE AND THE OTHERS ARE COMPLETELY DRUNK.
WHAT?
YEAH. THEY DRANK RUM.

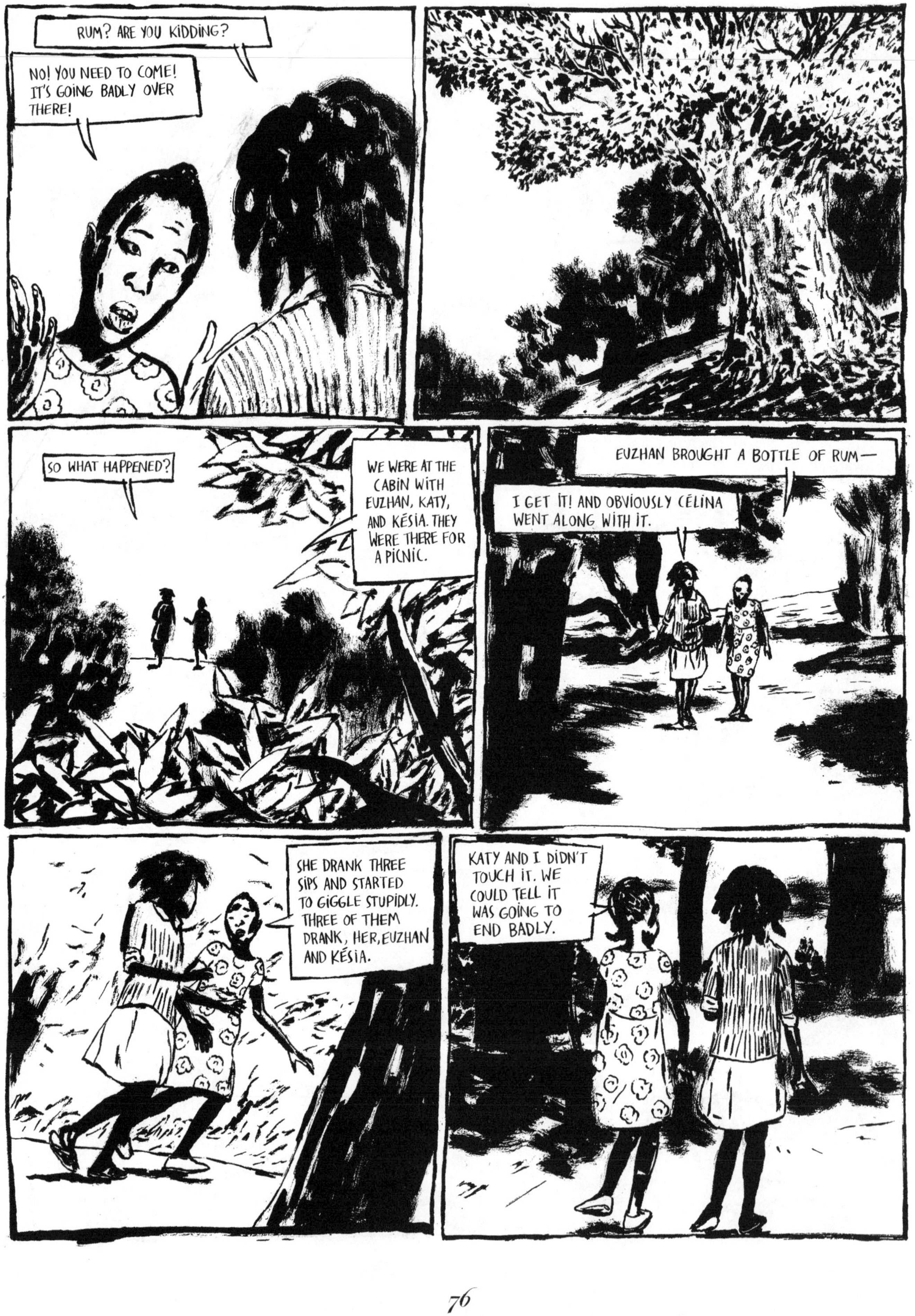
RUM? ARE YOU KIDDING?
NO! YOU NEED TO COME! IT'S GOING BADLY OVER THERE!
SO WHAT HAPPENED?
WE WERE AT THE CABIN WITH EUZHAN, KATY, AND KÉSIA. THEY WERE THERE FOR A PICNIC.
EUZHAN BROUGHT A BOTTLE OF RUM—
I GET IT! AND OBVIOUSLY CÉLINA WENT ALONG WITH IT.
SHE DRANK THREE SIPS AND STARTED TO GIGGLE STUPIDLY. THREE OF THEM DRANK, HER, EUZHAN AND KÉSIA.
KATY AND I DIDN'T TOUCH IT. WE COULD TELL IT WAS GOING TO END BADLY.

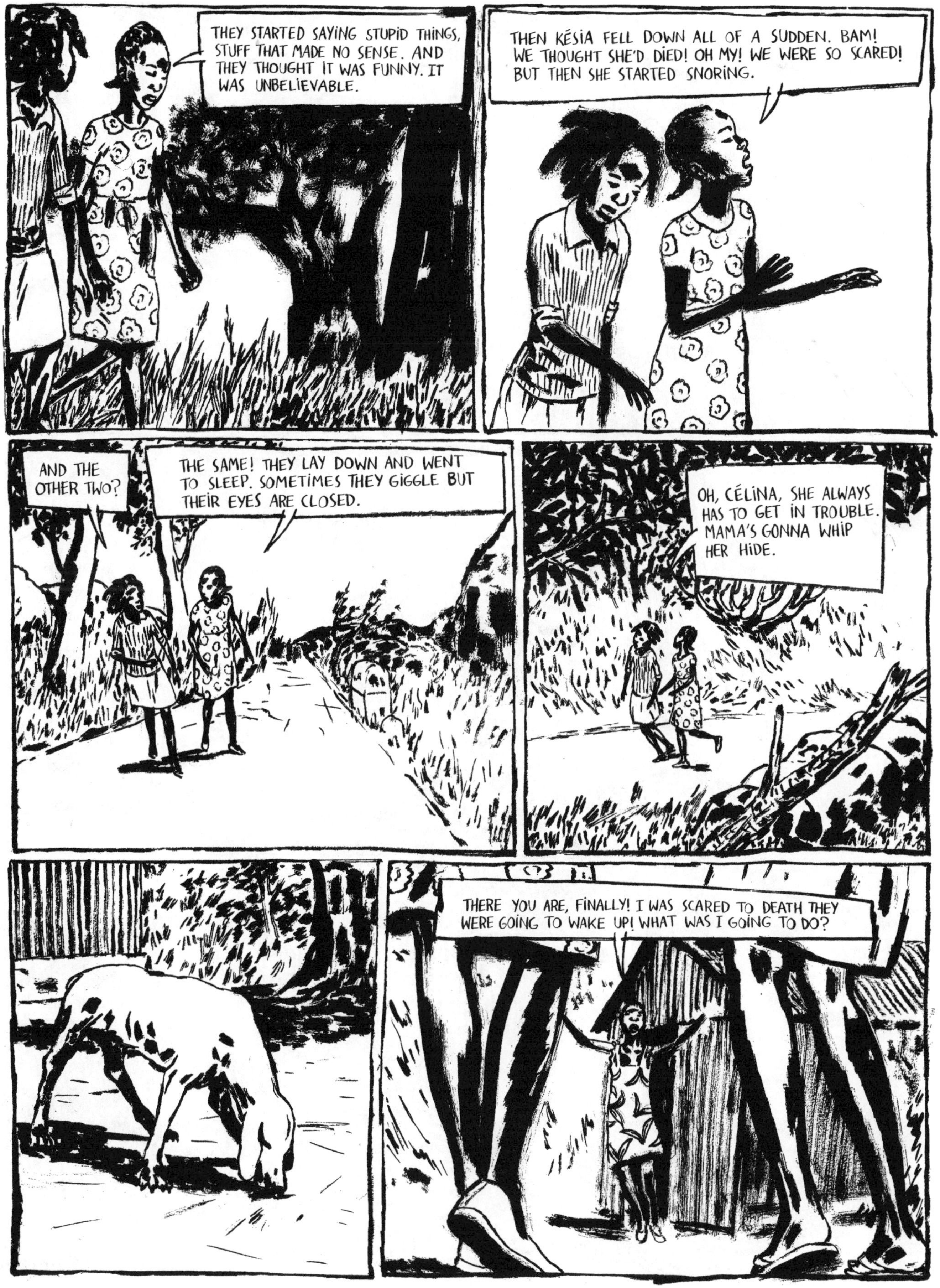
THEY STARTED SAYING STUPID THINGS, STUFF THAT MADE NO SENSE. AND THEY THOUGHT IT WAS FUNNY. IT WAS UNBELIEVABLE.
THEN KÉSIA FELL DOWN ALL OF A SUDDEN. BAM! WE THOUGHT SHE'D DIED! OH MY! WE WERE SO SCARED! BUT THEN SHE STARTED SNORING.
AND THE OTHER TWO?
THE SAME! THEY LAY DOWN AND WENT TO SLEEP. SOMETIMES THEY GIGGLE BUT THEIR EYES ARE CLOSED.
OH, CÉLINA, SHE ALWAYS HAS TO GET IN TROUBLE. MAMA'S GONNA WHIP HER HIDE.
THERE YOU ARE, FINALLY! I WAS SCARED TO DEATH THEY WERE GOING TO WAKE UP! WHAT WAS I GOING TO DO?

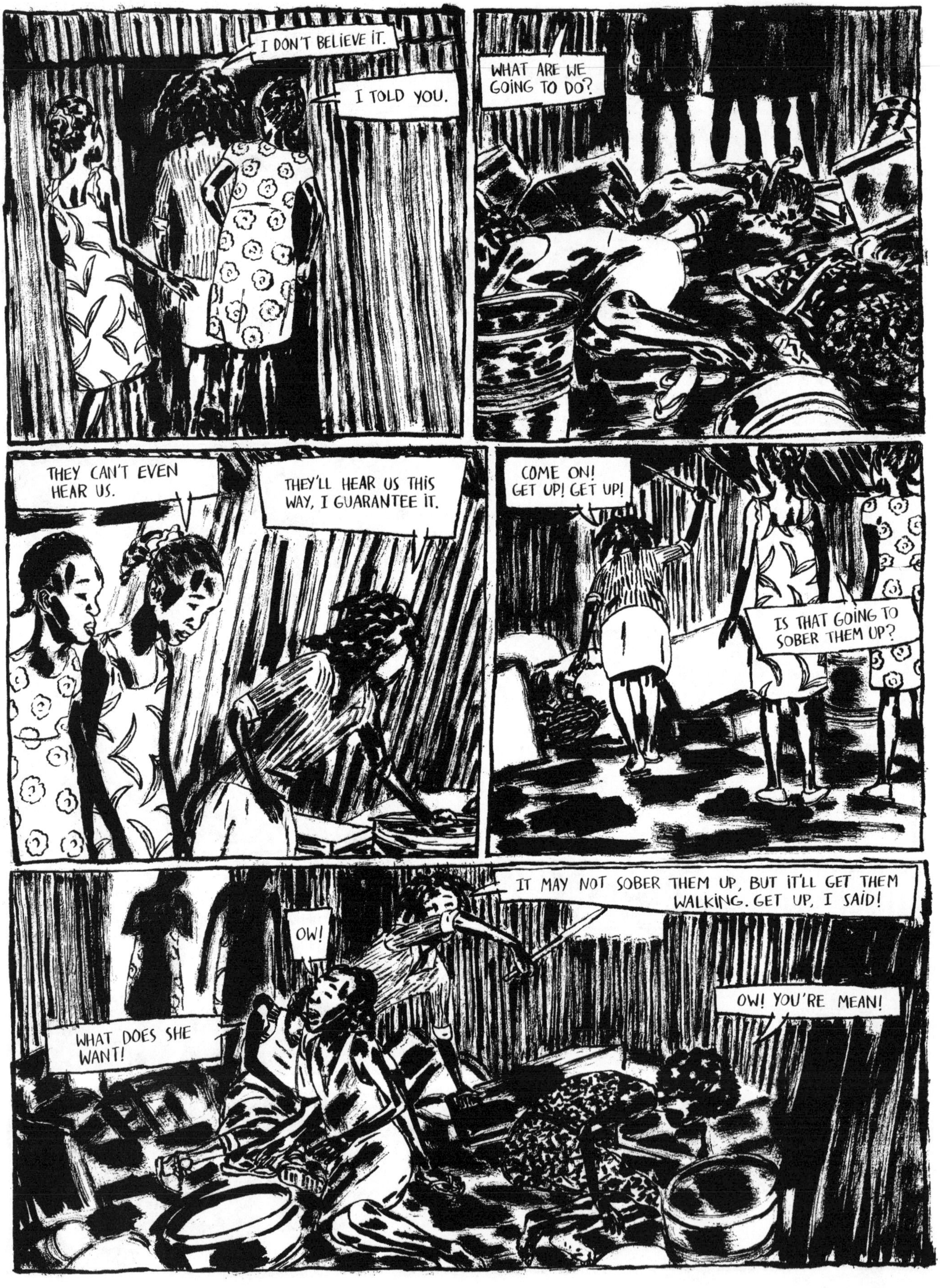
I DON'T BELIEVE IT.
I TOLD YOU.
WHAT ARE WE GOING TO DO?
THEY CAN'T EVEN HEAR US.
THEY'LL HEAR US THIS WAY, I GUARANTEE IT.
COME ON! GET UP! GET UP!
IS THAT GOING TO SOBER THEM UP?
IT MAY NOT SOBER THEM UP, BUT IT'LL GET THEM WALKING. GET UP, I SAID!
OW!
WHAT DOES SHE WANT!
OW! YOU'RE MEAN!

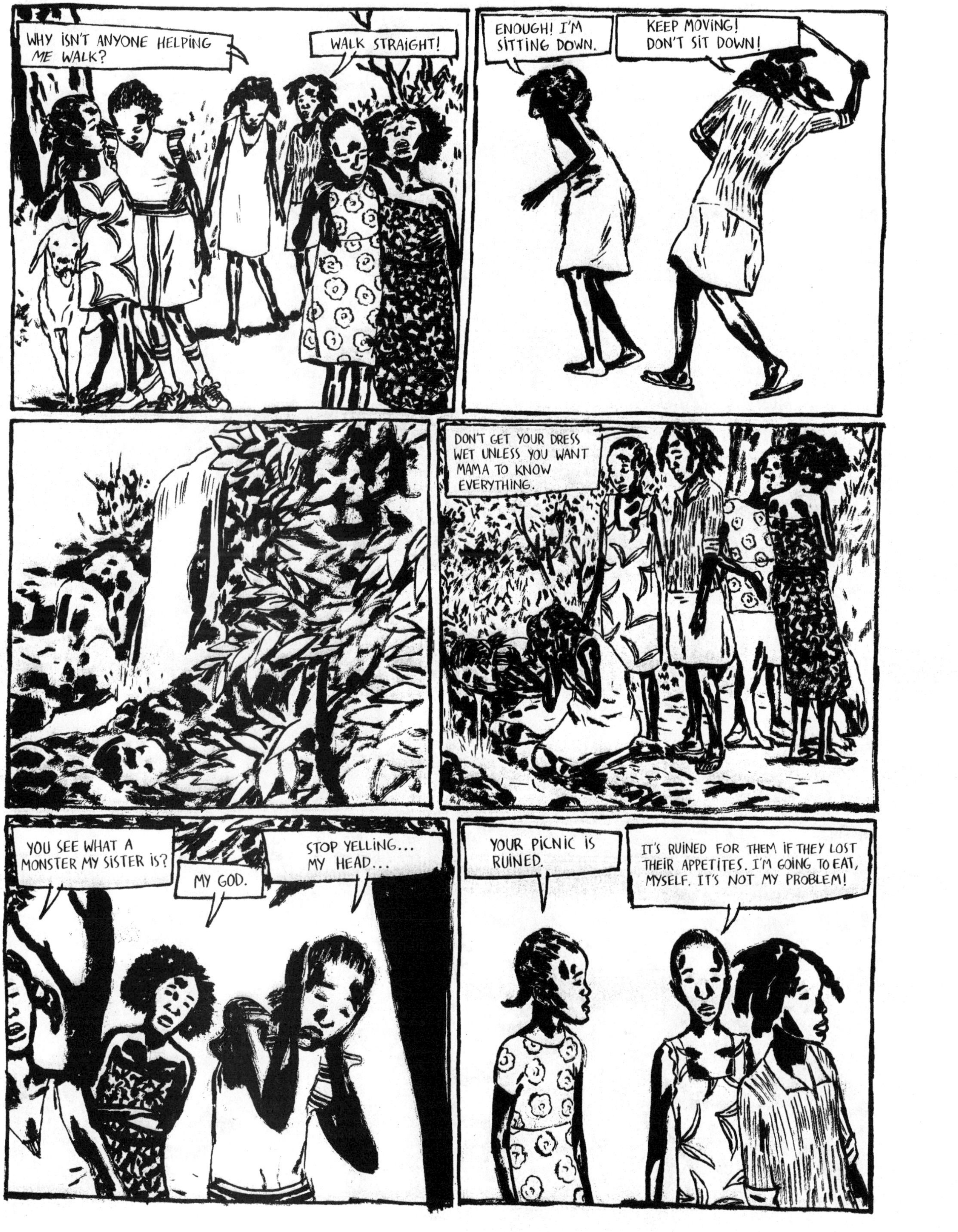
WHY ISN'T ANYONE HELPING ME WALK?
WALK STRAIGHT!
ENOUGH! I'M SITTING DOWN.
KEEP MOVING! DON'T SIT DOWN!
DON'T GET YOUR DRESS WET UNLESS YOU WANT MAMA TO KNOW EVERYTHING.
YOU SEE WHAT A MONSTER MY SISTER IS?
MY GOD.
STOP YELLING... MY HEAD...
YOUR PICNIC IS RUINED.
IT'S RUINED FOR THEM IF THEY LOST THEIR APPETITES. I'M GOING TO EAT, MYSELF. IT'S NOT MY PROBLEM!

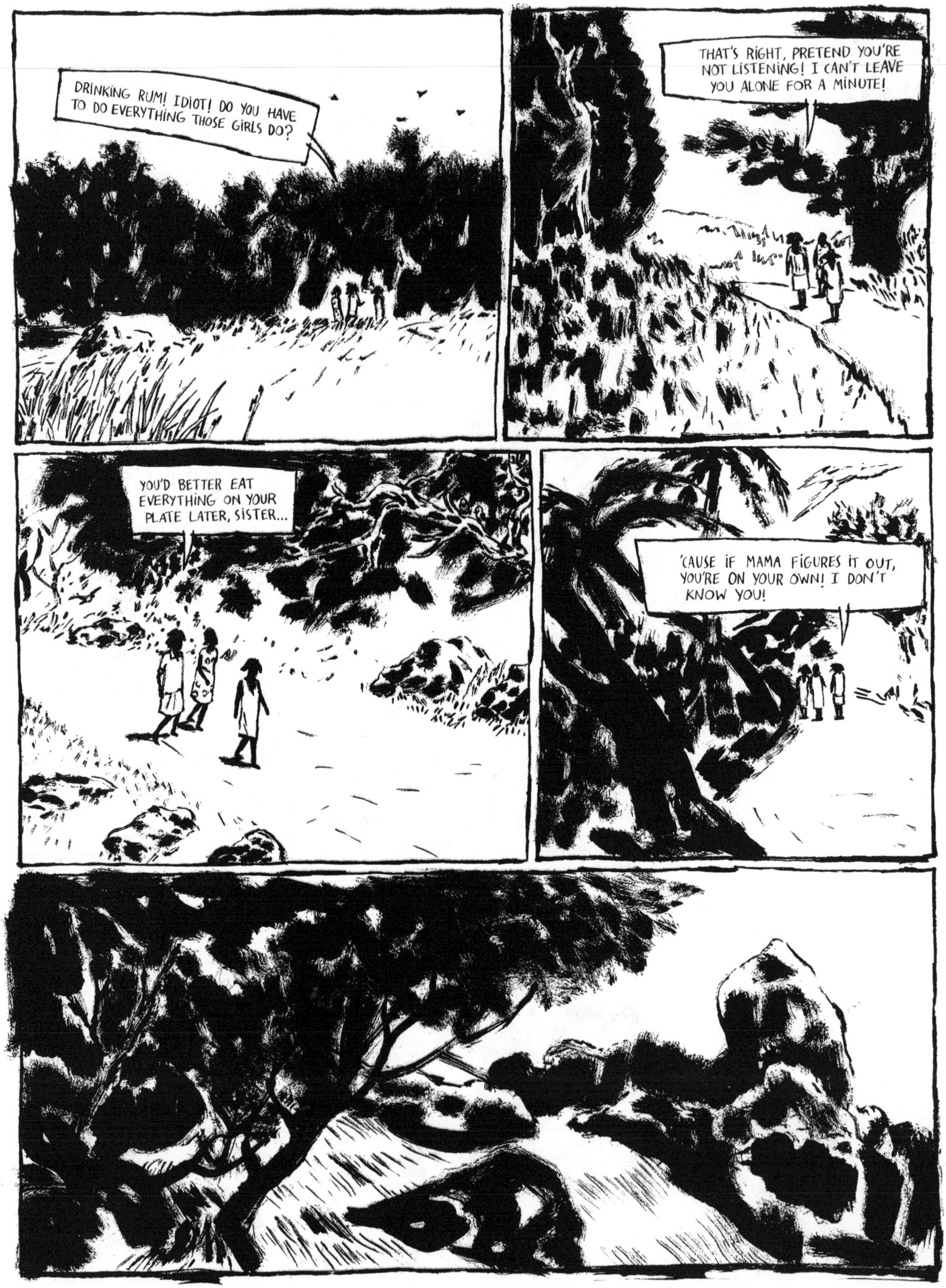
DRINKING RUM! IDIOT! DO YOU HAVE TO DO EVERYTHING THOSE GIRLS DO?
THAT'S RIGHT, PRETEND YOU'RE NOT LISTENING! I CAN'T LEAVE YOU ALONE FOR A MINUTE!
YOU'D BETTER EAT EVERYTHING ON YOUR PLATE LATER, SISTER...
'CAUSE IF MAMA FIGURES IT OUT, YOU'RE ON YOUR OWN! I DON'T KNOW YOU!

Afterword

by Matt Madden

*F*irmin Aristophane Boulon (1967–2004) dazzled the French independent comics scene of the 1990s with a series of intense, singular, and highly confident books and short stories. He was born in the francophone Carribean archipelago of Guadeloupe and moved to France first to study art in Paris and later to study comics in Angoulême.

I was captivated by Aristophane from the first time I set eyes on his work—a short story in an anthology where he effortlessly outshone his more established fellow contributors— and immediately set out to find whatever else of his I could get my hands on during my visits to France. His artwork is arresting for its rich textures and ever-shifting points of view, all brought about with his delicate, charcoal-like dry brush. His writing—and by that I mean his storytelling; his cartooning as a whole—is beguiling for its often casual, episodic structure which somehow conveys a sense of urgency, of truths being transmitted. Many of his early stories and books, like *Faune, ou l'histoire d'un immorale* and his epic *Conte Démoniaque,* are preoccupied with evil and frailty as viewed through the lives of demons and mythological creatures.

Les Soeurs Zabîme marks a different direction in his work, something like a new faith. The art continues the same explorations of texture and line as in his earlier books, but *Les Soeurs Zabîme* is suffused with a sometimes giddy lightness— even if it does not lack for a cool irony in the disinterested chronicling of the book's events by the narrator, the distancing effect of the continually odd framing, and the small miracle of telling a story about children that is neither cute nor sentimental. I have read the book countless times and I always find new shadings—both visual and narrative—to admire. Tragically, *Les Soeurs Zabîme*, published in 1996, was to be Aristophane's last published work. Like the filmmaker Jean Vigo, who shared some of his outsider's lyricism and sardonic humor, Aristophane left us with the gift of this small masterpiece as well as the pang of knowing we'll never see what he might have done next.

Books by Aristophane include:

1993 : *Logorrhée* (Le Lézard)

1995 : *Faune* (Amok)

1995 : "Un grand projet" in *Avoir 20 ans en l'an 2000* (Autrement)

1996 : *Conte Démoniaque* (L'Association)

1996 : *Les Soeurs Zabîme* (Ego Comme X)

Acknowledgments

Matt Madden would like to thank the following people for their support in bringing this book to an English-speaking public:

Nic Breutzman, Nate Doyle, Da Young Jung, Bob Mecoy, Thomas Ragon, Alexis Siegel, and Tim Sparvero.

Matt would especially like to acknowledge Domingos Isabelinhos and Ng Suat Tong for their initiative and efforts in getting this project underway in the first place.

:01

First Second

New York & London

Text and Illustrations Copyright © 2010 by Aristophane - Ego-Comme-X
Translation by Matt Madden
Translation Copyright © 2010 by First Second

Published by First Second
First Second is an imprint of Roaring Brook Press,
a division of Holtzbrinck Publishing Holdings Limited Partnership,
175 Fifth Avenue, New York, NY 10010

All rights reserved

Distributed in Canada by H. B. Fenn and Company Ltd.
distributed in the United Kingdom by Macmillan Children's Books,
a division of Pan Macmillan.

Design by Colleen AF Venable

Cataloging-in-Publication Data is on file at the Library of Congress.

ISBN: 978-1-59643-638-1

First Second books are available for special promotions and premiums.
For details, contact: Director of Special Markets, Holtzbrinck Publishers.

FIRST
EDITION

First Edition November 2010
Printed in the United States of America
10 9 8 7 6 5 4 3 2 1

BY ART
WE LIVE